all the

LITTLE CHOICES

★★★

STACEY RITZ

ROCKVILLE
PUBLISHING

ALSO BY STACEY RITZ

All The Little Choices

The Lost Years

REVIEWS FOR ALL THE LITTLE CHOICES

"This was my first book by this author. It was a wonderfully paced book that had me guessing!"

"I couldn't help but keep reading as I wanted to know what would happen next. I will say that as a reader who usually figures out the end well before I read it…the twist did take me by surprise."

"This is a suspenseful tale that will keep you turning pages all the way to the end. Well done!"

ALL THE LITTLE CHOICES

Prologue

ANTHONY

Present Day, 2017

How could this be happening to me? We watched the news together every night as we ate dinner; stories about tragedies happening to others. Others. Not us. Not her. Not me. Now I've stepped into my own personal horror movie. I'm the other. She's the other. We're the others. And there's nothing I can do to stop it now. It's happening and I'm helpless. Is she? My mind is spinning with questions. Who would do this? Did someone do this to her? Did she run away? Is she safe? Is she hurt? Is she trying to reach me? Is she dead? I'm sitting on the edge of the dirt brown La-Z-Boy recliner, the chair Abigail said she hated so much, the chair she had wanted to replace but I refused, standing my ground and letting her know I loved this chair too much to let it go. My legs are spread wide. My hands are holding up my head, placed against my forehead. I can't stop them from shaking. I'm going to be sick. Where is she? What is happening? How did everything change so quickly? Was it something I did? Didn't do? Something I said? Or didn't say?

"Abigail Victoria Parker, age twenty-six. A wife and mother living in Waterford, Indiana is missing and police need your help finding her." The newscasters nasally voice sounds so serious. This is serious, but Abigail? Really? None of it makes sense. We're happily married, we own a small but cozy brick cape cod on the edge of town. We are people of faith. We love each other. Abigail is following her dreams. Married. One child, with the hope of more to come. She's a wonderful mom to our son Gideon. She keeps the house spotless, she's a wonderful cook and she is the kindest soul I've ever met. Gentle, meek, and a smile that will melt even the hardest of hearts. Who would do this to her? How could someone take a grown adult? She'd told me once, two years ago

I think, that she wanted to take a self-defense class at the local YMCA. I told her she didn't need to do that because she had me. I told her that we live in a nice area, a safe neighborhood and that there was no reason for her to put bad thoughts in her head when everything was okay. Was I wrong? Is this my doing? By caring for my wife too much, have I caused her to be taken from me

I'd long since drowned out the nasally news reporters voice. Regardless of the channel or the reporter, they all started to sound the same after a while. They all stated my wife's name in a matter-of-fact manner. They all followed the same script, "wife and mother". But Abigail is so much more than those two words. I never meant to-

Gideon is beginning to cry from his room. I rub my hands across my forehead and over my closed eyelids before attempting to stand. I do not turn off the television. Although I'd heard the words play on repeat, something about them eerily comforts me. Somehow the words of strangers simply reporting Abigail's missing status gives me a loose sense of connection, a small taste of hope, regardless of how minute it is. I am willing to grab on to any thread of promise. And right now, the droning voices of reporters have become that tiny thread. Gideon's cries grow louder with each passing second. My knees are stiff as I push my hands against the sides of the La-Z-Boy and stand. Should I be this stiff at twenty-eight? Then again, should I be tending to our child while my wife is God only knows where and I'm waiting by the television like it's some kind of savior? I shake my head as I turn away from the glare of the screen and toward Gideon's wailing. I teeter back and forth between overwhelming depression and maddening anger. I'd never paid much attention to Gideon's schedule. I assumed he needed a diaper change or he was hungry. Surely, he was much too young at twelve months to understand what was happening in our lives. To understand that his mother was missing. I am quickly learning that his cries signal the need for sleep, diaper change, feeding, or the occasional holding session where I cradle him in my arms and sway him back and forth, like I'd seen Abigail do in the past. I am well aware Gideon knows I am not his mother. I don't have a soft touch like her, although I try to steady my hands and move him gently each time. I don't have the patience of a saint like she does. I am doing my best to pretend with the patience part, but I think Gideon knows the truth. I love being a father and a husband, but I never signed up to be a caretaker. How long would I be filling in for

Abigail? How long until she returns and we assume our normal every day roles? I ache at the missing of ordinary things, like coming down the stairs for breakfast and hearing the sizzling of the skillet and the soft humming of lullabies from my wife. I miss the way she folded back the blankets before bed at night and how she always plastered toothpaste on both of our toothbrushes, never just her own. I miss the sound of her bare feet padding down the hallway after waking up to feed or comfort Gideon in the middle of the night. I love feeling the warmth of her slender body as she quietly climbed back into bed and placed her arm around me as her breaths grew longer and deeper in the calm of sleep. I miss the way she hugged me every night when I walked in the door from work. Sure, our house might sound a little like *Leave it to Beaver*, but it works for us and that's all that really matters. We were happy. We *are* happy.

When I arrive to Gideon's room his face is red from screaming. I reach to pick him up and place his chest against mine, gently patting him on the back. "It's going to be okay little guy." I find it odd to be reassuring someone else when it's what I need myself right now. But it's just the two of us at the moment. Lois and Omar, Abigail's parents are busy working to arrange a candle-light vigil at the church. They'll be over later tonight to help with Gideon and to check in. My dad passed away in an accident before he was witness to our marriage and my mom is suffering from dementia and living out her days in a local nursing home. Both Abigail and I are only children; prized possessions in our respective families. Which is why, I believe, we both want to have a lot of children. Sure, we want them to all be prized, as they without a doubt will be in our family, but we want to have lots of them to spread our love around. The way we see it, there is no reason to have just one.

I sway back and forth with Gideon in my arms, and although it seems impossible, his cries only continue to grow louder. "Mommy's going to come home." I promise him through my own arrogant hope. "She'll be home soon, just watch." But my words do nothing to slow his frightful fit, nor my own.

Abigail never calls me Anthony. She's called me Tony ever since our first date. She is the only one who has ever called me by that name. When I was a child, my mom said proper boys were addressed by their full names, never shortened ones and for whatever reason, I took that to heart. Until Abigail entered my life. To be honest, it never bothered me. I kind of liked it from the start, I felt it was sort of a pet name she'd given to me and I never fought it. My mother, of course, could hardly stand to hear Abigail call me Tony and I still catch her rolling her eyes from time to time (even in her state of dementia) when she hears the name roll off Abigail's tongue, like she's saying some kind of curse word. It's almost as if Abigail calling me *Tony* in front of my mom, somehow brings my mom back to life, to her own self for that moment. During the first year of our relationship, my mother pulled me aside during the fourth of July picnic and asked me why I didn't start calling Abigail *Abby* instead. I laughed her off, never truly understanding why she had such a hang up on the whole name thing. I guess I'll never know now. This, like so many other things that once seemed small and trivial, have transformed into secrets now locked away; secrets I will never know the answers to because the woman I once knew as my mother is for the most part, no longer here. Now when I visit my mom in the quaint nursing home, I watch her slowly wilt away. She mirrors the tiny potted plants that sit on her window ledge and have turned brown at the edges, with the decay only continuing to creep deeper toward the plants center as the days pass. My mother still insists on calling me Anthony; that is, when she remembers who I am, which is sadly not often these days. More often than not, she thinks I am my father. She thinks Gideon is *her* child; that he is me. Sometimes I correct her, other times I don't. Is it really so wrong to let her feel comfortable and safe in the lies she tells? After all, it is what she believes to be true; so it's truth to her, is it not? My mother is clearly at her happiest when she thinks I am her husband and that Gideon is me, her own young son. Why disturb that when it won't change reality? Telling her again and again that I am someone she no longer knows or understands will only serve to upset her in every way. The fits she throws! She pulls out chunks of her hair with her wrinkled fists. Her eyes. Oh, those sad blue eyes. They look at me, in those awful fitful moments, as if I'm a murderer. As if I'm somehow poisoning her. But it is not me that is doing the poisoning; it is her own brain. The dementia. If she needs to be mad at a physical form for this awful debilitating disease, she can use me as the punching bag. I will take it. She is, after all, locked in the labyrinth of her own brain as it fills with a venom that is slowly wrapping itself into the coils of her flesh and blood, killing her with the creeping grip of a python as it curls its dark slithering self into every last corner of life. It will kill her. I know that. The doctors and nurses know. Abigail knows this too. Perhaps the only ones who don't know are the victim herself, my mother, and my son. The first, too ill to understand, the second too young and innocent to realize.

I'm thinking about my mother now as I change Gideon's diaper, again. He coo's softly as I grab a fresh one from the open Pampers box sitting on the floor beside my bare feet. My mother will never see my son grow in to a man. She'll never know her great grandchildren. She'll never know her grandchildren for that matter, because she has never recognized Gideon for who he really is. She will never make another memory; she is stuck with only a handful of the millions she made in the course of sixty-two short years. *Sixty-two.* She has been short changed by my measure.

My father and my mother had me later in life. She was thirty-four, late to becoming a mother for her generation. But it didn't bother her, or at least, she never showed it. She had seven miscarriages before I came along and from the day I was born, they quietly dubbed me the miracle. A high standard to live up to, if you ask me. But no one's ever inquired. With my mother in long-term care, my family has become Abigail, Gideon and Abigail's parents, Lois and Omar who are always gracious and kind to me. Abigail is the center of my world. She is the common thread to my only living and functioning family. I can't lose her. Where has she gone? Who has taken her? Is she coming back? I can't take this much longer. I keep trying to distract myself with thoughts of anything other than Abigail, but of course, like a broken record, my thoughts are consumed by the scratch that is me being worried sick about the whereabouts of my wife. I hear myself sigh and I watch in slow motion as Gideon rolls off the changing table where I've left him lay in his clean diaper. I throw myself to the ground, listening to a blood curling scream that comes from somewhere deep within me. My vocal cords vibrate as the sound fills the room, a horrific chorus that plays against Gideon's panicked wails. The tears burn my cheeks and lips as they fall beneath me and I see them traipse to the ground, staining the beige carpet. For a moment, I am caught in a haze. Logically I see my son crying in front of me as I am on my knees before him. I hear both of our shouts and cries. I am mesmerized by the weight of my own tears, by the bitter taste it leaves on my tongue. And then I think, this must be how my mother feels. Suffocated by her own body. When she throws her fits and pulls out her hair, this is how she must feel.

So overwhelmingly frustrated. So heartbroken. So terrified. So lost in the foreign world that has suddenly been created for her, a world she can never escape, no matter how hard she tries. Are our lives really that easily changed? Are we each so fragile that our house of cards, no matter how sturdy it appears to be, can collapse on us at any moment?

I force my stare away from the glare of my own tear stains that have plastered the beige carpet resting beneath my own flesh and instead I glare at my son. I have to help him. I need to do something. Maybe there is nothing I can do to save my mother, and the police tell me there is nothing more I can do to bring Abigail home. Nurses and doctors tell me I should let them handle it. Police and detectives tell me to let them handle it. So the only thing I am able to handle is Gideon. But at this moment, I'm not sure that I can even do that. At this moment I am beholden to the horror that has become my life. I am a prisoner in my own skin as I wait for the call that tells me my mother has gotten worse or that she has passed. As I wait for the call that says Abigail is dead or that she will never be found. My house of cards has fallen and I am helpless to stop the destruction that has occurred. As the tides in my life have so quickly changed, suddenly I am being held captive beneath the now unbearably heavy weight of those fallen cards. The cards that once made life so beautiful have transformed into a nightmare.

My mother worried about the ramifications of Abigail addressing me by the name of Tony instead of Anthony. When Abigail was here, I worried about silly things like when we would have our next child? How many children would we have? What would we have for dinner that night? Did I budget the money in the best possible way? But none of those worries really matter when everything falls to pieces. Right now I'm not sure what does matter anymore. I sit and ponder that as I stay kneeling on the floor in front of my screaming son. We are crying together, shouting for help that for some reason evades us both.

Gideon is wearing his blue t-shirt today. It is the shirt Abigail bought him three months ago. In white lettering the shirt reads: *Mr. ONEderful.* Abigail gushed over the shirt when she'd purchased it. She was so excited to celebrate Gideon's first birthday. She'd planned for a local family photographer to come to the house for the occasion and she talked about something called a smash cake for Gideon and of course blue and green balloons, which she said were Gideon's favorite colors. But Gideon is twelve months now and he had to celebrate without the festivities, and without his mother. Actually, there was no celebration at all. I didn't even give him this shirt until this morning. I wanted Abigail to give it to him. When I placed it over his blond head I wondered if I was doing the right thing. Should I have waited for Abigail to give him the shirt? Gideon outgrew things so quickly. I guessed that when Abigail was found and returned safely to us that she wouldn't care that I had given our son his special shirt. I guessed that something silly like a shirt wouldn't matter. Wherever Abigail is, I know she's thinking of us. I know she wants us to find her, to help her. I wonder if she knows we are trying? I wonder if she knows we'll find her? I wonder if she can hang on until we do? There is so much I wonder, but all to no avail. Because there are no answers to the mystery of a missing person. There are only questions that consume every corner of my mind.

"Abigail Victoria Parker, age twenty-six. A wife and mother living in Waterford, Indiana is missing and police need your help finding her." The story is now national news. However, whether the national or local news are reporting, they all use the same words to deliver their lines. *Wife. Mother. Missing. Age twenty-six. Needing your help.* And that we do. I do. Need everyone's help. Gideon needs it, too. We want her back. We want her to be okay; to be unharmed. I want to rewind the hands of time and hold her safe in my arms. But I can't do that now. I don't have that kind of power. Honestly, right now I'm depleted of any sense of power at all. But do we ever really have any power over our own lives or is that feeling simply a farce? If my mother could be cured of the awful dementia that plagues her, even for a moment, and be given the chance to speak freely, I have no doubt she would sadly laugh at the hand life has dealt her. She would tell me that her circumstances prove we have power over absolutely nothing except for our reaction to the situations we are presented. Talk about feeling powerless.

I hear the doorbell ring followed by the familiar creaking sound of the front door opening. "Hello?" I hear Lois' frail voice echo down the hall to where I am standing at the edge of Gideon's bedroom, watching him sleep and silently apologizing for the earlier fit and for not being able to find his mother just yet. My body pulses at the sudden sound, something other than the monotonous reporter's voices that echo throughout the house from the television screen. I use the back of my hands to wipe at my face. I turn to walk toward the living room to greet my in-laws. Hearing the click of Lois's heels on the linoleum floor that is made to look like hardwood I lean into her as we meet. Wrapping my arms around her small frame, I bow my head as the tears come again. Lois wraps her arms around me and pats my back with her hand. "There, there." She tries to comfort me with a loving mothers touch. After a moment I gather myself and stand upright, pulling away from her embrace. I hear Omar rummaging around in the kitchen; the opening of the refrigerator door. The sound of running water from the sink.

I draw in a deep breath before speaking softly, not wanting to wake Gideon. "How-"

Lois and I speak the same word at the same time. I motion with my hand for her to go ahead and so she does. "How are you holding up, dear? How is Gideon?"

The questions do not need answering. How would anyone be holding up when their wife has suddenly gone missing? But what else can be said? I nod, knowing that she knows there are no words that can be spoken in this moment to make anything better, other than "Abigail has been found and is safe." Outside of that, nothing else matters. The rest of it is just a jumble of random words; an attempt to pass the time and cling to hope.

Abigail's father, Omar, walks into the room carrying a tall glass of ice water. He nods to me before sitting on the couch, staring blankly at the television. "No, no, no." He mutters toward the screen. "Turn this garbage off." He reaches for the remote and flips the channel. More of the same news; another reporter's face stating that Abigail is missing and that help is needed. Omar flips the channel again and still, more of the same. We can't escape our reality. It's happening and we are engulfed by it; as it seems, the entire nation is now too. Except, they don't know Abigail. She isn't their daughter. Their mother. Their wife. She isn't real to them. She is merely a story line for the public to follow. Something the others can grab onto and silently be thankful it isn't happening to them. Just like Abigail and I used to feel when we watched the news at night. Those horrible stories only happened to *others*. Not us. Just, *others*. But now we're on the other side of the looking glass, helpless. We are a spectacle. A show. Entertainment. We are the unfortunate ones. We are the ones who make others feel lucky that they are not us. Omar switches the station four more times, only to find more of the same. It wears on him, as it is doing to all of us. A heavy cloak that we don't want to wear. He turns the television off and lightly tosses the remote to the side cushion of the couch and buries his head in his hands. His daughter, his only child, is missing. And none of us have the slightest clue as to where she might be or how we can help her. Now the monotonous sound has become the cries. Gideon's cries. My own cries. Omar's cries and now Lois joins in, too. The sobs are oddly almost comforting because I realize that we have each other. I am not alone in this. It is not Gideon and me alone. It is Abigail's family, together. It is the public: the television viewers, the police officers. It is all of us together, wanting to find Abigail safe and sound. Wanting to bring home my wife.

Omar, who is generally a man who uses silence and stares to communicate rather than words, breaks the pattern of our intertwined cries after several minutes have passed. "Who would do this to her?" He grits his teeth and I watch as his fists clench into the cushions of the couch. I pace back and forth knowing Omar's outburst is bound to wake Gideon. I don't know how to brace myself for the certain screams that are to come from my young son. Lois is now sitting on the couch beside her husband, her arm placed around his back. I can tell Omar is agitated and unable to calm down. His body continues to tense and the little spikes of gray hair that are sprinkled on the sides of his head seem to stand a bit taller. "Who?" This time his shout accompanies a smack of his fist against the wooden coffee table that sits in front of the couch. "Who would be so malicious to kidnap a grown adult? No less, a woman with a husband and a child at home! Who would have umbrage with my little girl?" When Omar says the words *my little girl,* he turns his head and stares at me, his dark brown eyes piercing deep into mine. His glare holds as he comes to a feeble stand. I watch as a broken father struggles to understand what I myself cannot.

How long do we hold on to hope? A month? Six months? A year? Ten years? Forever? I don't think I'll ever be able to turn it off; the hope, no matter how minute it seems. Otherwise, what else is there? Neither Lois nor I respond to Omar's desperate yowls. How can we? In the absence of our response, Gideon fills the void. As predicted, he begins to wail from his room and I watch, standing motionless as Lois jumps up and says she'll handle it. "I need to hold my grandson right now." She whispers faintly as she moves past me, her heels clicking down the hall. I am left with the heavy weight that quickly fills the room once Lois has disappeared. Now it is just Omar and me. Alone. Together. Weeping for the shared person that we both love the most in this world. I make my way over to the couch to sit next to my father in-law, but as I sit, he shifts away. Maybe he is making room, I think. When I turn to say something to him, his eyes meet mine and I watch as they turn cold. We speak without words; the way Omar prefers his interactions. I lean my back into the couch as we continue to hold our stare. Omar is sitting forward, his hands clenched on his pants, his back hovering above his thighs. There is something about his stare that chills me at my core and it only continues to grow worse. I hear Gideon's cries silence amidst the gentle humming of his grandma. I've always known that Abigail got her superior mothering skills from her own mom. They are gifted in a way I never will be. I should be thankful my son's cries have stopped, but instead the silence is piercing. I look away from Omar's intense glare, hoping he will do the same. But still his eyes are on me, as if they are trying to peer into my soul, as if he is questioning something. Questioning me? What? Me? Is he turning against me now? Does he think I had something to do with

Abigail's disappearance? Nothing could be further from the truth. Why is he turning on me? My darting eyes must be telling Omar my exact thoughts because he turns to me, his mouth the shape of an O as he prepares to speak. It is at that moment for some unknown reason, that I realize the room smells like cinnamon. Has it always smelled this way? I am jarred away from my roaming thoughts when Omar's voice sounds. He leans toward me and I can feel his hot breath against my cheek.

"If you had anything to do with Abigail's disappearance, I will kill you." He sits back after speaking, feeling satisfied with himself. A smile creeps across his aging face as he crosses his arms in front of his chest. The Atwell's have loved me from the start of our relationship. They've never been anything but welcoming and kind. This must be a nightmare, although I know it is not. I understand that things are taut right now, but there is no need to throw me into the fire. I'm on Omar's side. I'm on Abigail's side. How could he think any different? I draw in a deep breath, reminding myself that Omar does not mean what he's said. He's scared. I get that. If he needs someone to take it out on, let it be me. It will pass. Once Abigail is home and safe, all of this tension will fade away. Sour words will be forgotten. Our house of cards will be rebuilt, only stronger this time. We will prevail, because what other option is there? Abigail has to come home safely. We need her back.

Instead of responding to Omar's accusing statement, I reach out my arm to pat him on the leg. When he does not move I reach for his hand and hold it. His hand relaxes into mine. We are on the same team. We want the same thing; to find our Abigail.

One

ABIGAIL

2015

My art teacher once told me I could be an artist. I think I was seven or eight years old at the time. Instead of beaming a smile back at her, I asked, "but aren't I already an artist?" She laughed and nodded her head. "Well, I suppose you're right dear. I just meant that one day you might be able to sell your artistic items for money. You have talent." She winked at me and walked away, on to praise the next student's work and it occurred to me that was what *she* was paid to do. I had painted a picture of an apple with watercolors that day. I took it home and asked my mom if she would buy it from me. "How much will you pay me for my art work?" I asked innocently. She replied with a laugh, much as my art teacher had done when I'd asked her if I was already an artist. But then I thought I saw her reach into her pocket, I thought she was going to give me a dollar. I thought she was going to buy my art work and I could go back to school the next day and tell my art teacher that I was right, I was indeed already an artist and I sell my art for money. My dad walked in the door at that moment and tossed his bag onto the ground for my mom to pick up as she always did. His hands were waving in the air and he was ranting and raving about something at work. He was the principle at Saint Ann's Catholic School which served sixth through eighth grade students. As my dad stormed past the two of us, ignoring the fact that we were in the middle of a conversation, not to mention a sale, my mom quickly snatched my apple painting out of my hands and followed my dad into the kitchen. I knew better than to bring up the painting or discussion of my art work at the dinner table. That was dad's time to shine; that's what mom always told me. We ladies, she said, are to sit, eat and listen as the man of the room speaks. And so that's what we did. We sat with our legs crossed, ate with proper utensils and listened to him go on and on about how there's so many people in the world and none of them seem to have a brain. Those were his words, not mine. Sometimes I wondered if my mom genuinely took interest in his ramblings. To me, they were just a bunch of words strung together, delivered with an angry tone.

I waited patiently until my mom tucked me into bed that night. When she pulled the covers up to my chin and said "sweet dreams, dear" I kissed her cheek when she leaned forward, as I always did. And then I asked her about my apple painting. I whispered the question, trying my best to be polite. "Did you decide to buy my painting mom?"

She shifted uneasily as if she were trying to remember the painting. After a long pause, she spoke, "I will hang it on the refrigerator Abigail." She forced a smile to her lips, seeming distracted.

"But you won't buy it?" I asked once more.

"Dear, a painting or any work of art is just fun and games. It's not for selling." She'd told me quite frankly.

I tried to protest, telling her that my art teacher said real artist are able to sell their work and that's when she shook her head and said, "That art teacher of yours is filling your head with nonsense. Good girls grow up to be wives and mommies, not artists. Artists are nothing more than gypsies." She muttered the last part. I tried to ask her what a gypsy was, but she had stood and curtly said good-night before the sound could leave my lips, closing my bedroom door behind her. It has always been crystal clear to me that the expectations of my life were set by someone other than me. They were set by the two people I looked to for unconditional love; for survival. And when you depend on someone, no matter what age you are, I learned from an early age that you do as expected, lest there be hell to pay.

Using two Sharpie permanent markers, one black and one red, I wrote in the bottom of the plain white coffee mug. I'd purchased the mug yesterday while grocery shopping and I had already had the Sharpie markers on hand. I wrote the words so that when you looked inside of the mug, the writing was directly on the bottom. In other words, when the drink was finished and the cup was empty, the writing would become visible. Using the black marker I wrote: YOU + ME = and I wrote the answer, THREE with a tiny heart, in red. I placed the caps back on the markers and tossed them in the kitchen junk drawer. I blew inside of the cup, watching the ink dry. The next step was to bake the coffee mug in the oven for fifteen minutes so that the writing would become permanent. I set the oven to three-hundred and fifty degrees and placed the mug inside on a small tray. Admittedly, I was proud of myself for the creative way I was choosing to tell Tony that we're pregnant. We have been married just three months. As I had expected, getting pregnant didn't take long. As people of strong faith, we had agreed from the start to wait until we were married before we slept together.

I sit at the small kitchen table as I wait on the coffee mug to finish setting in the oven. With a pen and a notecard in hand, after a few taps on the table, I begin to write the second part of Tony's gift.

The only thing better than having you as
my husband is our children having you
as their dad. We're pregnant!
Yours, Abigail

Perfect. I let the blue ballpoint pen fall from my fingers, feeling satisfied with myself. I am doing everything right, I reassured myself as I watched it

from the center of the table to its edge, falling off
with a clink as the pen hit the floor. I rested my head
in my hands, letting my eyes wander throughout the
kitchen. I stare at the matching pair of red dishtowels
hanging from the side of the sink. I study the stainless
steel refrigerator, checking for the tenth time today
to be sure there are no fingerprints present. Another
scan reveals that there are not any. A child will have
her hands all over that refrigerator, I suddenly realize.
How in the world will I keep up with the cleaning?
With the mess? Drawing in a deep breath through
my nose, I sigh, reminding myself that everything
will be okay. I will be a good mother and Tony will
be a good dad. We live in a red brick cape cod on the
edge of town. It isn't much, but it is ours. The house
has three bedrooms, enough for a few kids before we
move into something larger. We have a fenced yard,
it's a five-foot tall privacy fence made of wood. We
have mature trees in the backyard, enough to provide
privacy from the neighbors. I'm sure we'll get a swing
set and maybe even a tree house for the kids to enjoy,
too. As I stare out the sliding glass doors leading
to the backyard, I can already hear the shouts and
laughter of our little ones. Placing a hand over my
stomach I rub back and forth twice, a smile creeping

onto my face. Our baby is growing inside of me. Our first baby is on the way.

I took a jewelry making class at the Waterford Public Library just before we were married. I didn't tell anyone about it. It wasn't a big deal, really. I've always been interested in creative endeavors and I've had this secret dream of owning my own jewelry shop. During our engagement, I foolishly made the mistake of telling Tony about my dream. I told him my secret after we had spent three hours sitting out at the lake, at dark. He held my hand the entire night as we stared out at the lake. It was a full moon that night, which served to illuminate the still waters beneath it; the ideal lighting for our rendezvous. Tony's fingers gently stroked the diamond engagement ring that clasped tightly to my finger. I still lived at home and although I didn't work, I did volunteer at Saint Ann's Catholic School, to help children with learning disabilities master subjects in which they might be struggling. I was a tutor of sorts. For free. But nevertheless, it was what I'd been doing since graduating high school. Now, at twenty-three, I was ready to leave home, as Tony and I would be purchasing our own house in Waterford as soon as we were married. A lot of my high school friends had gone away to college, and as much as I would have liked to do that myself, my parents had said they didn't see the point in wasting all of that money on an education I would never use. I was living rent and bill free. I ate my parent's food. They paid all of the bills. I still drove one of their cars. They paid for the gas and insurance. I have to say, it was a nice set up. And they assured me it would be this way until, as they put it, they "married me off." But I digress. When Tony and I were at the lake that night, he told me he loved his job. He worked in insurance and would soon be transferring into life insurance sales, rather than the hodge-podge of personal and small commercial policies that he sold now. Insurance didn't interest me at all, but Tony was particularly excited about the opportunity for large of amounts of money to be made.

"One day we'll be able to build a huge house for our family." He beamed, his white teeth glowing in the light of the moon. "This is our golden ticket Abigail. I'm good at this job and I'll be able to take care of you and our family…" Tony's voice trailed as I assumed he got lost somewhere in his own daydream of the future.

I smiled and nodded, having learned from my

mother how to be a good listener. "Do you want to have a lot of children?" I questioned, although I was sure I knew the answer already.

Tony's eyes widened as he turned toward me. His fingers stopped stroking my diamond engagement ring and instead he held one hand in each of his as he nodded. "Of course! Don't you?" For a moment I thought I saw a glimpse of fear jet through his eyes.

"Of course." I quickly agreed, feeling my hands fidget beneath the weight of his.

"You'll be such a good mother." He leaned forward, wrapping his arms around my frame and resting his head against my shoulder.

I closed my eyes, soaking in the relief that poured over me as I melted into Tony's strong embrace. "And you'll be such a good father." I echoed, smelling the scent of shampoo on his short spikey brown hair.

Tony held me for a few minutes longer before pulling away and brushing his fingers through my wavy black locks. "You are truly a dream come true Abigail Atwell." He cleared his throat, "Or should I say Abigail Parker." He winked as I obediently leaned forward to kiss his cheek. "It's always been my dream to find a girl like you, settle down and have a big family. You're everything I've always hoped for. I am the luckiest man alive."

I felt my face grow hot with embarrassment, feeling relived that Tony couldn't see me blush in the dark beneath the moon. Albeit my brash timidity, I couldn't help put replay his words through my mind. *A girl like me.* Any girl? Or was I the only one for him? *Like me* in that I would fulfill the role of wife and mother to his standards, or was I reading too much into his statement. It was, after all, meant to be a compliment, not a slight. I needed to let it pass. I was being too hard on him. We were having a nice time at the lake, enjoying the evening. Why ruin a good thing over my silly interpretation? Suddenly I heard the words coming from my mouth before I was able to stop them. "My dream is to open my own jewelry shop one day" I bit my lip knowing it was too late to stop now. "I've never told anyone that before."

Tony pulled back and studied my face, as if to see if I was serious or not.

"Of course I want to be the best wife and mother I can be. It's just a dream. Something I've thought about since I was a little girl. But like I said, I've never told anyone this before. It's not a big deal, really. It's just something I could maybe do on the side, to earn a little extra money. Maybe once the kids are in school I could do that while they're in class…" I couldn't stop the rambling. It all just kept spilling out of my mouth. "Just a little shop, you know? Nothing big. I've always thought I'd call it Holy Grail Jewelers. Just as a play on my life, being raised so religious and everything..."

"Holy Grail?" Tony's eyebrows raised, puzzled by my pun. Or maybe not puzzled so much as displeased. I knew I'd probably thrown him for a loop as I normally wasn't the funny type. I was typically serious and to the point. Innocent. Straight forward. Agreeable. Not funny. But here I was trying to be funny, or something along those lines.

I nodded, feeling sheepish. I pressed my lips down tightly, forcing myself to not jump back into the perceived comfort of rambling.

"Oh, your parents would love that." He added. Still, I wasn't sure if he was mocking me.

"It was just a childhood dream. That's all." I couldn't stop myself. I was raised to please and since I couldn't suck my words back in and make them disappear, I tried to lessen their strength. Like a sauce that's too spicy for some taste buds, I needed to dilute my words to make them acceptable. I knew what I had to do; I'd had years of practice.

Laughing, Tony answered, "I thought I wanted to be the guy who drove the garbage truck when I was a kid. Not so much now. When we're kids it's all about what we think will be fun. When we're adults, it's about making money and doing what's best to provide for a family. Things change." He said it as if he were sorry to have to be the one to break the news to me. It was as if he were telling a child that Santa Clause wasn't real. But I wasn't a child and my dream of making jewelry wasn't a farce. Nuzzling his nose against mine he kissed my cheek and then my forehead, followed by my closed eyelids, one after the other. "Abigail, I can see you now, making beaded necklaces with our daughter...or daughters."

I took the jewelry making class at the library, just for fun. There were only three people, including me, in the class. My two classmates were ages twelve and fourteen, respectively. The class was only one week; an hour each day. We each made a broach and a pair of earrings using an array of recycled materials that the instructor had brought with her. I was most proud of my earrings. A pair of petite dangle earrings made of blue Labradorite, they had a stormy appearance. The sterling silver wire was bent to fit through the ear. The Labradorite faceted cube dangled from the edge of the earring with a sterling silver daisy spacer and a tiny silver ball as the headpin. The small blue cubes caught the light when I placed them into my ears, glistening and reminiscent of a late evening summer storm. They measured just 1-1/8 inch in length. My broach was nothing extraordinary and had a little extra glue hanging off of its edges. I tossed it in the trash after class. But the earrings I kept, hidden safely in the back of my glass jewelry box. I'd wear them one day, just not today.

I am wearing a pair of navy blue flats with a pink dress. In my mind the outfit represents the possibility of a boy or a girl. My stomach swims with butterflies as I allow the giddiness to overwhelm me. Tony is going to be so excited! When I hear the familiar sound of the front door creaking open, I stroll to the entryway and take Tony's coat and bag and hang them on the black antique steel coat rack behind the door. Once the items are neatly hung I turn to Tony and hug him. "You're home!" I squeal, squeezing him tighter than usual. His lips touch my cheek in the usual fashion and I grab his hand. "Are you hungry?"

"You look nice." His eyes scour my body from head to toe. "New dress? What's the occasion?"

"No, not new. Have a seat!" I motion for him to hurry to the table. I am bursting to tell him, but I can't let it slip. I've spent all day preparing how to break the news to him.

"I'm going to flip on the news and sit in the living room while you get everything ready." Tony smiles and comes toward me, wrapping his arms around my waist as he stands behind me, whiffing in the scent of my homemade lasagna and freshly baked bread, each sitting carefully on the stove behind us. He softly kisses the left side of my neck until reaching the lobe of my ear. He whispers "love you" retreats to the comfort of his old La-Z-Boy chair.

Tingles race down my spine. But as Tony pulls away I can't help but state my piece about the chair, again. I can hop onto my soap box about that thing at any moment. "Tony, we need to get rid of that old thing. It is so tattered and worn. At the very least, we need to have it reupholstered." I know I sound like a broken record, but I hate that thing. The old chair doesn't go with the sofa or any of our other new furnishings.

"I love this old chair just the way it is." Tony laughed from the living room as I heard the sound of the television coming to life. "We got a new sofa…" his voice trailed, giving me the perfect opportunity to interject my two cents.

"We got a new sofa because we didn't have a sofa.

What were we going to do, just have that ratty old chair in our living room and nothing else?"

"Works for me babe." He chuckles again. I stick my head around the corner watching him lean back in his favorite chair, a smirk splattered across his face. He'd had the chair before he met me and he didn't want to let it go.

Winking, I add. "One day you'll give in. At least to reupholster the old thing. It needs…something." I motion to the ripped edge of the chair.

"I don't think so Abigail. I love this chair too much to let it be changed. I like her exactly as she is."

"Well, it's a chair. Not a *she*." Raising my eyebrows I turn back toward the kitchen to prepare our plates. "If you're not budging on the tired old chair, at least we should think about getting carpet or real hardwood in the living room instead of the cheap looking linoleum. Can I win that battle?" I tease back, although I really do want to replace that horrible linoleum. It is the kind that is supposed to look like thin boards of light hardwood flooring, only it doesn't. It looks exactly like linoleum that had been placed down in a hurry. I love our house, but that floor can go as far as I am concerned.

A moment later Tony walks into the room with freshly washed hands. He pulls out his chair and says that everything smells great. He is always complimenting the chef and I have to admit, I don't mind it a bit. I am proud to make meals we can enjoy together, like this one. Tony isn't much of a cook himself. He can make pancakes, toast, grilled cheese and spaghetti. Not bad, but not a wide variety either.

"How was your day?" I ask. I love hearing about his days at work. Sometimes he doesn't have much to say. But other times he tells stories about his clients or his co-workers that I find interesting. Like last week when Tony told me about a client named Peter. I don't know Peter's last name, but that's beside the point. Three months earlier Peter had called the office to increase the life insurance policy on his wife. Last month, Peter's wife was found dead. She was on the ground, lifeless in her own backyard. Later reports said that her death had been caused by an accidental overdose. The day after his wife passed, Peter called into the office wanting to collect the life insurance funds. Now the case is being investigated for insurance fraud and possible murder. Tony told me how police officers and detectives were coming into the insurance office and interviewing all of the agents who had spoken to Peter, as they tried to piece the puzzle together. It all just left me shaking my head. People are nuts! Would someone really do that to their wife? And if he did, was it because of the money? He valued money that much more than his own wife? Perhaps Peter was innocent. But with the way Tony told the story, it sure didn't seem like it.

"A lot of paperwork. Nothing too exciting." Tony runs his fingers through his buzz brown hair and I watch as his long lashes move upward while his eyes meet mine. "Anything going on here?"

I shake my head. Placing our two filled plates on the table, I sit across from my husband. Steam rises from the lasagna, hovering in the air for a moment before disappearing. The butter has melted into the warm slices of bread I'd placed for us in the center of the table. "Oh, I almost forgot, drinks! What would you like?"

"Ice water is fine." He smiles, motioning for me to stay seated. "I'll get it; you've already prepared the meal."

"Thanks." I stay seated, enjoying being served.

"My pleasure." Tony strolls back to the table setting two glasses of ice water in front of each of our plates, on the ceramic coasters I'd set out.

After bowing our heads for a short prayer expressing our gratitude for the food we are about to enjoy, we eat in silence for the first few minutes of our meal. The sounds of polite chewing fill the small room, until I speak. "Did you visit your mom at lunch today?" I say the words quietly, almost in a whisper, for fear of upsetting him. I ask the question from a place a genuine care and concern, but still, I know how hard the topic is for him. To see the woman who raised him, unable to care for herself, unable to remember her own son would be difficult for anyone.

He nods while chewing his food. After taking a drink of water, he elaborates. "I did. She's good. No fits while I was there today. Not like the last time." He concentrates on his food, too scared to meet my eyes or else he might tear up. Last week when Tony had visited his mom during lunch one afternoon, she went into a fit of screams, insisting he was a stranger trying to harm her. She pulled out fists of her hair and the nursing staff had to retrain her while they asked Tony to leave. Once a month we visit his mother, Lily, together. And once a week he goes to see her on his own, alone during his lunch break. He loves his mother, but he can't visit her any more often. It pains him too much to see her in this state, without her recognizing him as any type of family member or friend during most visits. He often wonders if he is harming his mother more than helping her with his visits.

"That's good to hear." I reply, sorry to see the sadness overtake his eyes.

"For a moment, she thought I was her husband." He laughs. Lily often thought Tony was her late husband, Thomas. Sometimes Tony corrected her, other times he just let her talk and be happy in the moment.

I smile back.

"She told me that she couldn't wait to marry me." He winks.

"Oh, did she?" We fall into easy laughter together. Sometimes it is easier to laugh over something so painful, rather than to drown in our own tears. Laughter feels better in the moment, even though it can't cure what is happening to his mother. "So, you're having lunch with other women who want to marry you, yet you're a newlywed yourself. Hmm…"

Tony reaches his hand out to touch mine. "You know you never have anything to worry about Abigail. I mean, I know we're just joking around about my mom and all, but seriously, I hope you know, I will never cheat on you." His hazel eyes dance as they glare into mine, our hands holding from across the table.

"I know." I answer bashfully. "You're so good to me, Tony."

"I hope you always think so." Raising his left eyebrow, he kisses the top of my hand before pulling away to continue his meal.

"On that note…hurry and finish eating. I have a surprise for you!"

This time, both brows raise and I know what he is thinking. "Oh, you do, do you?" He questions, a gleeful look across his face.

"Not *that!* Get your head out of the gutter."

Placing his hands in the air, palms facing me he gives in, "Okay, okay. I just thought…" He winks.

"Well, it's a surprise. It's not *that*. It's something else. But I think you'll be excited."

"Okay, I'm intrigued." He shoves the last few bites of food into his mouth. After gulping down the food and taking another drink to finish his glass of water, he leans back. "Are you just going to leave me in suspense?"

I stand and grab both of our empty plates and place them in the sink before reaching beneath the counter to grab the gifts. I fill the white ceramic coffee mug with just enough Hennessy Black to cover up my lettering at the bottom of the cup. Tony's friend, Michael Wentwell gifted the bottle of Hennessy to us for our wedding and Tony loves the taste. He calls it a stylish original cognac. I haven't consumed alcohol more than a handful of times in my life and don't know much about alcohol options to boot. In my opinion, the drink has a jasmine floral-type scent. I'd tried it a week after our wedding, one night after dinner with Tony and it tasted like fresh grapes with a hint of honey and citrus flavors. Come to think of it, that might have been *the* night this all happened. I didn't particularly like a drink that tasted like what I thought should be the scent of a household cleaner, but Tony adored it. I placed the mug in front of him. "Drink up!"

Inquisitively, Tony stares at me before his eyes move back to the mug. "New mug?"

"I didn't think you'd notice." I smirk.

"I don't care what I drink this in, it's my new favorite indulgence. Won't you have some with me?"

I shake my head, sitting back and letting the wooden chair swallow me. "Not tonight. Go ahead. After you drink, I'll give you the gift."

"Oh, the surprise is a gift?" He picks up the mug, downing the liquid. "I'll drink to that. Hennessy Black poured by my beautiful wife and then a gift?" Tony closes his eyes as he lets the liquid trickle down his throat. "That is good." He can't help himself. The man loves the drink. I wouldn't be surprised if he'd thanked Michael for it every time he'd seen him since the wedding, three months ago. He places the mug back on the table and stares up at me, waiting for his gift. I want him to look inside of the mug, to see what I've written. I want him to ask me if I am pregnant. But instead, he just sits, smiling and waiting.

I clear my throat, hoping somehow that will prompt Tony to look into his cup. But my efforts are to no avail. I take the thin square box from my lap and place it in front of him. "For you." I beam. "But first, look inside of your mug...don't say anything. Just look. And then open the box."

Following instructions, Tony's eyes light up as he peers inside of the mug and reads what I've written.

YOU + ME = THREE

He pauses to look up at me before opening the box in front of him. His hazel eyes are sparkling after what he's just read. He opens his mouth, ready to speak.

"Nope. No. Open the box before you say anything." I prod.

He does as I say and turns his attention back to the box, although I see him peak up at me a half a dozen times before he pulls the lid off to reveal the contents. Tony stares into the box that sits open in front of him.

Inside of the box is a small white onesie. On the front of the onesie, written in black cursive lettering, says:

HELLO DAD!

I watch, feeling proud. Proud of the pregnancy. Proud of making him so happy. Proud of the creative way in which I've chosen to spring the news on him. Just, proud. Tony's mouth forms an O and he tries to speak several times before his words are accompanied by a sound. "Abigail," he gasps. "We're going to be parents?"

I nod and keep my eyes on his as he stands, holding the onesie in one hand and bending down to hug me with the other. "We're going to be parents!" I echo before letting my smiling lips find his. I am everything I am meant to be and I know it in this very moment. It feels good. I am a good wife. Tony is a good husband. We are going to be great parents. We are going to be a happy family. We are going to turn our parents into grandparents. It pains me to think that Tony's father is missing this and his mother, although still alive, is missing this too. It isn't fair to have a life cut too short, to miss out on big moments like this. I turn my attention back to the optimism and mirth that fills the room. This is a time to celebrate, a time to take it all in. This is our time as newlyweds and I don't want to let anything change that. Thinking of Tony's parents reminds me that we never know how long we have. Tomorrow is never promised to any of us. We must enjoy the here and now. And that's exactly what we're going to do. Tony, me and *our little peanut.*

Two

ANTHONY

Present Day, 2016

There must be thousands of candles lighting the walkways surrounding Saint Ann's Catholic Church. My eyes blur as I gaze around, realizing how the glow from the flames brings so much light in the darkness of the night. I clutch Gideon in my arms, a diaper bag held over my opposite shoulder. Gideon is also mesmerized by the light that overtakes the night. Abigail once called this place her home away from home. We went to Sunday Mass each week, we were married here. She went to CCD here. (In the

Catholic church CCD stands for the Confraternity of Christian Doctrine. It is a religious education program for children, provided by the church.) She was baptized here. She received first communion here. Her dad was the former principle of St. Ann's School. She'd volunteered at the school after graduating high school herself, helping special needs students. I could see why she felt it was a place she could call home. A lot had happened here. And now, if she only knew, we are holding a candle light vigil for her here. We are all here, with a thousand bright candles, praying and hoping for her safe return. For a moment I am so lost in thought I forget that Gideon is in my arms until he coos at the flickering flames and reaches his arms out toward their alluring dance.

A hand comes to rest on my shoulder and I turn, trying to force a grin. "How are you holding up honey?" Mrs. Botsworth, an elderly woman from the parish looks up at me with concern.

I nod and politely thank her for coming tonight.

"You'll find her soon Anthony. Hang in there." She leans forward to kiss my cheek and then Gideon's. Gideon begins to cry and Mrs. Botsworth waves good-bye as she files herself back into the crowd that has gathered in Abigail's name.

"Hey buddy." My friend Michael comes to stand

next to me. "Need a drink?" He offers up a shiny flask that he pulls from inside of his coat.

Shaking my head I nod toward Gideon who is still crying. "Thanks but no thanks." I answer.

We stand together. I let my eyes blur as Gideon's cries slow to a dull murmur against the muffled sounds of the crowd. As many candles as there are, there must be more people. On the opposite edge of the church I spot a news van. A female reporter with red hair is standing in front of the burning candles, poised toward the camera, telling the world, no doubt, that Abigail is still missing.

There are flyers going around with Abigail's photo. It's a photo from last Christmas, taken by her mom. I am cropped out and the picture shows Abigail's flawless face. Her ivory skin. Her lips blotted with a shade of red lipstick. Her shoulder length wavy black hair and her easy smile. Her big brown eyes are looking into the camera, telling the world that everything is perfect. Not in an overconfident kind of way, but in a natural one. In the photo her eyes are relaxed and I can tell she's just finished laughing. I wonder if her mom said something funny, or maybe she was laughing at something I'd said. I wish I could remember. The photo is a headshot. I remember she wore a red dress with a thin strand of white pearls her mother had given her on her sixteenth birthday. I drew in a deep breath of night air, wanting so badly to return to that day. To keep Abigail safe. To keep her with me. What am I missing? Where is she? Who has her? As my mind enters into the spirals of insanity once again, my attention is drawn to the right.

Lost in thought, I have forgotten Michael is standing next to me until he clears his throat, "Hey man…" he points and my throat catches as I see the sight coming toward me. My eyes fill with heaviness as Lois and Omar push a wheelchair that carries my mom, in my direction. Overcome with emotions I stand still as they approach. Michael offers to take Gideon from my arms, but that only makes me hold my son tighter. When my mother sits just a foot in front of me I drop to my knees and without a word I place Gideon in her arms.

"Oh, he is beautiful Anthony." She beamed. *Anthony.* She said my name. She knows who I am. She understands that this is *my* son. The tears fall from my face like a storm, soaking my cheeks with salt. Gideon holds still as his grandmother clutches him in her arms. Not wanting to lose my mother, I quickly grab her frail hand.

"Mom." I whisper. "Mom, we have to find Abigail." I bow my head, trying not to be consumed by the moment. The light of the candles filling the night. The crowd of people who had come for support. The prayers being said. My son in my arms. My missing wife. My mother sitting before me and remembering my name.

A tap on my shoulder shakes me back to life. As I turn I see Father Henry standing behind me. I glance back at my mom and then at Gideon in her arms. His little mouth has turned into a knotted frown and the wails began to pour out of his thin lips. At the same time my mom begins to shout, "Where am I? Someone tell me where I am? Where's Thomas? I need Thomas!" She grows more restless with each new word. My gaze bounces from Father Henry, to my mother, to Gideon, to Lois and Omar, to the candles surrounding us. I don't know where to turn. In a daze, I watch as Lois leans forward to remove Gideon from my mother's arms. Omar releases the brake on my mother's wheelchair and starts to move her a few feet away in what I assume is an attempt to calm her nerves. Father Henry looks bewildered as he offers his help. My world is spinning faster and faster and I am helpless to stop it.

I turn to say something to Father Henry, but find myself unable to form a proper word, only a line of random stutters that serve to furrow his brow. I wave

my hand and make my way over to where Omar
has wheeled my mother. Within the ten short steps it
would have taken to reach my mom, a man places his
hands on my shoulders and stands squarely in front of
me. "Excuse me, are you Anthony? Are you Abigail's
husband?"

I nod. "Yes." I answer, trying to look past him at
my mother who is still shouting questions at Omar.

"Anthony Parker?"

"Yes." I answer again, feeling agitated. Can't this
man tell that I need to tend to my mother?

"So *you're* Abigail's husband." He replies, matter-
of-factly.

I stop and look at the man. Something about the
way he's said those words sends a chill down my
spine. "I am." I state firmly, placing my chin a bit
higher than usual. "Do you know where Abigail is?"
I question hastily.

For a moment, the world around us goes radio
silent. I can't hear my mother's shouts. I can't hear
Gideon crying or the sounds of Lois comforting him.
I can't hear the murmur among the crowd that has
gathered for the vigil. I can no longer feel the weight
of Father Henry's glare on my back. I can only stare
back at the man who stands before me, asking me

about my wife as if he knows her. "Are you a friend of Abigail's?" I ask, my words slow.

He pauses and considers the question before answering. I am not sure what there was to think about. He either is or isn't an acquaintance of my wife's. "No."

"Then, how can I help *you*, Mr.-?" I draw out the Mister in hopes that he will introduce himself and maybe his name will ring a bell.

"I'm just passing through town and wanted to stop by and offer my condolences, Mr. Parker." He places emphasis on my name as if it leaves a bad taste on his tongue. "I've been following Abigail's disappearance on the news and…"

"What did you say your name was?" I interrupt.

He laughs. "I didn't." The man stands a foot taller than myself and has dark hair. It looks as if he hasn't seen a razor in at least a week.

"And your name?" I try again, growing incredibly impatient. I push my head back and feel my neck crack as I catch a glimpse of the stars resting above us.

The gruff man sticks out his hand in an attempt to shake mine like gentleman. "Any leads?"

"Excuse me?"

"Do you know who might have taken her? Or do you think she ran off? What do you think? What are your leads?" The questions roll off his tongue with ease.

"Are you a detective or something?" I ask, growing more defensive with each word he speaks.

"Na." He chuckles again. "Just a concerned citizen. You know, husbands are often responsible in these sort of cases." He winks and walks away, muttering something as he leaves about how the truth will come out eventually.

Father Henry is at my side once again, his hands placed on either side of my shoulders. "Walk with me."

I am plagued with nightmares. Tonight is no different. I am drenched in a cold sweat. The perspiration does not stop at my forehead, but covers every inch of my skin. I sleep only in my boxer shorts. I have one thin sheet pulled up to my waist, nothing more. Yet, I am trembling like a frightened child. I am dripping as if I just pulled myself out of a pool. I am gasping for air like someone has been holding me beneath the water's surface for too long. I am desperate for relief. My eyes still dart around our bedroom, hoping to find a clue, an answer. Hoping to find my wife.

I have woken in a panic, thinking I have heard Abigail knocking at the bedroom window, calling my name. I hear her voice as clear as day. She shouts for help as she taps against the glass. Racing to the window I pull back the curtains and scour the yard against the night sky. Abigail is not there. She is not here. I do not know where she is, despite what some are subtly and others not so subtly, accusing me of doing. I have lost my wife. Sitting back in bed does me no good. I throw the sheet off my nearly naked body and slide my bare feet into my sandals which are sitting near the full hamper, just at the edge of the bed. The hamper is always full now. Gideon goes through so many clothes. I put off doing laundry for as long as I can. Sometimes when Lois and Omar are at the house, Lois will do a few loads of laundry for me and for that I am always grateful.

I grab the black flash light that is stored in the top drawer of our dresser, hidden beneath my dress socks. As I push the dresser drawer closed, I hold the flash light in my opposite hand and shake it to confirm there are indeed batteries inside. I slide the button to turn it on and watch as a dull light illuminates itself from the device. I try my best to walk softly as I pad down the linoleum floor in the hall. I hold my breath as I go past Gideon's room, careful not to wake him in the middle of the night. I make it to the kitchen and still opt to use my flashlight rather than chance turning on an overhead light. I push the sliding glass door open that leads from the kitchen to the fenced back yard and shine my dim light around the yard as I continue to walk out into the dark. "Abigail?" I whisper at first. "Are you there?" The night air is chilly against my bare chest. I detect the sound of rustling debris beyond the fence. Probably a family of raccoons or some other small animal running from the sound of my voice, I think. "Abigail?" My voice grows louder with each new call. Logically, I know my wife is not hiding in our small backyard, in the middle of the night. I know this. But something inside of me is making me check to be sure. If the neighbors hear me, they'll think I've lost my mind. I don't care. I miss my wife. If I need to call for her in the middle of the night, so be it. They don't know what this feels like. They don't know how terrified I am. They just don't know. I hear myself sigh as I wish I didn't know what it felt like, either. "Is anyone there?" Now my voice has grown to a full shout. I have nearly reached the back right corner of the yard. Next, I will walk to the left back corner. I will check the entire yard. I have to before I can go back inside. Glancing back up at the house from the rear of the yard, I see the open sliding glass door. I hear the crickets chirping all around me. There are several clusters of stars in the sky hanging just above our little roof. The moon is covered by a thick night cloud. It all looks so peaceful and serene; our own little slice of Heaven. Only, I know that reality can't be escaped. And reality is that I am losing my mind. I have a child inside who may never know his mother. We bought this house for us, for our family. It is not complete without Abigail. I reach the left corner of our backyard and of course Abigail is not there, either. Defeated, I hang my head and stumble back to the house and slip into the open sliding glass door. The batteries in my flashlight must be dying because the light flickers a few more times and then goes dark. "Useless piece of crap!" I mutter to myself as I toss the flashlight into a kitchen drawer. I turn to close and lock the sliding glass door before leaving the kitchen and heading back to bed. Going to bed is one of the worst parts of life now. I always keep Abigail's side of the bed made, her covers tucked in neatly until she returns to us. Sometimes I swear I can see the indent from her head, in the contours of her white pillow case that rests beside mine. Sometimes I wake in the morning thinking I smell a hint of her shampoo next to me, although I always wake to emptiness. To her absence.

I walk through the kitchen, into the living room and turn toward the hallway, careful to keep my steps quiet. Before I get past the living room, I hear a rustling at the front door. Pausing something catches in my throat. Is someone there? The door makes a sound. I know it is locked, but it sounds as if someone is jiggling the doorknob. Could they be? At this hour? I glance at the small digital clock glowing with blue numbers just beneath the quiet black television screen. It is three thirty in the morning. My heart begins to race as I quickly think about what I should do next. Do I hold the doorknob and say nothing so that the intruder knows I am on the other side? Do I rush back to the bedroom, grab my phone and call 9-1-1? Do I wake Gideon? His bedroom faces the front of the house and although I'm sure I locked his window and closed his curtain, I am petrified someone will take him from me the way they've taken my wife. Could it be Abigail trying to come home? She wouldn't have a key. Her purse and all of her belongings are still here because she disappeared without a trace. Am I having another nightmare? Is any of this real? I decide to walk toward the door. I will put my hand on the knob to make sure this is happening. I feel the wetness on the palm of my hand when I grasp the door handle. And then it moves. Someone is trying to come inside of our house. I hold tightly even though I know the door is locked in two places. The deadbolt is secure and the chain lock is on. I've always thought of our neighborhood as a safe one. With Abigail missing and now this, whatever this is, I'm beginning to think otherwise. I should give up wondering why this is happening and just focus on keeping what's left of our family together. But my wife is missing and there isn't a trace of her to be found. And now there's someone at our door in the middle of the night. Our happy little world has fallen apart so quickly. We don't have a peephole on our door or else I would steal a glance. I want to go to the front window in the living room and get a look, but I'm too scared to leave the door. I hear the heavy heaving of my own breaths. The doorknob has stopped moving and so I hop over the couch and rush to the front window to see if I can figure out who is outside. I pull back the thick curtain and catch a glimpse of a figure in all black. I can't tell for sure but it looks as if they are carrying a large camera. My body sighs, realizing it was probably just someone looking for a photo of the Parker house that they could sell to the media.

The day after Abigail went missing, when the media caught wind of her disappearance, they came in swarms to our front lawn. I kept the shades drawn and we stayed indoors, only coming and going when we absolutely had to. We used the garage, so we didn't have to fight the crowd walking up to our own doorstep. But when police made it clear that I, her husband, may have nothing to do with Abigail's disappearance, the media faded away quickly, off to chase another story. The police had warned me, however, that if public opinion, or if their ongoing search lead them to believe I had anything at all to do with my wife's disappearance, they would not put a halt to the media frenzy. If public opinion was changing, as it was beginning to feel as of late, the tides might be changing. The media might be back with a vengeance this time. Media outlets love a good *husband murders wife* story. But they won't find that here. They won't find anything but a husband desperately looking for his wife, frantic to hold onto his sanity.

"Mr. Parker?" A voice questioned.

"Mr. Parker?" Another echoed the first.

"Mr. Parker, do you know where your wife is? You sell life insurance Mr. Parker, correct? Did you murder your wife, Abigail, for money?"

"Can we have a moment of your time Anthony?"

"Mr. Parker, do you have any idea where your wife is? Do you have any leads?"

"What are you doing to help in the search for your wife, sir?"

"Do you believe your wife is still alive?"

"Did someone take your wife? Does she have any enemies?"

The questions fall around me like autumn leaves as I grasp Gideon in my arms, pressing his face into my chest in an attempt to shield him from the vengeance of the reporters who think they've found a story to put themselves into the spotlight. We are in our driveway, trying to get to our car which I'd parked outside the night before. We are on our way to Sunday service. My silver Honda Accord is oozing with runny egg yolks and the reporters are swarming like an angry hive of bees that have been antagonized. Their questions don't even make sense. If I had a lead, wouldn't the police be on it? If I murdered my wife, wouldn't I have run away and hidden myself somewhere? If I knew that someone wanted to harm my wife, the police would know that, too. The reporters are so desperate for a story, but the only story here is one of an innocent husband doing his best to hold everything together while his wife is missing. Isn't that a story enough in itself? Why do they have to blame the husband? There is absolutely no evidence that I've done anything wrong. I told the police from the start that I am willing to cooperate with them in any way they think would be helpful. Of course, I hired a lawyer to make sure my rights were looked after. I offered to take a lie-detector test at any time. I have given them every bit of information I can recall. In my mind, we are a team; the police and me. We all want to find Abigail, so why shouldn't we be a team? Of course I'm a little skeptical of their motives when I wake up to find a lawn full of reporters, once again ready to pounce on me for their next meal. I suppose the police may be a little skeptical of me, too. Just like the great Agatha Christie mystery novels, no one ever knows who to really trust. No one ever really knows what secrets the others are hiding from them. I get that. And I respect that the media and the police want to check every angle of the case, including me: the husband. If only I could make it clear to them that they do not need to waste their time looking at me. Oh, I'd so much rather they look into *real* leads. If I am so blunt to say that to them, however, I know it will only turn them on me like a pack of angry wolves. There is no manual in existence that tells a man how to behave or how to cope with this situation I am in. How does an innocent man keep hoping for the best? How will I ever find my wife if everyone decides to turn against me? I don't want them to stop looking. I won't stop looking, I can't. Every night I scour the internet for any possible lead. Neither of us ever had a Facebook account, but I've created one now called FIND ABIGIAL PARKER and there are already over a million *Likes* since the story of her disappearance went national. We've held candlelight vigils, we've held large volunteer search teams in all of the local forests and wooded areas. We've sent divers into the lakes and rivers throughout the county. We've plastered my wife's photo on every telephone pole, in every grocery store, on every news station, on internet sites for missing persons...I am doing everything I can think of, everything I know how to do. If there is something else I can do that will help me find my wife, I wish someone would tell me. No one has any answers and as frustrated as they think they feel about the case, they want to turn against someone and they must figure that I am an easy target; the husband.

Last night, I picked up my wife's e-reader. It's sat lifeless on her nightstand since she disappeared. At first, I felt full of guilt for touching her device. We never looked at each other's phones or checked up on each other in this way; it wasn't how our relationship was structured. I shouldn't snoop. But it's been too long. I have to now. If there is a clue on here, I can't leave it unseen. I scroll through the books she'd read or was reading, hoping that something would speak to me or maybe give me a clue into her thoughts in those weeks leading up to her kidnapping. The books were mostly of the romance genre. I saw a book by Martha Beck, a collection of essays for creating your right life; an uplifting, inspiring read. I saw a few mystery books, but nothing that made me think that Abigail was trying to learn how to protect herself from someone who was making her nervous. Of course there were countless books on pregnancy and caring for a new baby. I don't know if I'd been hoping to find a book titled something like, "How to Keep Yourself Safe". I really don't know what I was looking for. I was grabbing at straws, because there was nothing left to grab. What more could I do but wait, hope and pray? I talk to Gideon every day about his beautiful mother, even though I am sure he can't understand a word of what I am saying to him. I keep telling him how amazing his mom is. I keep telling our son that his mom and dad both love him so much. I tell him that we'll find her soon. I tell him that she used to call him "our little peanut". And I weep when I tell him, every single day, how much I miss her and how much she means to me and to our little family.

I try not to allow myself to become too agitated with the reporters as I carefully place Gideon into his car seat. I close the door and watch his wide innocent blue eyes staring up at the reporters. At the moment, they fascinate him with their expensive cameras and bulky equipment. Elbows shove at me as I press against my car and reach for the driver side door handle. The questions haven't stopped, but I've blocked them from my mind. My lawyer has instructed me to keep quiet and to say nothing at all if this should happen. It's happening and I'm heeding his advice, my lips are in a thin tight line as I climb into the car with our son and lock the doors, even though I know locking them can't keep us safe anymore. Pressing the lock button is only a farce, a pretend peace of mind. The reporters are banging on the car windows and as I turn the engine to life and creep the car backwards to attempt leaving my own driveway. I am consumed with hate for their witch hunt. I am not the enemy, but we each think the other is the one doing wrong.

Gideon begins to cry and I know how it goes. It starts out as a slow whine and will quickly progress to a blood curling wail. It is coming and his breakdown will be in full swing, I am certain, before we are out of our own driveway. We need to make it to Sunday service. It is, after all, the place Abigail called her home away from home. We need to be where Abigail would want to be. We need to be as near to her as we possibly can. I don't know how else to do that except to place myself in our home or in church. I try to stick to our normal routine as much as possible, but nothing is normal anymore. The shouting reporters aren't normal. My wife disappearing out of nowhere is not normal. Eating dinner without Abigail is so far from normal. All of this cannot possibly be my new normal. I can't accept it. I won't. If the reporters won't help me find my wife, if the police are letting the media place the blame where there isn't any, I'll have to find another way to search for her myself. Someone needs to be doing something productive. Someone needs to find a legitimate lead. I have no idea what to do next, but I'll think of something. I have to, what other choice do I have if I want to find my wife? Unlike the rest of the world, I don't care about a story filled with twists and turns and drama. I care about finding Abigail and bringing her back to her home, safe and alive.

Three

ABIGAIL

2015

Although she is not the size of a peanut yet, I've started calling our child, *little peanut*. I am seven weeks pregnant now. My baby's heart has formed her webbed fingers and toes are developing. All of the books say that our little peanut is the size of a blueberry. A blueberry! So small, yet she will grow into a human being, which is beyond amazing. Using an old earring box, I placed a single blueberry inside and set the box at Tony's chair for dinner. On the top of the box lid, when the box is opened, I write *our baby is a blueberry!*

Two days ago I am certain I started to get morning sickness. They never show this sort of thing on television or in the movies. Mothers and mothers-to-be are always happy and peaceful looking, never draped over a toilet trying to pull themselves together. I began feeling a bit queasy at the end of last week and dismissed it to something I'd eaten, but now I am sure it is morning sickness; although the nausea is not strict about sticking to the morning hours. It strikes me at any time, day or night. I ordered something called Preggie Pops online at Babies-R-Us yesterday and they should arrive today or tomorrow. It is made with natural ingredients and calms the morning sickness. The online reviews swear by these things, but I'll believe it when it actually works for me. I wonder if it will do anything to help with the fatigue that accompanies this nausea and vomiting routine. I really hope it does. I don't have a lot of friends my age, as my time has been spent at church, with my parents or devoting myself to my husband, so I don't have anyone to really talk to as far as comparing pregnancies or what to look for in the coming weeks and months as the baby develops. That's why I've been reading a lot of books. I have an entire stack I checked out from the library and I have all of the time in the world each day. As long as I keep the house clean and prepare the meals, I can read the rest of the day away and fill up with helpful (and admittedly, sometimes frightening) information on the pregnancy, delivery, and the first year of our baby's life. Sometimes when I'm reading I fall asleep on the couch, only to quickly wake within the hour, jolted by the fear that Tony will return home from work and I'll be lazily napping the day away, without dinner warm and ready on the table. I know what you're thinking, that it's terrible for a husband in this day and age to expect a wife to cater to him and cook for him. But it's the arrangement we've made and it works for us. It wasn't because of his demands, it was the way we'd both grown up; it was how both of our parents had been and how we wanted our own family to be. We each had our own roles and albeit they were traditional roles, we both knew what we expected from the other and the lines didn't get blurred. The housework and cooking are mine. The money for bills and insurance are his. Maybe one day we would evolve and change our ways, but in all honesty, I didn't see that happening. I wanted to be a good wife and he wanted to be a good husband. We both wanted to be good for each other.

Walking back to the kitchen I move the box with the small blueberry just slightly to the right. It looks better there, although I've moved the box over less than a half-an-inch from where I first placed it. Smiling, I hear myself humming as life pulses through me like a warm generator. I am doing everything right. The wife thing. The mother-to-be-thing. As I hum, strolling through the kitchen, putting the dishes from the clean dishwasher away to their rightful places, I think of the Kacey Musgraves song, "Follow Your Arrow" and begin humming its catchy tune. The song talks about how quick people are to label other people and how, no matter what you do in life, you'll be labeled, so you may as well do what you want. In the song, the singer says if you don't go to church you're a horrible person and if you do go to church and sit in the front pew the world calls you a goody-goody, something along those lines. That's me, a goody-goody. I've been called it before once or twice and never took it as a slight. It's who I am. It feels good to be good, to fulfill my role in life to my best ability. Maybe I'm corny. Or maybe it's the pregnancy. Whatever it is, right now I feel good, dancing around the kitchen with clean dishes and utensils in my hands. The world is at my fingertips and no one can take it from me. I feel alive. I am grateful not to be nauseous at this moment. I am happy, and isn't that what we all want; happiness? If only I could capture this feeling in a bottle and spray it on myself like perfume whenever I need a little lift, that would be grand. But happiness can't be captured, only enjoyed. So I'll hang onto it as long as I can. I'll keep dancing in the kitchen, barefoot and humming. This goody-goody has a little blueberry growing inside of her and surely that is enough happiness to last a lifetime.

It's Wednesday and normally on Wednesday's I do what I do on all the weekdays while Tony is away at work, selling insurance. I scrub the toilets. The floors are vacuumed and steamed. I take everything out of the refrigerator and wipe down the shelves. I wipe and sanitize all of the kitchen and bathroom counters and I check all of the windows to make sure there are no smudges or fingerprints. I make my own cleaner for the windows; a simple mixture of distilled white vinegar, water and an essential oil to dilute the scent of vinegar. I usually use a lemon scent. It works well, hardly costs anything and it is better for our health and the environment (no toxic chemicals). I'd found the do-it-yourself ingredient list for the window cleaner on the internet shortly after we were married and I've been using it ever since. I'm not a total health nut, but I do like to do the best I can at any given task and being a wife and mother is no different for me. I want to be the best I can be; which means learning about safe cleaners for the home and keeping a variety of vegetables in the rotation of meals I prepare.

I usually do the cleaning in the morning; take a break for a short lunch, usually a turkey sandwich and some fruit with a glass of water. And then I begin preparing dinner and I pack a lunch for Tony to take to work with him the following day. I listen to the radio a lot when I'm cleaning or preparing meals. Sometimes I listen to audio books, too. I always enjoy a good mystery novel. I've just recently finished listening to *The Betrayal* by Laura Elliot. By the time I'm done preparing meals, Tony is usually home. If I finish early I use that time to read my baby-to-be books. I want to have as much knowledge as I can so that I can try and be prepared for our little peanut's arrival.

Today instead of eating lunch alone at home, I am meeting my parents at First Watch. We haven't told them about the pregnancy yet. We plan to share the news that they will soon be grandparents once we're past the eight week mark; and we want to tell them together. Tony doesn't have his own parents to tell and I want him to feel as excited as I do to tell mine. Because of the lunch with my parents I will be starting dinner preparations late today. I have already packed Tony's lunch for tomorrow and placed the brown bag in the refrigerator. For dinner, I'm making chicken noodle soup in the Crockpot, which I've already turned on and we'll be having deluxe grilled cheese sandwiches, too. I've already made the homemade white bread for the sandwiches, so it will only take a small amount of time to cook them on the cast iron skillet when I return home. I'll have plenty of time, I reassure myself, trying to choke back the anxiety that creeps into my skin as I pull out a chair across from my parents at the restaurant table.

"Abigail, you look well." My dad glances at my outfit and then up to my face and hair. I am wearing a casual pale blue dress that reaches just above my knees. The top has a collar around the neck and three petite decorative buttons. I am wearing my black hair loose, as I usually do. It falls just past my shoulders in waves. My face is dotted with a hint of mascara and a touch of red lip stick, my signature look. My dad makes a comment about my appearance every time we see each other. Sometimes I *look well.* Other times, by his judgment, I look *healthy*; which I always take to mean that I look a bit pudgy. It's something in the way he says the word healthy, the hesitation he makes just before the word leaves his mouth. At times he'll tell me I look tired or run down. So looking *well* is the highest form of compliment coming from him.

"Thank you, dad." I reply studying his thinning gray hair and wondering when it turned from black to silver and when the baldness on the top of his head began. "Hi Mom." I turn my gaze to my mother's pale blue eyes. Her hair matches my dad's in color, only it is thick, full and pulled back into a neat low bun. She is wearing the gray scarf I gave her last year for her birthday; it looks nice in contrast to the black top she has on.

"Hi dear." She meets my eyes and with a lack of enthusiasm focuses her attention to placing a straw into her glass of Pepsi.

"Did you hear that Michelle Lindrum is having her second child?" My dad's attempt at starting a conversation.

Feigning interest, I try to force a smile as I nod my head. "Good for her." My parents were always reporting updates on the lives of others my age who I'd gone to school or CCD with. They were people

I had fallen out of touch with years ago or that I'd never been close with at all (or even had a conversation with). Yet, my parents loved to give me the updates as if they were reporting breaking news. They especially loved to tell me who was having children and how many; their way, I am certain, of letting me know they are ready for grandchildren of their own.

"Also, Norman Munchins mother passed away. Breast cancer." My mother added, shaking her head.

I nod, looking back and forth at each of them. They will continue with the reports at least until our food is served. I am grateful when the waitress arrives to take our order. I order a plain omelet with cheese and spinach with a side of hash browns.

"Breakfast for lunch?" My dad questions, raising his silver eye brows and bringing a dozen wrinkles marching to his forehead.

"I'm just in the mood for an omelet today." I smile, knowing the conversation will quickly turn back to reports of marriages, babies and deaths. And without missing a beat, my mother chimes in, letting me know that my assumption is correct.

"Sally Harvey's husband has been cheating on her and they're getting a divorce. It's especially heartbreaking because they have two children under the age of five. How are they going to raise two little ones in two separate households? I don't know how divorced couples do it…" Her words continue to flow as I allow myself to drift off in a daydream, careful to keep nodding my head and moving my eyes to each parent every once and a while. Maybe it's part of the pregnancy; this daydreaming thing. I've noticed I've been doing it more and more. I've also been having strange dreams; the type of dreams where you wake wondering if it was real or imagined. Sometimes the dreams are pleasant and I am running through a flowery meadow and when I come to a stream I dip my legs in its cool water and lay my head back into the tall grass giving my weight to its embrace. The warm rays of sun hitting my face, the gentle breeze dancing against my skin and the babble of the stream leave me blissfully happy. But other nights the dreams are terrors. I am being chased by a man who has been watching me. I am running as fast as I can but I can't get away. I never see the man's face; it's always dark or covered. The dreams are always dramatic in one way or another. I want to ask my mom if she remembers having nightmares when she was pregnant with me, but they are still reporting their list of updates and shaking their heads. I cannot interrupt. Perhaps I'll ask her another time.

A few minutes later the waitress brings out our food and sets the warm plates in front of each of us. "Does everything look to your liking?" She asks.

"Yes, thank you." I answer before I hear my mother asking for a new glass of water and my dad asking for more napkins to be brought to the table.

"I heard that Chuck Palmento moved to Florida and he's getting engaged to the Tina girl he's been dating for a few years. Good for him. Poor boy, you broke his heart. I didn't know if the boy would ever get over you." My mother's eyes meet mine. She had always liked Chuck and she'd never stopped bringing him up in conversation since the two of us went steady in fifth grade, for five weeks. It was a million years ago, but she would never let it go. She was well aware that Chuck was my first kiss and for whatever reason, she wished that I had stayed with Chuck. A long shot, I always thought. A fifth grade romance (if you can call it that) leading to marriage. I almost laugh out loud at the thought. Chuck and I were never meant to be. But he came from a proper family. His parents vote the way my parents do. They attend our parish. Chuck's mother taught at Saint Ann's where my dad was the principal. The family has donated substantial money to the church. In my mom's heart, she always hoped I'd end up with

Chuck. She loved Tony, I knew that, but there was always something about Chuck that tugged at her heartstrings.

"Our little heartbreaker." My dad chuckles before grabbing his next bite of mashed potatoes.

"And what about Gram Nelson, speaking of heartbreakers?" My mom's eye brows rise, showing interest. "That boy was a looker!" Her face grows flush.

"If you liked him so much, you should have dated him." I am quick to answer and after the words had been said I bite down on my tongue, something I should have done before I've spoken.

My mother's mouth forms an O in shock at my all too quick and unexpected comeback. "Someone's on edge." She tosses a look my way. "Or have I touched a nerve?"

Narrowing my eyes I look from my dad to my mom. "Hardly, mom. It's just that I shouldn't have to remind you, I'm married. To Tony." I add, ready to return home. I don't know what I've expected. This is fairly typical of our meals together. Me listening, them reporting. Why do I ever think it will change? Did I really think that because I am pregnant, that the conversation would somehow turn more uplifting? That the conversation would focus on us, on our family, instead of on random gossip about the rest of the world? I guess I had thought that. My mistake. Tony's skin would crawl if he heard my parents bringing up Chuck or Gram. He hated talking about our former lives, before we met each other. Especially when the conversation turned to others that we'd dated. Hearing them bring up the past makes me feel uneasy, unfaithful in some way, although I am not doing anything wrong. I am merely having lunch with my parents. And, for the most part, politely listening. Having lunch with my parents often reminds me of how picky and strict they'd been while I was growing up. Tony had been such a relief. Right from the start he put me on a golden pedestal and always told me how much he appreciated me. Instead of picking on me to be better, he praised me for being me and that felt good, like a breath of fresh air.

An outsider might believe that my parents are gentle and kind. After all, they met on a mission trip for the church, in Botswana. They do have big hearts, but I would not use the words gentle or kind to describe them as individuals or as a couple. My dad went from a student on mission trips to becoming the principal of Saint Ann's Catholic School. Although he is now retired, he still attends church every Sunday and holds himself and those around him to a strict book of rules. Those rules are his firm interpretation of *God's will*. I was raised in a no-nonsense traditionalist home under the strict influence of the Catholic religion. My mom agreed with everything my dad said and did. My dad is full of advice. While growing up, I was told, "We've got to get braces on your teeth young lady. If we don't get braces for you we'll never get you married off." My other favorites included, "Girls with slouched backs won't be tolerated in this house. Keep straight and be dainty like a proper lady." And "...life is meaningless without children," which makes me wonder now if my dad thinks my mom is useless now that her only child is grown. And maybe one of my favorites was this one: "Find a proper boy to take care of you, and find one sooner rather than later." But all I ever saw growing up was my mom taking care of me and my dad. So why should I have found a boy to take care of me? Don't we take care of each other? Isn't that what a relationship is? As my parents eat their meals and shake their heads at the news they are reporting to me, my head shakes in unison with theirs, only I'm shaking mine at the past.

At the earlier mention of Gram's name I think back to our seven month relationship, prior to meeting Tony. Gram did a brief stint of volunteering at Saint

Ann's, which is how we met. By brief, I mean to say seven months. We started dating soon after we met. We had both been trying to grab for a highlighter in the school's supply closet when our hands brushed against each other's and prompted a clumsy conversation. I felt a shock of electricity pulse through me from the first touch and for seven months we were inseparable. With wavy blond hair and bright blue eyes, he is the physical opposite of Tony's dark buzzed hair and deep hazel eyes. As time moved forward our relationship grew serious and when Gram proposed to me and I hesitated, it ended. It wasn't an immediate break-up, but it was a whirlwind. One moment we were together and everything was great, the next it all fell apart. We broke up. He quit volunteering and that was the end of us. A month later I met Tony at a charity dinner and silent auction fundraiser for the local Big Brothers Big Sisters organization. My heart mended as I focused my energy and attention on new love and life went on, as it always does. Gram was always pushing me to become more independent, to be a little wild and crazy; to think about really opening up my own jewelry shop. But Tony liked me just as I was; as I am. With Tony there was no pressure, things were easier. I shake my mind back to the present moment as I hear my mom call out my name more than once.

"Abigail?"

"Yes?" I answer brightly, realizing I have finished my omelet and am ready to move on to my dish of hash browns. I squirt a dab of ketchup onto the plate for dipping and reach for my fork.

"You seem a bit distant this afternoon. Is everything okay?" My mom only asks questions when she smells gossip. She's like a hound dog, with a nose to find the buried bone in any situation.

"Of course." I reply a little too quickly. Her eyes find mine and drop to my stomach and then back up to meet my smile. She's on to me. She knows. But Tony and I want to tell my parents together, I don't want her to spoil the surprise. "Just a little tired" I add, trying to find a way to throw her off the scent.

"Tired? Are you nauseous too?"

My dad turns to my mom and asks her why she's being a pest. She waves him away and he returns to his meal, oblivious to our hidden conversation that sits between the spoken words.

"No. Why do you ask?" I do my best to sound innocent.

"You do have quite a good appetite today." Her eyes move to my empty plate.

"I didn't eat breakfast. I was hungry." I shrug and then find an invisible hair on my dress and pretend to pick it off and toss it to the side.

Moments later our plates our cleared and my dad pays the bill.

"Thank you for lunch dad." We all stand, I grab my purse and we head toward the exit door.

"My treat, honey." He pats my back and wraps his arm around my shoulders as we push open the door and move to the outdoors. There is not a single cloud in the sky as we walk to our cars. My dad is talking about oil changes and gas prices, his arm still around me while my mom is walking off to the side a few feet away, stumbling through her purse in an attempt to find the car keys. A chill runs down my spine as I look to the left and see a man wearing a black leather jacket and dark glasses. Is he staring at me? I look away, still feeling the weight of his gaze on my face. When we reach the car, my dad hugs me and closes the door for me as I turn on the engine. "Don't forget to lock the doors." It's another one of those things he always says. I see my mother nodding from behind as she dangles the car keys from one hand and waves to me with the other. I wave back before putting the car in reverse.

"Love you." I roll down the window and wave

back. I see my parents at least once a week, in addition to every Sunday at church. But we still say I love you every time we leave. With all of the interest in local gossip, they are always quick to remind me that we can't predict the future and we never know what will happen each time we leave each other. I always think they are being a bit crazy, but then I realize they are growing older; we all are, and there are no guarantees. So we say I love you each time we leave, because we never know when it might be our last. A grim outlook on life? Maybe, but we say the words regardless. We are a family no matter how old we are.

I turn out of the parking lot and check my rear view mirror. I see my parents slowly pulling out of the opposite exit of the parking lot; they are heading to the grocery store. A chore my mom used to do alone, now they do together. I am waiting for an opening to come in traffic before I can pull out and as I glance back in my rear view mirror once again, I see the man in the black jacket and dark glasses. He is in the car behind me. When I turn right, he turns right too. At the first light, when I turn right again, he follows. There is less than an inch between our cars. My heart begins to pound as I reach to turn the radio down. I need silence. I need to think. Is this man really following me or am I being paranoid? I make three more turns, just to check, and still, he follows closely. I reach to grab my sunglasses, not wanting him to see my eyes peering at him in the mirror, but when I look again before my glasses are on, he smirks at me. He knows that I am checking on him. I look at my dashboard and see that my gas tank is on empty. Tony always fills the gas for me. I hate going to gas stations. He must have forgotten to fill up the car this week, he's been putting in extra hours by going into the office on Saturday's since he found out we're pregnant. I am no more than three miles from home. I am hoping the man in black will turn off and I will be free of him soon. If not, I'll have to go home with him on my tail and I don't want this man to see where I live. Even if he's just out for a joy ride (do adult men do that?) I don't want this stranger knowing where I live. Tony still won't be home for hours. The car begins to beep, alerting me that I am on low fuel. My anxiety spikes, pulsing through my skin. I have to head home. I turn left at the next light as does the man in black. When I can see our house in the distance I check my rear view mirror once again and to my relief, the man is gone. Reaching the driveway I press the button to open the garage door, still looking around to be sure I am not being followed. It must have been a coincidence, that's all. I draw in a deep breath as I pull into the safety of the garage and watch the door close tight behind me before I open my car door. My nightmares have been feeling more real lately, but I don't want them to make me paranoid to live life. They're only nightmares, after all. I am safe eating lunch with my parents. I am safe in my own home.

Four

ANTHONY

Present Day, 2016

Never in my life did I think I would use the term *private investigator* when referring to myself. Life is never really what we expect, I am learning. We cannot control what happens, only how we react to the things that do occur. Lois and Omar have hired an investigator to search for Abigail, since the police and the media are not getting anywhere. It has been four months. Four incredibly long grueling months. And we still have no leads. The media has grabbed onto me as their lead, convinced ours is another husband murders wife and dumps her in the lake story. I don't know how many ways I can assure them this is not that story. I am not that guy. I love my wife. I love our child. I would never knowingly do something to put either of them in harm's way, believe me. Admittedly, at first I was worried that the Atwell's hired the private investigator to follow me. There have been those small moments, especially in the last month or so when Lois and Omar will say something that insinuates I know something about Abigail's disappearance and I'm withholding information. If anything, at least the investigator will disprove the all too popular belief that I had anything to do with Abigail's disappearance. On a more hopeful note, I would love for private investigator Todd Blaine to find my wife and bring her back to us safely; at the very least, I hope he can start finding viable clues to lead us to her. I will follow a trail of breadcrumbs if I have to. Anything to help us find Abigail; although I hope we find her sooner rather than later. Each day that passes weighs me down more. I know it is having the same heavy impact on the Atwell's. There is no way to escape the constant bubbling pressure that is felt when your loved one is missing. It's like a terrible blister beneath your toenail, giving you constant pain. Every step you take, you feel the blister. You always want it to pop and heal. I always hope we will be given a clue to help us find her. But much like a nagging blister, the pain will never stop until she is found. I spend every day wishing for our yesterdays, not able to live in the present or in the future because I need her with me. If only we could go back to our yesterdays. If only we could have a do-over and I could keep Abigail safe in my arms and free from harm. The *if onlys* are piling up as the clock keeps ticking.

With all of the technology in today's world, how can my wife be missing for four months? There are cameras at stop-lights and in gas stations. We have cell phones with tracking devices. Credit cards and checks can be traced. It's been one hundred and twenty three days without her. One hundred and twenty three days that she's been dead somewhere or is being tortured by someone. I can hardly bear either thought. Abigail is so innocent and naive. She is so sweet and trusting. She is, I realize now, the perfect target of a heinous crime. How did I not realize this before? How did I not realize how fragile she is? My thoughts are taking over as they do these days, but before they can go any further I am interrupted by the ring on my office phone. I am at work, sitting in my small windowless office on my lunch break, with no lunch. I have a bottle of Ice Mountain water and a bottle of Pepsi on my desk. Both are still unopened. I haven't had much of an appetite and I know I am losing weight because I have to wear a belt with all of my pants and my shirts make me appear to be a child wearing my father's attire. Friends from church and work bring over Tupperware containers full of casseroles; our refrigerator is filled with enough to feed an army. It's not for lack of food that I am losing weight.

"Anthony Parker" I answer professionally.

It is one of my existing clients, Andrew Germain, wanting to raise the amount on his and his wife's life insurance policies. He also wants to know who he should speak to in order to create a will and trust. I pull up his information in the computer system and let him know I'll send him a quote in two weeks. I follow up by offering him the name and number of an individual within our office who works on wills and trusts. Before we hang up, my client stumbles on his words before saying, "I'm really sorry about your wife, having gone missing and all.

No one ever really knows what to say and sadly I'm getting used to these awkward exchanges. I am just grateful when they are kind words, when someone tries to understand what I am feeling, rather than insisting I murdered my wife or that I have Abigail hidden away somewhere. I have lost some clients because of the media firestorm, but I have kept a lot of them too. I think the people who call me a murderer or who believe I am in some way responsible for my wife's disappearance only do so out of their own fear. They don't know me. They don't know us as a couple or a family. They just need an answer for their own hearts and minds. They want to think that it was *the husband* because then they can sleep better at night, telling themselves that there is not a kidnapper on the loose, telling themselves that they have a good spouse who would never hurt them; telling themselves that they are not us and they will never be. "I'm just really sorry. I hope you find her soon."

I thank him for his words and as we end our call I fight back the tears that try to force themselves forward. I open my warm bottle of water and take a drink, a lousy attempt at distracting myself. In this business, I understand that there is a level of comfort people have in securing life insurance policies, wills and trusts. But from personal experience, I can now say that no amount of money can buy the security everyone is looking for. No amount of money can promise to keep us and our loved ones safe from harm's way. Surely money can help with expenses when the unthinkable strikes, but it cannot, in any way, ease the emotional pain.

I used to feel so excited for my work, for the prospect of earning a good living through insurance sales. I used to feel a lightness when I thought about the future; our growing family. And now I'm destroyed; the feeling only grows with each passing day. After taking another sip of warm water I look down at my desk and realize I did not place the office phone fully back into its cradle. I wiggle the phone to make it fit and as I do my elbow hits the bottle of water. I had not replaced the cap on the bottle and the liquid quickly takes over my desk, spilling on my array of statements and papers. I hear myself gasp as I pick up the bottle, realizing it has already emptied itself all over my things. I grab my soaked papers and toss them to the safety of the dry floor, knowing they are ruined and that I have no one to blame but myself. I have never been a person who is quick to anger but I have become one. There is only so much a person can take before they burst. And I am beginning to burst. I can't take it anymore. My dad is not here to help. My mom is rotting away in the nursing home, never knowing who she is or what is happening to her poor mind. My wife has been missing for one hundred and twenty three days. I am raising my young son, alone. I eat very little, when I do eat, I have meals given to me by community members and strangers, from Tupperware containers. My son cries, a lot. I do not know if he misses his mother or if he just enjoys a good scream and wail; either way, the sound is horrendous and I go to bed with a throbbing head every night. I dodge media and other naysayers nearly every time I leave the house. Our quiet little brick house that was meant to be the place we raised our family has been egged, toilet papered, littered with hate signs, and riddled with media personnel and protestors. I have terrible nightmares when I do fall asleep, but mostly I stay awake and think about where Abigail might be and how I can find her. Where would a deranged kidnapper take my wife? Is she within our town? Our state? Our country? With as long as it has been, she could be anywhere.

I pull my black plastic waste basket out from beneath my desk and cup my hands together, brushing the water on top of my desk into the bucket. Once the bulk of water has made its way into the bin, I break off a wad of paper towels from the roll that sits in my bottom drawer and finish drying the mess. I'd forgotten about the roll of paper towels until now. Abigail had given me a three-pack of them to keep in my office, since she packed my lunch each day. She said I would need them someday and that I'd be grateful to have them. I had rolled my eyes at her and told her I would never need them and that I was sure I'd forget about them. Remembering the conversation brings back the sound of Abigail's voice. I can hear her so clearly, as if she has just said the words to me this morning. Instead of bringing me comfort, my anxiety spikes. If she is never found, I don't want to forget her voice. I replay her voice again and again in my mind wanting to hold it carefully in my hands. My body sighs as I try to push away the thought. She has to come back. We have to find her. I don't want to forget anything about her; the way her black wavy hair falls across her shoulders, the ease of her wide mouthed smile, the gentleness of her kiss, the sparkle in her eyes. The way she called Gideon our little peanut before he was born. The way her laugh made me laugh just by its sound; it was more of a shy giggle than a laugh. She was never one to make a scene or to draw attention to herself. I plop back into my office chair and roll back a few inches so that I can prop my feet onto my desk. The good memories keep me feeling close to Abigail; they help me think that she is still alive and trying to get back to us. I hope she knows we are trying to find her, we are doing everything we can think of. But as quickly as the good memories have flooded my mind and the edges of my mouth crack as they turn up because it's been so long, the bad memories rush in like an angry army taking over without remorse. My body tenses, bracing for the war, but no matter how much I tighten my muscles, the painful memories still come back with a vengeance. This time they start with the moment I realized Abigail was missing; when I knew something was terribly wrong.

It was a Friday night and I had come home from work an hour early, hoping to surprise Abigail. With Gideon being so little at the time, I knew it was hard if not impossible for Abigail to leave the house. I'd wanted to take them out for a nice meal, even though I knew she'd have dinner prepared. Her eyes had been looking a bit dreary that week. I'd asked her the night before why she looked so sad and she had insisted that it was only because she was so tired from getting up at night to feed Gideon. I believed her, but looking back now, maybe I should have kept digging. Maybe there was something else there. What were her eyes trying to say, or to hide? Friday when I arrived home, I noticed that the front door was ajar. Abigail was so neat and tidy I sometimes wondered to myself if she had undiagnosed obsessive compulsive disorder.

She would never leave the door ajar. Immediately my guard was up and I hurried to put the car in park, turn off the ignition and run into the house. Maybe she'd overcooked something and was airing out the house? A quick glance at the windows in the front of the house told me that probably wasn't the case. The windows were all closed. As I approached the door I shouted Abigail's name and heard nothing. I did not smell smoke. But as my feet took me into the house and my eyes grazed the living room, I knew with certainty that everything was not okay. The rug was turned upside-down, the coffee table thrown against the far wall. The light on the ceiling fan had been busted with what I could only assume was a baseball bat. Shattered glass lay on top of the La-Z-Boy chair, the couch and the linoleum floor as if it had just snowed. The house smelled angry. Abigail's purse had been tossed on the floor, its contents scattered around the room. Later, I realized that her cell phone and her wallet were among the scattered items. Her credit cards were still there. There was still cash in the wallet. Nothing was missing, except my wife.

In shock, I had briefly forgotten about Gideon, after all he was so new to us. When I heard his muffled shouts from the bedroom I ran to him only to trip and rip the knee in my pants. Blood oozed through the tear and trickled down to my shoe, which tracked on the linoleum as I rushed to find my son. Trembling, I hoped to find Abigail and Gideon safely hiding in his room together. When I reached his door and found it closed, I shouted Abigail's name and turned the knob. The door was locked. We'd never locked the door. Surely Abigail was inside if it was locked? After a few tries I rushed across the hall to grab a wire coat hanger and opened the door. The room was dark. The shades were drawn and the small radio in the corner of the room played *Hush Little Baby* on repeat. Abigail was not in the room. Gideon was. He was in his crib, on his back, screaming for his parents. It seemed, for all he knew, nothing was out of the ordinary. He needed a diaper change and was ready to be fed. Cradling Gideon in my arms I raced across the room and threw back the heavy curtains, letting in the evening light. When we bought the house, one of the things Abigail liked so much was that the evening sun hit the front of the house, which she said would allow us a comfortable shaded back yard to enjoy in the evenings. With Gideon still cradled in my arms, screaming, I shouted Abigail's name a hundred more times as I opened every closet door and checked every room in the house to no avail. By the time I reached the kitchen

I knew she was gone and every nerve in my body danced on its edge. A cold chill ran down my spine and I felt the hot beads of sweat forming on my forehead. In the kitchen I saw my bottle of Hennessy Black sitting on the counter. It was open and empty. Like a fool, I searched for a letter, hoping for a clue. But I knew Abigail would never leave Gideon home alone. There was no letter to be found. My wife had disappeared without a trace.

Grabbing my cell phone I dialed 9-1-1, all the while Gideon screamed his heart out in the background of that unthinkable conversation. "We need her to come home." I told the woman on the other end of the phone. "She's missing and we need her back. Who would take my wife?" I cannot remember a single word the 9-1-1 operator said to me that evening. I can only remember the sinking feeling in my gut.

When I was eleven my dog Biscuit was hit by a car. I got off the school bus at the start of the road, with four other kids. I was three hundred meters from my house. I waved good-bye to my bus mates as we all scattered and went our separate ways toward home. A few steps later I saw him. Biscuit, my collie mix was splattered in the middle of the road. His eyes were hanging outside of his head. His tail was lifeless.

Dark red blood covered his thick tan and white fur. I rushed to Biscuit's side, shouting his name, hoping for him to come back to life. Hoping for a miracle, although in my gut I knew it wasn't possible. I crouched down in the center of the road and pressed my head against Biscuit's messy side. A heard a car honk, but I didn't make an attempt to move until someone must have told my mom and she came to pry me off of him and retrieve his body. Come to think of it now, it was a Friday afternoon when I found him. Why do bad things always happen on Fridays? I had a sinking feeling in my gut when I found Biscuit in the road that day, and I had it when I called 9-1-1 to report my missing wife, with our screaming son in my arms. I silently prayed for a miracle for Abigail, but I realized that when you're praying for a miracle it's because something terrible has already happened.

When I hung up with the 9-1-1 operator, they had assured me they would send an officer out to gather more information and to look through the house. I immediately called Lois and Omar. As horrific as the 9-1-1 call had been the call to the Atwell's was even more painful. How do you tell someone that their daughter is missing and you don't have a clue what's happened to her? I didn't know what to say and I stumbled horribly on my words.

"Hello?" Lois answered.

Gideon was still screaming uncontrollably. I hadn't changed his diaper or attempted to feed him amongst the chaos. I couldn't catch my breath at the sound of her voice. I didn't want to tell her the news. I didn't want to be living this gut wrenching nightmare.

"Hello?" She asked again. "Is anyone there? Abigail, is that you?"

Clearing my throat, I mustered up the strength to speak. I pressed my eyes closed and drew in a deep breath that expanded through the top of my ribs. "Lois? It's Anthony." My voice sounded quieter than usual and I felt as if I were watching myself go through the motions, as if I had no control over my words or actions. I was floating above myself, knowing there was nothing I could do to soothe the pain; mine or anyone else's for that matter.

"Anthony, hi dear. Is everything okay? Where's Abigail?" She didn't sound overly concerned, and why should she be? At this moment, to her, everything was as it should be, only I was about to shatter that idealistic reality.

"No. No, Lois." My voice shook. "Everything is not okay. Is Omar with you?"

I heard the sound of her gasping on the other end of the line and my heart pulsed, hating that I was hurting her. "What's going on? Omar is here, he's just in the other room watching television. Tell me what's going on…please. Is it Gideon? Is something wrong?"

"Gideon's fine. It's Abigail." I stared breathlessly, feeling weak. I pulled out a chair from the kitchen table and sat, bouncing Gideon in my right arm while holding the phone with my left.

"Please, what's happened? Is she in the hospital? Is everything okay?" Her voice was rushed and I heard Omar join her, only his tone was much louder and abrupt. I heard his muffled words in the background, and then taking the phone, his voice boomed on the line.

"Anthony? What's going on? What's happening? Tell us this instant!" He demanded.

"It's Abigail, sir. She's missing." My voice quivered.

"What do you mean…missing? Where is she?" Omar was trying to be patient.

"That's just it. I don't know. She's not here. She's not at home. I came home a little early from work and the front door was open…" Before I could finish he interrupted.

"We'll be there in five minutes. Don't go anywhere. Call 9-1-1!" I tried to answer but the line had already gone dead. The Atwell's were one of very few families who still used a landline rather than cell phones. Omar insisted that cell phones caused brain cancer. Placing my phone in my pocket I rocked Gideon using both arms before finding the strength to stand and walk through the ransacked house and back to his room to grab a clean diaper. I would change him first, and then figure out what and how to feed him; something I'd never done. One thing at a time, I told myself. Just keep breathing. Keep moving. We'll find her. The police will find her. She can't be far. She'll be okay. I desperately tried to reassure myself of these things, although it did nothing to ease my fear. When the team of police showed up at our house and I watched their eyes go from the ransacked interior to the empty bottle of alcohol on the kitchen counter, to my torn pants and moist bloody knee, I knew what they were thinking. I kissed Gideon's head noticing that he smelled like lavender as they asked me to come down to the police station for further questioning. Lois and Omar arrived in time to take Gideon, snatching him from me so quickly that it felt in that moment that they thought I was a brutal killer. From the very start, I offered to answer any questions, to help in any way I could. During the hours of questioning, I pleaded again and again with each of the officers, shouldn't we be out looking for my wife? Aren't the first hours and days the ones that matter most when a person has gone missing? Isn't that our best chance to save her? But the police were more concerned with questioning me, the easy target. I felt like a wild animal, tranquilized and caged at the zoo; a crude spectacle for all to see. An innocent life held captive and being callously driven to the point of insanity. A once peaceful creature forced to turn savage against the isolation and chaos.

After being detained for seven hours of questioning, hours that could have been spent searching for my missing wife, the police asked me to complete a missing persons report. They asked for photos of my wife, which I had a half a dozen of on my cell phone. They asked for a list of nicknames or aliases that Abigail used. She didn't have either. I didn't even call her Abby. She has always been Abigail to me and everyone in our world. I gave them a physical description of Abigail: black wavy hair that falls just past her shoulders, she often wears red lip stick. Twenty-six years old, brown eyes, five foot four and a thin build of one hundred and twenty-five pounds. No tattoos or noticeable scars that would be an identifying characteristic. She is not on any medications nor does she have any medical conditions. They asked me what she'd been wearing when I last saw her. I last saw her before I left for work in the morning and she was still wearing her pajamas: a white shirt and baggy red and blue flannel pants. But surely she'd changed into her day outfit after I'd left, as she always did. I didn't have a clue what she would have worn today since I hadn't been home. When they asked me what possessions she might have on her I couldn't answer that either. Her purse, phone and keys were still in the house. Her car was still in the garage. When they asked for a list of places Abigail frequently visits I told them that she is mostly home with our son Gideon but does visit our church, the grocery store, hair salon, and the library. I don't know of anywhere else she goes because she is mostly home, taking care of Gideon. When her car is on low fuel I take it to the gas station for her to fill it up. She isn't out and about much. She also has lunch with her parents from time to time and visits my mom, with me, in the nursing home. I provided a short list of relatives and friends, when requested. The list contained a few people from church and her parents. I hadn't realized until now that she didn't have any close friends. The final question to complete the missing persons report was to tell the police what the situation was surrounding my wife's disappearance. Another question I couldn't answer. "She's just gone." I stated flatly. "If I could explain it, I could find her! Don't you understand that?" I was trying hard not to lose my cool, but it was difficult. I ground my teeth, desperately wanting the police to help me find her. I had given them all of the information I had; I wanted to take action, to do something to bring her back, not sit and fill out paperwork or be questioned again: always the same questions phrased in different ways. I was told that Officer Danny Herring was in charge of the case, for the time being. I asked for a copy of the missing persons report so I could be sure they didn't twist my words. Although they said they had cleared me as a suspect, I knew instinctually that the tables could turn at any moment. I needed to keep myself safe for Gideon and for Abigail. With the way the police had reacted so far, questioning me and not having gone out to search for her, I knew Abigail was going to need me to lead the search if we were ever going to find her. Before I left the police station, Officer Herring glared into my eyes and said, "It is not illegal for an adult to go missing. You should know that, Mr. Parker." All afternoon the officers had tried to pin me for kidnapping or murdering my wife. When that wasn't getting them anywhere, they switched tactics and tried to convince me that Abigail had run away. When I pressed back and asked why she would do such a thing when everything in our life was good, they didn't have an answer. They tried to find holes in our marriage, evidence of infidelity. But there were none. They tried to unofficially diagnose Abigail with post-partum depression, but again, they could not cite any evidence of that, nor could I.

The next morning I contacted the National Missing and Unidentified Persons System (NameUs), operated by the United States Department of Justice. I registered with any missing persons databases I could find. I drove to the church, to the hospital, the library and even to the Waterford jail and the coroner. I knew Abigail wouldn't be in any of those places, but I had to check and I left my name and number with every person I spoke. I showed each of them a photo of Abigail on my phone, begging and hoping they'd seen her. Every person shook their head. Every person widened their eyes in disbelief that something this awful could happen in Waterford. And I know they were all looking at me shaking their heads, grateful they weren't me. I scoured social media sites. Neither Abigail nor I had social media accounts. Abigail did have a Pinterest account, but otherwise nothing else. Nevertheless I got on Facebook, Twitter, Instagram and every other social media site I could find and I looked for anything that might be a clue to Abigail's whereabouts. We had a shared email account at home and I checked sent and deleted mail to be sure I wasn't missing something that was right in front of my eyes. No clues there, either. I knew there wouldn't be. How could there be a clue when she'd been taken? If someone broke into the house and came after her, she wouldn't have had time to think about leaving a clue. She's kept Gideon safe. Somehow his door had been locked from the inside. But where was she? How was I going to find her? I wanted to have faith in the police force, but I couldn't. I couldn't just sit back and hope they would find her, especially when they didn't seem that interested in the case once they spoke with me and told me I was not a suspect.

I created flyers with her photo and left them at

local gas stations, the library, church, and the hospital, everywhere I could think of. I left piles of flyers at each location, stunned that the photo staring back at me with the word MISSING written above her face was my wife. It was after midnight before I slowed my pace. The time on the clock shook me back to life and I quickly dialed Lois and Omar's number, wanting to check on Gideon. I knew it was late, but surely they were not in bed, in the wake of all that had happened today.

"Abigail?" Omar answer the phone before the end of the first ring. His voice sounded frail and meek.

"Omar, it's me. It's Anthony. I'm sorry it's so late-"

"Did you find her? Tell me she's okay." He begged. I heard a rustling in the background and muffled words from Lois that I couldn't quite hear.

Shaking my head I forced myself to say the words. "No. We haven't found her yet. But we will. We will…" My voice trailed as I stumbled, choking on my own tears.

"If you know where our daughter is, please, tell us. Please Anthony." Omar separated himself from me by calling Abigail *our daughter*. He wanted to remind me that she was their flesh and blood; she was their little girl.

"Omar, I swear. I have no idea where she could

be. I have no idea what's happened to Abigail. I will
answer any questions you have. I will do anything
I can to find her." I went on to list the myriad of
places I'd been this afternoon, looking for Abigail. I
told him about filing the missing person's report and
scouring the internet. I told him about distributing
the flyers. The words fell out of my mouth like a
running facet. Once I started, I couldn't stop. Like a
giant boulder rolling down a hill, I just kept going. I
was too afraid to stop. Too afraid to hear the silence
because it sounded like the shrill of a horrid scream
that would never end.

Eventually Omar interrupted me, his voice
growing stronger with each word. "You say you'll
answer any question?"

"Yes. Yes, of course. Anything."

"Okay, Anthony. Then tell us this: why did you
leave work early yesterday? Was it to harm our
daughter? Why was there an open, empty bottle of
your favorite drink on the kitchen counter, amongst
the mess? Why is Gideon safe without a scratch to
show on his little body? Why were your pants torn,
your knee dripping with blood? We're ready to listen.
Go on with your answers. You said you'd tell us
whatever we had to ask." He dropped the questions
in my lap like a loaded gun. "Go ahead young man.

We're listening." Omar cleared his throat and I heard Lois whispering something to him in the background again.

"Omar. Please." Now it was my turn to beg. "We're on the same side. Can't you see that? I didn't do anything to Abigail, I swear. You have to believe me. You have to."

"Those aren't answers Anthony." His voice booms, jolting a chill down my spine.

"Okay, okay. I'm answering…" I draw in a deep breath. "I left work early because I could, which is rare. I saw an opportunity to get home a little earlier than normal and I took it. I wanted to surprise Abigail and take her and Gideon to dinner. I knew she'd been cooped up at the house lately and I thought it would be good for us to go out as a family." My words rushed together.

"Did you have reservations somewhere?" Omar quickly inquires.

"No." I stutter. "It was a spur of the moment thing."

"I see. Go on…"

I thought about his questions, making sure not to skip any. It was important to let the Atwell's know we were in this together. I wasn't the bad guy here. We needed to work together if we were going to have a chance at finding Abigail. And right now, my words were the only thing that could save me from being ostracized by my only remaining family. "Okay, the bottle of Hennessy Black. Yes, that is my favorite drink. Yes, I had that in the house. But no, I did not drink it. It was open and empty when I arrived home. You must believe me, you must. Did I seem drunk when I called you or when you took Gideon from me before I headed to the police station? I wasn't. The police even gave me a breathalyzer test when I got there and I passed. I didn't have any alcohol in my system and they have the proof." How many times would I have to answer these same questions? First it was the police, now the Atwell's.

"Okay. A breathalyzer test by the police is a good start." Omar's voice slightly lightens.

"And my pants tore when I was running around the house in a panic. I had just gotten home and saw the destruction and I was rushing around calling out to Abigail and Gideon. I tripped and fell and the knee in my pants ripped. I didn't notice I was bleeding until after I'd found Gideon." I sighed, feeling a deep ache in my lower back. "You see, I'm on your side here. I'm innocent in all of this. I swear. I have no idea where Abigail is or who has taken her." I wanted Omar to say he believed me and I wanted to believe him when he said it.

I sat silently waiting for his response, while he waited for me to continue talking. After what felt like an eternity, he spoke. His voice was full of sadness and I could tell he'd been crying in the quiet moment that existed between us. "And?"

Am I forgetting something? What else does he want to know? "I'm sorry Omar. Was there another question? It's been a long day and it's late." I yawn as I glance again at the clock on the kitchen wall.

"You didn't tell us, why was Gideon locked safely in his room? How do you explain that one?" There was a hard edge to his voice, although I tried not to take it personally. I knew he wanted answers just as much as I did. He was trying, like me, to understand the impossible situation we found ourselves in.

"My apologies." I cleared my throat and leaned forward in my chair, feeling my shoulders round and my head hang. "I have no idea. My only guess is that somehow Abigail locked the door and closed it before the kidnapper knew she had a child in the house. It would make sense that she was sure to keep our son safe. I only wish she'd been hiding safely in his room with him." My voice cracks as I try desperately to stop the inevitable tears. My eyes are red and swollen. Exhaustion takes over every muscle in my body.

Instead of replying to my answers, Lois took the

phone from Omar and as she came on the line, her voice overwhelms me. I've never noticed how much she sounds like Abigail. "Anthony, we believe you. We trust you. We know you love our Abigail." She was doing her best to sound strong, but like me, I could tell she was a wreck.

Relief washed over me at her words. Although a small part of me wondered if Lois had merely said those nice things to make me think they were on my side. I recall the old saying, keep your friends close and your enemies closer. Is that what she was doing? Surely not. I opted to think positively and believe that her words were honest. "Thank you." I cried. "Thank you. I promise I'm innocent. I promise I know nothing more than I've told you. I promise I'll do everything I can to find her."

"We'll keep Gideon with us for a few days so that you can focus on the search. Call us tomorrow and keep us posted on any updates. Call any hour."

"I will." I answer dotingly. "I will, I promise Lois."

"And Anthony?" She adds.

"Yes?"

"Anthony, we have to find her. She's our only daughter."

"I know. I know we have to find her. We have to." I agree, rolling my neck from side to side, trying to fight off the numbness. "She is my only wife." I add, trying to lighten the moment for a reason unbeknownst to me. It was a poor choice of words and poor timing. I want to suck the words back in just as soon as they've left my lips, but it is too late.

Lois greets me on the other end of the line with a long silence.

"I'll call you tomorrow." I try to sound strong and redeem myself, although I know I can't. There is no redemption to be found in this horrible, miserable situation.

The next day I hire a lawyer, just to be sure someone is truly looking out for me.

Five

Our little peanut is now the size of a peach! I am thirteen weeks into the pregnancy. Thankfully, last week my awful symptoms of morning sickness began to subside. The nausea and the vomiting were nearly unbearable from week seven to twelve. I want to celebrate the diminishing symptoms. I think I'll download a new book on my e-reader tonight; maybe a novel by Alice Hoffman. With the nausea the last few weeks, reading only made me feel worse.

It's a small, low cost reward I can give myself, without guilt. Week thirteen may hold promise.

Each week I've given Tony a fruit or vegetable that represents the size of our little peanut. At week five it was an apple seed. Week six, a sweet pea. Week seven, a blueberry. Week eight, a raspberry. Week nine, a green olive. Week ten, a prune. Week eleven, a lime. And last week, week twelve, a beautiful deep purple plum. Next week it will be a lemon. I already have one hidden away in the back of the refrigerator for the occasion.

Although I am thrilled that the nausea and vomiting have subsided, I have started experiencing some sharp lower abdominal pains when I change positions too quickly. I called the doctor and she said it's called round ligament pain and it's happening because my uterus is continuing its rapid growth. She said it's harmless unless the pain is accompanied by fever, chills or bleeding; none of which I have. I can withstand this pain more than enduring the sickness during the prior few weeks. At least it is progress. The other change this week is that my breasts have started leaking a light orange, thick and sticky discharge from time to time. Again, the doctor tells me it's nothing to worry about and it's just happening because my body is starting to produce colostrum, which is the precursor to breast milk. She said it's a "normal, albeit annoying part of pregnancy." I laughed when she said the word annoying, thinking that was an understatement.

In the next few weeks we'll be able to identify our little peanut's sex with an ultrasound, but Tony and I have decided we want to be surprised. We have another prenatal appointment soon. I'm excited to hear the little one's heartbeat with the Doppler machine. Tony said he won't be able to make the doctor's appointment with me, again, because it's more important for him to work and make more money before the baby is born. He reminds me daily that a baby is expensive. Yet, his eyes dance when he talks about having a house full of children one day. Part of me wishes we were finding out the sex of our little one. We are going to paint the nursery yellow so that it will work for a boy or a girl, but it would be nice to not have everything be so gender neutral as we're planning for his or her arrival. I told Tony I would record the sound of our little one's heartbeat with my iPhone, during the doctor's appointment. This way he can listen to the heartbeat we've created when we have dinner together later that night. He grinned and told me that I was always thinking of others and planning ahead and how great of a mom I am going to be, which of course made me beam with excitement.

It's Monday and I've been busy cleaning and organizing the house. I don't know how I'll have time to keep up with everything once our little peanut is born. Tony says that we'll eventually need a bigger house for all of our children, but I am always quietly bewildered, wondering how I'll keep up with the housework of a larger house. There will of course be more food to prepare with more people and more beds to make and a lot more laundry, too. Also, Tony is stressed out about making more money before our first baby is born; how anxious will he be when we have a house full of little ones running around, needing new shoes, clothes, toys and food? I try not to let my mind wander to worries like these. After all, what will worrying about the future do? Worrying won't help. It can't slow down time. It can't solve any problems that haven't yet happened. It's just that my mind wanders from daydreaming about an idyllic life with our little peanut, to those crazy worries that I won't be able to be a good enough wife or mother. I force my mind back on the task at hand. On Monday's I am on my hands and knees scrubbing the tub and shower. After that I take a short break for breakfast, usually a glass of orange juice, a banana and a few handfuls of mixed nuts. Then I head outdoors to pull weeds. Why do they always come back so quickly? I guess that's where the expression comes from when someone's talking about how fast a child grows and they tell them, *you're growing like a weed.* It's a saying with a world of truth behind it, because let me tell you, the weeds come back with a vengeance each week. When that's done I move on to the outdoor lights. They are always filled with deceased insects such as the brown moths and June bugs that splatter, so I take the glass off and empty them of insect shells and clean them with my homemade vinegar mixture; the same cleaner I use to clean the windows. Tony never asks what I do each day. I know he has no idea the small details I tend to, but I like to keep everything perfect. It's how we separate our duties; it's my job and I take it seriously. I want to do the best job I can. I know that Tony is not going to come home and say "Wow, those are amazingly clean outdoor lights!" But it's enough to know that he's happy and I know he's proud of me and our house if, by chance, his co-workers stop by or the neighbors compliment him on our curb appeal. He always says that if his mom were of sound mind and if his dad were still on this Earth that they would be so pleased to see the life he's built. And I know they would. Tony has everything he's dreamed of; a wife, a nice home, a good job and his first child is on the way.

The sun feels good on my neck and back as I pull out the pesky weeds that have popped up throughout our landscaping. I always wear gardening gloves to keep the dirt from pressing too far beneath my nails; it is so difficult to clean out the dark spots. I wear long socks and put a small navy blue towel on the ground for my knees. When I reach to pull a greater plantain from the ground I notice that a few inches from its base is a smaller version of the weed. *A mother and baby*, I think quietly to myself. The oval-shaped foliage has pronounced rib markings. This perennial weed is broad and continues to come back again and again, its big leaves smothering anything that falls beneath its shadow. Our yard brings so many of the greater plantain weeds that I Googled the best way to remove them before coming outside to weed the yard today. I learned that instead of just yanking them from the ground, I need to dig them out by the roots, pulling the entire plant from its home so it will, hopefully disappear and never return. If it has grown in a grassy area I then need to mow over it to prevent the seeds from spreading. I use my small trowel to dig around the mother and baby set of weeds and pull them from the Earth, watching the roots rise with them. I toss them eagerly into the plastic bag I have waiting behind me. I continue the process until I round the right corner of the house and along the side I watch the daisies dance in the subtle breath of air drifting past. I am well aware that the most common perennial weed is a daisy with white petals and a yellow center. But this is one weed that makes me smile and I just can't bring myself to remove them. They dance so freely on the breeze as they stand tall, reaching for the warmth of the sun. There is a cluster of rosettes along this side of the brick wall of our home. I come off my knees and sit back on the towel, placing a hand over my stomach. Will our little peanut dance wild and free like the daisies? Or will she drift toward the comfort of conformity, preferring a weed free lawn that is sprayed and manicured to the idea of perfection? I decide at that moment that I want to give our baby a strong name, a name with meaning. I make a mental note to find a few baby name books to begin the search. I run the open palm of my hand along the small lump that has become my stomach. I wonder when I'll feel the little one start kicking. I suppose, at the size of a mere peach, she can't start pumping her legs against me just yet.

I let my eyes wander upwards to the blue sky. There are only a few clouds today and I let myself drift along with them as they slowly pass. I realize I should be pulling the weeds, but right now I am going to enjoy Mother Nature. I am going to soak in Vitamin D and listen to the rustling of the patch of wild daisies as they shake like an instrument against the next gentle gust of air that passes by.

When our baby is born, I think, I'll take her outside with me and she can watch or help me pull the weeds, depending on her age. I find myself lost in a vision of rubbing our noses together and laughing at everything and nothing. I imagine singing to our little girl and watching her eyes light up as I do. I don't have a great singing voice, I know I'm a bit tone deaf, really, but that will only make our days even better. That will only make our children laugh with me even more. Because we don't have to be perfect. Right now I want to be. I try to be. I keep up with a million chores, I pack Tony's lunch, I hug him each day when he walks in the door. I have dinner ready every night and I keep a bottle of Hennessey Black on hand, his favorite drink to enjoy after a day at work. But maybe, once our little one comes, I won't have to be this perfect anymore. Maybe I'll already be more because I will have our first child in my arms and by my side. I'll already be enough because of our baby. The outside lights being cleaned of insect carcasses each week won't matter anymore. Right? Cleaning the shelves inside of the refrigerator won't be so important when I have a little life to care for. So then I can relax. Then I'll take a breather. Then I'll know it's all enough; I am enough.

My head is turned upward toward the sun, just like the dancing daisies. My hand falls from my stomach and catches on the grass. I open my eyes and adjust my neck so that my eyes fall back to the lively daisies, once again. I hear the plastic bag rustling behind me, although I know it won't blow away because it is too heavy from the weeds I have already plucked. But it isn't the plastic bag that has caught my attention and shaken me from my daydream, back to reality. I feel the weight of a stare. Someone is looking at me and I lean forward and turn my head to peer around the front corner of our house. No one is at the front door. A chill races down my spine from the nape of my neck. And then I see the car parked in front of our house. People do park on the road from time to time, but why has this car chosen to park directly in front of our house? I squint my eyes trying to peer through the dark passenger side window; the windows are too tinted for me to see anyone. Suddenly a jolt jumps my heart; could it be the man who followed me home from lunch with my parents? Has he been watching me? If he has been watching, he knows that I spend my days at home, alone. I continue staring back at the dark car. It is a black Lexus. I don't know much about cars but I can see the circled L logo displayed prominently at the front of the car. I cannot make out the license plate number from this angle. My heart is racing now. I look away, wondering if the person or people inside are staring back at me. I grab my trowel, the navy blue towel I was using for my knees and my plastic bag full of discarded weeds. "Protect me." I whisper, looking up at the sky. I walk quickly to the front door, all of my items in tow. I don't want to run and make it obvious that I am trying to get away, in case I am being watched. But I do want to get inside as fast as I can. I shut the door behind me and lock the deadbolt once I am inside. I see my cell phone sitting on the living room coffee table, something else to make me feel safe. *I am okay*, I tell myself. *I am fine.* My heart is still racing when I peer out the big window in the living room. I hide behind the heavy curtains and only dare to peak. The black car with the tinted windows is gone now. Were they discouraged I'd gone inside? Maybe they weren't looking at me at all. Maybe the pregnancy hormones are just making me paranoid. That's probably it. I run my hand over my stomach in an attempt to reassure our little peanut that they are safe, too. I check once more out the front window, the road is clear except for a few scattered cars passing by. I am okay, I remind myself. There's no need for me to tell Tony about the dark car. No need to worry about anything. I will keep this to myself, as I did with the man I thought was following me home from lunch a few weeks ago. I leave my shoes on the mat by the front door and walk back to the kitchen. I find the fuzzy peach I bought to give to Tony tonight; a reminder of the size of our growing little one. I hold the fruit in my hands and let its soft flesh graze my skin. Its perfect; no bumps, bruises, scratches or flat areas. I draw in its tropical smell and like magic, somehow it slows my breath and my heart begins to calm. *We'll be okay*, I reassure myself again, careful not to hold the delicate peach too tight.

Merry means redemption. At least that's what one book I read tells me. I'm drawn to the name and now find myself hoping for a little girl. Merry Violet Parker. Tony said the name Merry is okay. He said he would think about it. However, I know that Tony is hoping for a boy, although he says he'll be happy either way as long as the baby and I are healthy.

He wants to name a boy Gideon Simon. When I looked up Gideon in the baby book it says that it means destroyer. In my opinion, not such a great name for our little peanut. I know that the so-called meanings of names are just for fun and there is probably no real significance behind them. Maybe it's just my pregnancy hormones, but I am feeling sentimental and I want our child's name to have a positive meaning associated with it, if only for my own peace of mind. I know if I tell Tony that the name Gideon means destroyer he'll tell me I'm ridiculous and spin it somehow, maybe telling me that it means he destroys all things bad, so really it's a good, strong name. I'll keep leafing through the name book. We have plenty of time before our little one comes. Hopefully it will be enough time to find names we can agree on.

I'm twenty weeks pregnant now. Our little peanut is much bigger than a peanut! She is the size of a banana. When I drove to the grocery to choose a banana to set out for Tony tonight, showing him the current size of our baby, I couldn't decide which one to bring home. The organic bananas were half of the size of those sprayed with chemicals. Some were as long as my forearms while others were only the length of my outstretched index. In the end, I decided on a mid-size organic banana. After all, this game I am playing by setting out a food the size of the baby each week, is just for fun.

For dinner tonight I've made salad and added chickpeas for their extra health benefit. Using soft whole-wheat tortillas, I have prepared simple quesadillas filled with smoked turkey, Monterey Jack cheese and a bit of spinach. And for dessert, I've tried something new from a recipe I found online for Raspberry Fool. It's just a cup of raspberries, a half of a cup of raspberry jam and a little bit of heavy cream and granulated sugar. I like to stick to simple recipes; things I know will taste good once I've finished preparing them. I don't like taking risks on recipes that take all day to prepare when it could turn out to be a colossal waste of time if the taste isn't palatable. I am putting the finishing touches on our meal. I glance at the clock hanging on the kitchen wall and note that Tony should be home within the next ten minutes. I always have dinner ready when he walks in the door and that pleases him. I take a clean spoon and steal a few stray raspberries, enjoying the burst of flavor as they hit my tongue. After one more bite of raspberries I grab a clean spoon and scoop our dessert into two separate serving bowls. Next, I add garnish, a sprinkling of raspberries, maybe three or four on each dish, and a cookie to top it off. I stand back, licking my fingers and smiling at a job well done. It looks perfect and I know from my small trial that it tastes divine. I should photograph my accomplishment, I think. But I have no one to share it with. I don't have any social media pages other than Pinterest (which gives me great ideas for recipes and do-it-yourself cleaning supplies), and my parents don't use cell phones and can't begin to understand how my phone can take pictures. I sigh, still standing back and admiring the meal and dessert I have made before grabbing the two dishes of Raspberry Fool and placing them carefully on the second shelf in the refrigerator. I put our two plates of quesadillas in the oven to keep warm and place the salads on each of our placemats at the dinner table, next to each glass of ice water. Wiping my hands on the dish towel at the sink I tuck my black wavy hair behind my ears and grab my red lipstick from my pocket, run the makeup across my lips and smack my lips twice to spread the color evenly.

If our little peanut is a girl, I know she'll see me putting on my signature cherry red lipstick each

night and she'll want to put some on too. The corners
of my mouth press upward at the thought. I wonder
if she'll have black wavy hair like me or hazel eyes like
Tony. If we have a boy, I wonder if he'll respect me
as much as he does his father. I wonder if he'll enjoy
spending time with me. Tony and I have already
talked about putting a swing set in the backyard, one
that has a slide and a little gymnastics bar they can
climb around on. A boy or a girl will like that. I want
to put a sandbox in the backyard too so they can dig
around and find buried treasures. Maybe once our
first born is a few years old, we'll adopt a dog from
the animal shelter and they can grow up together,
romping around the house and the yard. I find myself
lost in daydreams a lot these days. It's quiet here at
the house and most of my days are spent alone until
Tony comes home. Sure, I have the occasional human
interaction when I'm grocery shopping or running
errands. But mostly it's just pleasantries. *How are you?*
It's a beautiful day. That sort of thing. No one ever
really cares to hear my response, which sometimes
makes me feel invisible. But when Tony gets home
I am seen. I always ask about his day and hope he
has a story to tell. He always tells me how nice the
house looks and how good the meal is, which makes
my efforts feel worthwhile. I admit, I do miss the days

before we were married and had a house, when we spent more time doing things together like feeding the ducks at the pond, hiking on a wooded trail or wading in the creek and seeing who could skip a flat stone the furthest. I always won. Tony said he didn't understand how to skip rocks and I told him it's all in the flick of the wrist, but he never quite got it. Living at home carried its own set of expectations and pressures and meeting Tony was like a breath of fresh air. But being in this house alone day after day can, at times, play tricks on my mind. I think it's the silence, that's all. I listen to audio books a lot of the time and listen to music when I'm cleaning and cooking. The words of others keep me company, although they do nothing for a sense of connection. I'm always relieved when Tony gets home from work. I'm eager and ready to listen and talk. But he is always worn out and quiet, ready for sleep. We are living two very different lives these days; I guess that is part of growing up. I guess that is parenthood in a nutshell. Two adults living separate lives and finding a way to come together as one to raise the little ones. Nevertheless, I miss having more time with Tony before life became so serious and structured. He's so worried about working more hours before the baby comes, so we can save up as much money as possible to provide for our child. It would be wrong of me to complain about missing him. He's working so hard and he's tired, and I respect what he is doing for our future. Selfishly I wish he was here more. I wish we could relax on the couch together and maybe he would rub my aching feet. I wish I could put my head on his shoulder and run my fingers through his short buzzed brown hair. I wish we both felt tired at the same time, instead of becoming opposites. I wish he was as excited to see me when he came home from work, as I am to see him. Sometimes I fear he is more excited for the meals I've prepared than for me, his wife. When I wrap my arms around his neck and hug him, I sense he is relieved to be home, but I do not feel excitement. Maybe that wears off over time in a marriage. It's understandable, given our busy lives and all.

My cell phone vibrates from the inside of my pocket and I reach for it. Mostly my calls only come from Tony or my parents. Texts are only from Tony and on rare occasion, someone from church asking me to bring a specific dish the following weekend. Tony's name is flashing on the screen. I look at the time and notice that he should be home.

"Hello? Tony?" I answer, hoping he hasn't gotten into an accident on his drive home. The office is only a half-an-hour from our house, but he does drive the Interstate and there are always semi-drivers causing accidents on that stretch of road. Just last week a semi-driver dozed off at the wheel, a line of five cars were stopped at the red light ahead of him. The truck driver didn't notice the stopped cars or the red light and crashed into all of them while driving fifty-five miles per hour. Four people died in that horrible accident and several are still in critical condition, per the last news report. I shudder at the thought, thinking that if Tony is calling me, at least I know he is alive and well.

"Hey Abigail…I'm so sorry." His voice trails.

"Is everything okay?" I follow up. "Are you on your way home?"

"Everything is fine. I'm really sorry Abigail. I'm running late and I'm still here at work."

I take a moment to digest his words as I open the refrigerator and look at the two decadent dishes of Raspberry Fool I've proudly made. I sigh, feeling my chest rise and fall. "Will you be home soon?" I ask, hopeful.

"I'm sorry." He is saying I'm sorry an awful lot these days and I am beginning to hate the word. What is so important that he has to stay late to work on? Can't it wait until tomorrow? I tap my foot as I pull out a chair at the kitchen table and take a seat.

"Dinner is ready Tony. I was really hoping you'd be home soon." I tried to keep my voice even, soft and with a lack of accusation but I wasn't sure I was pulling it off.

"I know. That's why I'm calling. You're so good to me Abigail. I'm really sorry. It'll be a few more hours. I'm really not sure what time I'll get home tonight. You can go ahead and eat without me. There's no need to wait up. I am working with a new client and the meeting is running long. My hands are tied here-"

"I get it." I interrupt. "It's fine." Biting my bottom lip, I try to hold back tears. It's not as if this is the first time I've eaten dinner alone since we've been married. The number of quiet dinners has grown to more than I can count on my fingers and toes. "I'll wrap up your meal and keep it in the refrigerator for whenever you get home."

"No need to do that. The boss is ordering pizza for everyone who's working late tonight. I'll just have a few slices here." I know he doesn't mean to hurt me but his words sting. He doesn't realize that I've spent time and energy making a nice meal for the two of us.

My presence, our clean house, the meals, he is taking it all for granted it seems.

"It will be here, if you get hungry later." I clear my throat. "I miss you."

"Miss you too, honey." His words are rushed and I hear several muffled voices in the background and know he needs to get back to his client. He's told me before that when he is at work he has to be focused. A part of me hopes he will ask what I've made for dinner or how my day was. The other part of me puts up a wall as I brace myself for the lack of interest in my ghostly life.

We say good-bye and I place my phone back in my pocket, hop up from the chair and grab both dishes of Raspberry Fool and plop back down, propping my feet up on the chair sitting opposite of me at the kitchen table. If I am going to eat alone, I am going to eat dessert first. And I am eating for two, after all, so I may as well enjoy both desserts. As I spoon the first bite of dessert into my mouth I find my eyes gazing at the banana sitting on Tony's placemat. I will leave it there for him to see when he comes home, whenever that might be. Whether or not he chooses to spend time at work or with me, I am growing our child inside of me and our little peanut is growing by leaps and bounds each week.

Tony might not be close by, but I am. Unlike him, I don't have a choice. I am the incubator for this new little life. I can't walk away and tell our little peanut I am too busy.

When I am half-way through the first dish of dessert I feel a jolt. Kicking my legs off of the spare chair and placing them on the ground beneath me, I sit straight with my back pressed against the wooden chair, feeling the jolt once again. It feels like someone is popping popcorn inside of my stomach. My obstetrician told me that I should start feeling the baby kick soon. Is this the baby kicking? I lift my shirt and press both of my hands against my naked stomach, trying to feel a hard kick. I only feel the flutters of butterflies and then little jumps like popcorn being made inside of my stomach. It almost tickles and my eyes well up with tears, thinking that Tony should be here for this. He should be here to eat dinner with me and he should be here to feel these flutters happening. Our little one is really coming to life. Our little peanut is moving. Maybe she doesn't want me to think I am eating alone tonight. After all, I'm not really alone. Or maybe our little peanut really likes the raspberry dessert.

As the popping and fluttering settle down, I draw my hands away from my stomach and let my shirt fall back into place as I sit tall in my chair and reach for another bite of dessert. After the next bite, the sensations return. It must be the raspberries. She like raspberries; I smile to myself feeling close to our baby. A personality must already be forming in there, to have likes and dislikes. At least I am close to someone. I've been nostalgic about the past, about life before a house and marriage. I've been lonely. I'm not going to be lonely anymore, though.

Six

ANTHONY

Present Day, 2017

How do you hold the interest of someone who has grown bored with you? I am desperate. The police and media have given up on us. At this point, they're no longer interested in any part of the case. Every day I call the police station, begging them to stay on the case, to keep searching, but all of my efforts are to no avail. Lois and Omar of are course still doing what they can to keep the story alive, but their efforts are limited with their lack of appreciation for modern technology. This week they've made new flyers, which I'm having printed today and we'll hang them throughout Waterford once again. But Abigail could be anywhere by now. She might not even be in Waterford. If she was here, why hasn't anyone found her?

If someone has kidnaped her, surely they'll slip up at some point. If a neighbor or someone sees her, I want them to have seen her photo and realize that she is a missing person. It's our only chance. I don't know what else to do with so little manpower behind the hunt. We've held searches in all of the local woods; I have the hospital and coroner's office on alert. I feel like I'm banging my head against a cement wall. I keep trying, and getting absolutely nowhere.

Between work, caring for Gideon and trying to find my missing wife, I think I've aged two decades in the past few months. The house is a wreck. I never clean. Sometimes Lois does when she stops by to pick up Gideon to babysit him while I'm at work. I'm eating the last of the Tupperware casseroles given to Gideon and me by fellow church-goers. When I open a container today, the noodles are filled with mold and I toss it, wondering if I am supposed to be keeping the Tupperware containers to wash and return them. I've tossed each one in the trash after consuming its contents.

When I'm at home with Gideon I always keep the television on, hoping for a breaking news update telling me that Abigail has been found. I keep my cell phone in my pocket, too. Even when I'm in the shower I keep it on the counter with the ringer turned on high, just in case. If it wasn't for the television I think I would completely lose my mind. There is too much silence in this house. Of course the silence is interrupted by Gideon's cries, but that doesn't dull the silence in the way I'd like it. Instead, his cries only serve to agitate me. Sometimes it gets to the point where I think I can feel the pain seething through my veins, poisoning my very existence. I spend time with Gideon, but I don't think I am a good dad. I change his diapers and feed him when he cries. Mostly I do the essential things. I don't know what else to do with a small child. This was never the role I imagined for myself. Abigail is so good at being a mother and now I worry that Gideon will never know her.

The torment of not knowing if Abigail is dead or alive weakens me more with each passing day. And if she is alive, will we ever find her? Or will she ever find a way to get a signal of some sort back to us? Am I missing something obvious? Who took her from us? How long had they planned the attack? Did they try to take Gideon, too? I lean back in the old La-Z-Boy chair and reach for my bottle of Hennessy Black on the end table. I do not bother to pour it in the glass, instead I drink straight from the bottle. In the midst of so much pain, I need an outlet and this bottle is it. I have to find a way to escape from reality, even if just for a little while; a way to feel sane for a moment, rather than suffocated by the pain of this unbearable distress.

Taking another sip from the dark bottle, my weight gives way to the chair. I allow myself to drift to sleep, the monotonous voices of news reporters run together in the background like a box fan. My mom always placed a box fan in my bedroom at night when I was a kid. She said it would keep the monsters at bay. I believed her, and so it worked. Now the consistent sound of reporters on the television serve the same purpose, to block out the demons while I fall into a dream.

With the police and media, and therefore the general public, losing interest in the search for my missing wife, the Internet has become my greatest ally these days. Between social media sites and search engines like Google, I am doing everything I can to keep the story alive. *Find Abigail.* The online communities can be harsh, though. There are thousands of supportive people, but for every kind person there's a handful of unkind ones. For whatever reason some people leave comments saying I murdered my wife and hid her body. Others say I'm not doing enough to find her and that a good husband would have found their missing wife by now. Some comments are much worse and I don't care to rehash them because they hurt too much. The people leaving the comments don't know me. They don't know Abigail or Gideon. They don't know us at all. But they write their anonymous words and think they have all of the answers. I don't respond to the negative ones, although I always want to write back and ask what they would do if they were me. I know they can't possibly imagine being me. A year ago, I was them. I was quick to judge. I thought I had all of the answers. I was above this, whatever *this* is. This was something that might happen to *them,* but never to me. Look where I am now. Now it's me. One day it might be them. I don't wish this on anyone, but I do wish people would take a moment to put themselves in my shoes before leaving a quick comment as an attempt to harm me.

Knowing that Abigail could be anywhere in the world by now, I figure the Internet is my best chance at helping her. Flyers can only reach locally, but the Internet can reach across the globe if people share our story. The lack of clues in her case is quite frankly, driving me crazy. There are no leads. Police haven't found any crazy serial killers on the run who they think may have come through our area and taken Abigail. Once they'd cleared my name from the short suspect list (short, meaning my name was the only one they put on the list), they tried to find evidence that Abigail had simply run away. No concrete evidence has been found. Next, they had wanted to prove that she was experiencing postpartum depression and that she'd ran away for that reason; simply being overwhelmed by Gideon. Again, no evidence was found to match that claim, either. They went on to help conduct volunteer searches in the local forests. Nothing. Not even the smallest clue has been found. After that, they went back to looking for a suspect, or so they told me, and they've never added another name to that list. They're at a standstill. Nothing is happening. No one is looking, except for her family; Lois, Omar and me. The flyers we continue to post throughout Waterford always crumble and disappear like I'm afraid the case itself will do if we don't at least find a small clue soon.

The night Abigail went missing, I checked her phone, looking at recent calls; there was nothing out of the ordinary. Police checked, too. If only she had her phone with her now, it's possible we could track her. With her iPhone I could have logged into iCloud to find the location of the phone. I can't tell you how many nights I've sat awake, wishing she'd grabbed her phone. I try and remind myself that she did keep Gideon safe. He was untouched; unharmed. She did what she could, I know that. I am not mad at her; I am simply frustrated with the situation; with the fact that this is our life. Everything changed so quickly.

Today I'm trying to convince a local newspaper columnist to spread the word about Abigail's disappearance. Each email I send and call I place, I am told sorry, but no. I try calling all of the local radio stations and either leave a voice mail or am told no. I call the news stations, too and again I am quickly told no. They story has already been reported, they tell me as if I don't know this. One station tells me that if we find a clue to Abigail's disappearance they will re-report the story. I take down the name and number of the individual I speak with and place it behind a small round magnet on the refrigerator.

Lois and Omar are handling the private investigator they've hired. They've told me they will keep me apprised of anything they learn, but so far it has been radio silence. They are paying good money for the investigator; my fingers are crossed that clues will start to be found. Not knowing what else to do, I decide to take out an ad in the Waterford newspaper. I know it's only reaching locals, but my zooming mind reminds me that we never know who might be passing through to pick up a paper. Semi-truck drivers, for example, travel the country. What if they see the ad and tell us they've seen Abigail recently on their travels? I'll take anything at this point. I'm like an ant dying of dehydration and sitting beneath a faucet, waiting desperately for it to drip. One drip can change everything, it might save our lives. But if it is dry, if no drip comes, I will die.

I kissed Abigail on our second date and I knew instantly that I wanted her to be my partner in life. She's told me more than once she knew it at that moment, too. I think I may have known this on our first date, but I was certain when we kissed on our second. We went to the Waterford Potato festival and walked around. It wasn't a particularly fancy date, although it was comfortable having so many people around us and so many items to look at and booths to visit. We did the dinner and movie thing on our first date. That's where I'd noticed she had a small dimple on the right side of her face when she laughed. And that's where I learned she loved to make jewelry; and now that I recall those early moments in our relationship, I realize Abigail had stopped making jewelry a long time ago. I suppose she'd gotten too busy with married life and the upkeep of the house and then the arrival of our little Gideon. I shake my head, going back to the happy memories. They seem so distant and I desperately want to grab them and pull them back. Sadly, I am all too well aware of the fact that I can do no such thing. You can't hold on to a moment. It's not a material thing, it's fleeting. All any of us have left of a moment is the memory that has burned into our minds. I can replay those memories like a short film, listening to her words, watching her laughter and the sparkle in her eyes. I can analyze it for errors. I can play it forward and backward. I can play it in slow motion. I can play it a million times or a billion, and still, I can't touch it. We can't get those moments back, because they are gone. We only have the residue of the movie that remains in our minds. I don't know if I keep trying to replay the early moments of our relationship to not forget, to leave a stain amongst the crevices of my brain, so that Abigail's voice is still with me, or if I replay those memories to try and find a clue. Regardless of the reason, I am foolhardy to get there. I need to remember the good times.

We walked around the Waterford Potato festival holding hands and stuffing our faces with French fries, loaded potato skins and even potato soup. It was a full year later before Abigail told me she actually hated French fries. When I asked her why she ate them that day she told me that's what love does. "Love makes you do crazy things." She'd said, looking me directly in the eyes and pressing the tip of her index finger against my bottom lip. I'd just leaned my head back and laughed. How had I not known she hated French fries? I couldn't believe she'd waited a full year before she told me. We sat in the grass and listened to a local band perform. Abigail's legs grew itchy with a splattering of small red dots where her skin met the grass. I was the one to point it out and when I did she said it was no big deal and quickly plopped down in the center of my lap, leaning her head back against my bicep. I couldn't help it at that moment. She was looking up at me with her big brown eyes, her wavy black hair falling loosely across my arm as I held her. I bent down and closed my eyes as our lips met. I felt a grand finale of fireworks release in the pit of my stomach. My mouth tingled with excitement. After a few seconds I pulled away, opening my eyes. Had she wanted me to kiss her? Did I catch her off guard? The worries started dancing through my mind until my eyes focused on her face and I watched her long dark lashes flutter to life, her brown eyes dreamily met mine. That's when I knew we were meant to be. There was something magic in that kiss and I knew I wanted to kiss her, and only her, for the rest of my life.

Normally a first and second date brought so much anxiety. But ours was different from the start. We just fit together, like we were meant to find each other. We got each other's jokes. We held hands as if we'd done it a thousand times, her petite palm fit like a glove in my hand. Abigail rested her head on my shoulder and it felt like home. When her eyes found mine from across a crowd, I felt like I could read her mind. She was the one who'd said it that day, just after we kissed for the first time, she told me, "I think you really get me." At the time I didn't know exactly what she meant, but looking back, I do. I'd thought she was telling me I could read her thoughts because being with her felt so easy and natural. But now what I think she really meant was a bit deeper than that. I think she was telling me that I was seeing her for her. When we were engaged, she once kissed me a half a dozen times behind my ear and down the side of my neck before meeting her lips with mine. We were on the front porch of her parents' house, saying goodnight. I told her I couldn't wait until we were married. I wanted to marry her for every possible reason, but in that moment I especially wanted to marry her so that we could consummate our vows. We had both agreed, due to our upbringing and religious beliefs that we would wait to have sex after we said I do. After we finished kissing that night on the porch, Abigail pulled away from me and she leaned in and whispered so softly in my ear that it tickled when she spoke the words, "I'll be your everything if you promise to be mine." We wound up kissing again, not wanting to pull ourselves away from each other.

My eyes swell with tears at the memory. This is supposed to be a happy movie playing in my head, not a sad one. But everything is sad when your wife is missing. She was my everything. Was I hers? Did I fulfill my end of the bargain? Had I made a mistake? I'm constantly searching for clues and since we haven't found any physical clues to Abigail's whereabouts, I am manically scouring my brain for one that might be rooted in body language or words. I know I am not in the most rational state of mind right now. When the love of your life is missing, I don't think that's even possible. I am trying to analyze the past with a microscope, but my microscope is blurry. Memories can't be captured because they are fleeting. We can't hold them any more than we can hold a dream in the palm of our hands. We can only replay them, but to whose narration? Tell five different people to watch the same ten minute play and then tell you their interpretations. I guarantee you each person will have a totally different one. So what does that mean for me? Which of the five people are correct? Are they all right? Is only one of them right? Are none of them right? I am dizzy thinking of the possibilities. Where is she? Surely factual information can't be interpreted differently. Facts are facts, right? So, where is she? Where is my wife? How am I going to find her? Is she being harmed? Is she dead? Is she trying to send me a sign to help her? Am I missing something obvious? My thoughts are racing faster than my pulsing heart until the phone rings and I find myself holding my breath.

"Hello?" I answer, breathless. "Abigail?" I know it

won't be her, but I'm caught up in the moment and I want more than anything for it to be her. I'm losing my mind. I've lost my wife. I need some relief. I want to beg the caller to bring me that relief.

"Anthony Parker?" The voice is stern and bold.

"Yes, this is Anthony Parker. Who is this?" My voice cracks.

After a short pause and what I imagine to be a rustling of papers the voice comes back on the line. "This is your neighbor. I live two houses down from yours. My name is Fred Welleby."

"Yes, Fred. Hello." My words are curt. I don't know who he is, we haven't spent much time getting to know our neighbors since we moved here.

"I might know something about your missing wife, Abigail. Would now be a good time to come by and talk?"

My mouth nearly drops to the floor. "Yes. Yes! Of course. Come over. I'll put the porch light on. I'll be waiting Mr. – ?" I couldn't recall his last name, I was too floored with the possibility of a clue.

"Fred Welleby." He repeated. "I'll be right there."

Seven

"I think there is a man watching me." I tell Tony during our quiet dinner at home. We have been eating in silence for ten minutes. I wasn't sure I was going to tell him about my paranoia, because I'm sure that's all it is. But I have to break the silence. And maybe, I admit secretly to myself, I want to know he is here to protect me. I want to know that Tony still really cares. Because lately I've felt so alone, so separate. He tells me it's the pregnancy. Everything that's not sunshine and roses, Tony tells me, is because of the pregnancy. What if it's still like this, feeling so isolated and separate from my husband, once our little peanut is born? Will it be because of the baby? Will he always blame it on something or someone? Is he right?

As expected, Tony smiles and looks up from his plate, into my eyes. Behind the smile I sense annoyance. And I think I hear a small grunt, but then he clears his throat before he speaks. "Abigail" he sighs before continuing, as if he is going to say one thing and then changes his mind before the words come out. "Tell me what happened." He places his fork down, on his napkin and lends his attention on me as he leans forward. "Are you okay?"

Instantly a rush of calm rushes over me. We are okay. I am okay. Tony still loves me. He is right, it is the pregnancy hormones that are getting to me. I am just being paranoid, surely. I love having his full attention and a smile comes to my lips, although I'm not entirely sure that is the appropriate gesture after what I've just told my husband. "I'm sure it's nothing." I wave my hand in the air as if I can just bat my paranoia away. It's that easy, only it isn't.

"What happened?" His voice is soft and gentle; he is concerned and wants to hear what I have to say.

Lately he can't see me, he looks through me. But right now I know he sees me. He loves me.

"Well, I'm probably just being paranoid. It's that dark car, the one with the tinted windows. It was sitting outside of the house again today." I pick up my fork and go back to eating my food, showing him that it is not a big deal and I am sure I am worried for no good reason.

"Did you see anyone? Did anyone get out of the car? Knock on the door, anything like that?"

I shake my head. "No. The car just sat there. It gives me the creeps."

"Would you feel more comfortable if we adopted a dog now?" We had talked about adopting a rescue dog once our little peanut was born and mobile. We both thought it would be a good idea, but I don't want to bring a dog into our house now. Not yet. It's too soon. It will be too much for me to handle. Our baby will be here shortly and I need to figure out the routine with her first, and then we can add a dog to the family. It's only fair to do things in this order; for my own sanity, and for the care of our baby. I need to devote time to our little one and figure out how in the world to raise a child before I can raise anyone else.

I shake my head again. "Not yet Tony. I want to wait until our baby is a year or so."

"Okay." He scratches the top of his head. "An alarm system then…would you feel more comfortable if we had one installed?"

"Yes. I think that's a good idea. I like that idea." I smile again, thankful that Tony cares enough about me to placate me, even if he thinks my worry is not a true concern.

"I'll start calling around for estimates tomorrow. It might take a bit, but just be sure to always keep your cell phone with you. You can call me anytime. And always keep the front door locked." His forehead is crinkled as he tries to think of ways to ease my mind.

"I'll keep the curtains closed on the front windows too." I add.

Tony nods in agreement. I know I'll need to remind him to call for price estimates. I'll wait a few weeks and then remind him then. I don't want to be a nagging wife. "Thank you." I add, biting my lower lip.

Another round of silence ensues as we both finish our lasagna dinner which I have made from scratch. I added spinach before baking it, but Tony did not notice. He never notices the little things. I stand to clear the plates from the table and Tony reaches for his bottle of Hennessey Black and pours a small amount in his glass. I rinse each dish and utensil before placing them in the dishwasher. When I open the refrigerator to return the pitcher of filtered water to its rightful place, I spot the cucumber. "Oh!" I exclaim, grabbing the cucumber and turning toward Tony, still sitting at the table with his glass of Hennessy Black. I think he has poured a second bit into his glass. "I almost forgot! This week, our little peanut is the size of a cucumber. Can you believe it Tony?" I hold the green fruit up against my swollen stomach as I stand before him.

Tony looks up from his glass. "Wow!" He smiles and nods, finishing his drink. "Our little one is sure getting big. He will be here any day now." He winks. "Do you think it will be a boy? Gideon Simon Parker?"

I shrug my shoulders and toss the cucumber to him to hold. "Maybe. Or maybe a girl...Merry Violet." I squish the right corner of my mouth to the side. We tease each other sometimes about the sex of the baby. The truth is we'll both be happy whether our little one is a boy or a girl. It's just that Tony picked out the boy name and I picked out the girl name, so in an odd way we are in a competition and we won't know who wins until the day I give birth. Regardless of our silly game, it's just that. Silly. We're both excited for our baby to arrive, to meet him or her. To hold them in our arms and to see them look into our eyes.

"Come over here." He motions me closer and places the cucumber on the table. I take a few steps toward him and he reaches his hands out to place them on my stomach. "Hey there little one." He stares at my stomach and presses his palms against my shirt. "We can't wait to meet you." Tony looks up at me and winks. "We love you already." He draws his hands back to his lap and I lean down to kiss his forehead.

"I love you Tony." I whisper before taking his glass and clearing the rest of the table.

"Love you, too. Both of you." He stands, pushing his chair away from him and heads to the living room. I know he is plopping down into the La-Z-Boy chair when I hear the click of the television turn on.

Tony may now know that our baby is the size of a cucumber, but I didn't get a chance to tell him that the little one is close to weighing three pounds and that she will be adding weight at the rate of a half a pound per week for the next seven weeks. How amazing is that? He also doesn't know that lately I feel like I have a flamethrower in my chest. I've read online and in my pregnancy books that indigestion is normal. Something about my expanding uterus putting pressure on my stomach. That is certainly happening. I gently pat my stomach, as I finish cleaning up the kitchen. I would tell him these things, but he never really asks. What I mean by *really* is that on the rare occasion he asks specifically about how I'm feeling with the pregnancy, he doesn't wait long for an answer. I usually have time to give him a one or two word reply. After that he moves on to something else, leaves the room or has wandered off somewhere different in his mind and I can tell he's not really listening, even if he is looking at me.

It's unreal to think that there is truly another human growing inside of me! I've been a bit klutzy lately, tripping on things. Maybe it's my protruding stomach that is throwing me off balance. My heels are collecting dust and I am sure to wear flats or tennis shoes each day. I'm keeping it as comfortable as I can with my attire. I've been putting moisturizer on my stomach before bed each night. My stomach itches from all of the expanding and growth. Speaking of bed time routines, the last few nights I've had to prop my pillows against my back. I sleep semi-seated so that I can catch my breath. The articles online tell me that this too is normal and it's because our little peanut is growing and pressing against my diaphragm, which can bring about breathlessness. Ah, the beauty of pregnancy!

Tony's voice breaks my thoughts as he calls to me from the living room. I wipe my hands on the red dish towel hanging over the kitchen sink and head toward him. Tony has moved from his chair to the couch and when I arrive he mutes the television. I notice the local news is on. He pats the side of the couch and I sit next to him. "Sit with me." He puts his arm around my back and pulls me in close. My head drifts easily to his shoulder although I am wondering now if he somehow read my thoughts from the kitchen. "We never take time to hang out together anymore."

I let my eyes close. It's nice to take the pressure off my feet and I slip my flats off so that my bare feet are now hovering just above the linoleum floor. It feels good to be held. Tony pulls me in closer and kisses the top of my head before leaning his own head back against the couch. We are a couple and I haven't felt this way with him in what seems like forever. These days, I am generally swollen and uncomfortable in my own skin. But right now I am cared for and cozy. I want this moment to last forever, although I know it won't. I want to tell Tony thank you for this moment, but before I can, my breath grows deeper and I drift off to sleep in his arms. This is the way I want it to always be. This is the way I want to feel forever. Safe and loved.

Annoying sellers frequently call my phone. They always show up as unlisted callers. Several times a month, at least. I don't know how they obtain my cell phone number, but they do. I have not and will not buy anything from them. Most of the time I answer the call and tell them to not call again; *add me to your do not call list*, I quickly tell them. Does anyone seriously buy something from over the phone? I'm sure most of them are gimmicks anyway. Last week the caller tried to tell me that he could give us a better deal on life insurance. Tony sells life insurance. I didn't bother to tell the seller this, I just told them again to add me to their do not call list and then I hung up. They are not listening anyway, but by law they have to stop calling if I request to be on that list.

I am in the middle of dusting the ceiling fans in the house when my phone rings. Most likely a seller, I think. And then I realize I should probably not be standing on the small ladder when I am so pregnant.

Oh well. I'm already up here, cleaning the fans. It needs to be done. The ladder is sturdy enough, I will be fine. I answer, prepared to give my usual spiel. "Hello?"

I only hear heavy breathing in reply.

"Hello?" I am well aware of the fact that I now sound annoyed. So many times I have to say hello two or three times before the seller even begins to speak.

I wait another few seconds. "Hello? I am hanging up now."

The breathing is still heavy and I hear a muffled voice, but cannot make out the words. It is a male voice, deep and raspy. It sends chills down my spine and I quickly hang up the phone. I toss my dusting rag to the floor and slowly climb down the three steps on the ladder. Instinctively I walk to the living room, my eyes scan the door to be sure it is locked. The curtains on the front window are closed but I walk up to them and pull them slightly back at the side and peer out, expecting the dark car with tinted windows to be sitting in front of our house again. There is no car. Only the mailman pulling up to our box. He looks up at the house, smiles and waves. My peeking must not be very good, I think. I pull the curtains back a little more, letting the light flood the living room and I wave back to him. Paranoia, I tell myself. That's all it is.

Black Cat Books is a hidden gem in Waterford. I hadn't heard of it until now, not that I get out much. I'm an avid reader and visit the library several times a month. I leave with stacks of books so high that I use my chin to hold them down until I get to the car. I toss them into a laundry basket that sits in my back seat for this very purpose. I buy e-books on my Kindle reader, too. I don't belong to a book club, nor am I an aspiring writer, I just love a good story. I've submersed myself in books since I could read. I've always reasoned that growing up without siblings, I needed the comfort of friends in some form; albeit fictional friends, I found them in books. I found the bookstore today after finishing the weekly grocery shopping. There was construction on the main road and traffic was rerouted. The grocery store is on the opposite side of town from our house and I don't know the roads as well in that section of town. I got twisted after the signs for the detour abruptly ended; I followed the two cars directly in front of me, thinking they would head back to the main road.

I was wrong. Each car turned off in different directions, neither of which was to the main road. My heart started racing, although I told myself to calm down. I was only in Waterford, surely I would find my way home, eventually. And anyway, what is the hurry? I have sesame chicken in the slow cooker at home. All I need to do before dinner is make the salad, and that will only take a few minutes. I tap my finger against my lips as I turn down one street after another, hoping to pop out in a recognizable part of town. After one more turn I realize I am behind a small strip mall, it's the one where my hair salon is located. And then my eyes light up at the sight of the sign. *OPEN. Black Cat Books. New and Used Book Sales.* I generally don't feel adventurous, I like to stick to my routine. Maybe it's realizing that our little peanut will be here so soon that makes me pull into the parking lot. I won't be able to venture out much once she is here. I put my car in park, undo my seatbelt, grab my purse and look back at the bags of groceries in the backseat. It's cool outside today. The radio said it is fifty-two degrees and being that it is cloudy, I decide a few minutes in the bookstore won't harm the groceries. I step out of the car, locking the doors behind me and head toward the front door. There are only a handful of cars in the lot. The store is admittedly, off the beaten path. This, to me, only makes it a richer find.

I open the store door and hear a small bell ring above my head. I draw in a deep breath of air, blissful at the scent of so many books waiting to be read. My eyes wander through the wide aisles, wondering where I should start. I check my watch and give myself thirty minutes before I have to leave. The groceries should be fine until then, I assure myself. I am not someone who deviates from routine, but it is intoxicating. For this moment in time, no one knows where I am. In this moment I am no one except a browsing shopper. When I go to the library or the grocery, the employees who have been around for a while all know my name. Waterford is a fairly small town. And while familiarity is comforting, anonymity can be too.

My feet and hands are swollen. I'm sure my face is too, although whenever I ask Tony he promises I look as thin as ever. He is lying to try and make me feel better. But I know the truth. I can look in any mirror and see that my body has drastically changed from a once small frame, to now bloated and bulgy. My body is like a balloon that is too full of air and ready to burst with even the tiniest prick. I am wearing unsightly soccer sandals today, not exactly a fashion statement, but my feet fit into them, unlike so many of my other shoes right now, and therefore they were the chosen shoes before I headed out today.

I decide to wander over to the far right side of the store where a sign hangs from the ceiling saying "New Authors". It's always a thrill to discover a new author because that means they'll be many more books to read in the future. I am already smitten with this hidden gem of a store. As I browse through the titles lining the tall shelves, running my index finger across each of the books spines while doing so I nearly jump out of my skin when a voice hovers above my shoulder.

"Can I help you with anything today?" It's an ordinary question coming from a familiar voice.

I glance over my shoulder to meet the eyes of the questioner, not wanting to lose my place of browsing. "Just looking, thanks." I say quickly, although my eyes catch the questioners and I realize there is a reason the voice sounds so familiar. My breath catches in my throat as I drop my finger from the book spines and turn to stand and face the familiar eyes.

"Abby!" It is not stated in a question, it is instead, with absolute excitement.

"Oh my gosh, it's you!" I hear myself squeal like a school girl. My arms flail open and we hug.

"You're pregnant?" This, in the form of a question.

I nod, looking down at my protruding stomach.

"Congratulations!"

"Thank you." I reply, still studying the face for signs of change. There are a few small wrinkles around the eyes, but otherwise everything has been well preserved. "You look great." I smile, I have to say it.

"You too."

A rush of heat hits my face. "How long have you worked here?" I change the subject, wanting to bring my face back to its normal pale color.

"Oh, I've been a manager here for a handful of months. I left town for a few years, did some traveling. Now I'm back in Waterford." I couldn't help but wonder if being back in Waterford brought happiness or it's opposite.

"I saw your dad, actually. Did he tell you? It was probably three months ago at Last Stop." Last Stop was a tavern in Beativille, just outside of Waterford.

My face squeezes together, unable to hide the look of confusion. "My dad?"

"Yep. I told him to tell you hello for me. I'm guessing he didn't?"

I shake my head. "I had no idea." As far as I knew my dad never visited bars. It is incredibly out of character for him and I am intrigued.

"When did your folks divorce?"

My face crinkles even more. "I'm sorry?"

"Your dad was pretty smitten with Blair Palmento that night. I figured they were an item now..."

"What? Blair Palmento?"

"Yep. It was her. I spoke with both of them that night. Are they not together anymore?"

It takes a moment before I can form proper words. "Blair and my dad? They were never together. My parents are still married."

"Oops. I may have misspoken. I'm so sorry Abby."

Something tickles the bottom of my leg and bend forward, thankful for the distraction. A black cat rubs my feet back and forth and I hear her gentle purr as her green eyes look up to meet mine. I smile and reach my hand down to pet her. She climbs my leg, stretching her front paws out to meet my fingers and rubs her nose against my skin. "She's cute."

"That's Elise. She's one of the two black cats who live here at the store."

I laugh. "Of course. I get it, Black Cat Books. The store wouldn't be complete without one or two." For a moment I've forgotten I've just been told that my dad was cheating on my mom.

A sharp pain hits my lower back and I reach to grab at it with both hands.

"Are you okay Abby?

Taking in three deep breaths and then letting them out slowly, I don't bother to answer, thinking the answer is quite clear.

"What can I do? Do you need to sit down?"

After a moment of squeezing my eyes shut and grabbing at my back I nod in agreement. A chair will be nice.

The level of care I am receiving goes above and beyond. I can't say thank you enough. I am brought a cool glass of water, a damp cloth, something to prop my legs up on and a few books that I am told are on the house. It is nothing short of the royal treatment. I haven't left the store and I already can't wait to come back. I call my obstetrician from the comfort of the chair and am told that back pains are normal and are expected during this phase. It is always the same thing with pregnancy. One annoying pain will subside only to be replaced by a new one. Surprise, its back pain! It is always something. I've come to realize that I have to find ways to cope with the pain at each stage, and to know that if I am not having some kind of pain, that's when I should question things.

The pain in my back is lessening as I relaxed in the chair. In fact, I think I have laughed more this afternoon than I have since I've been pregnant. I have even laughed at the fact that my dad was a cheater. Is a cheater. A lying cheater. I don't know if I will confront him about it or let it be. I'll figure that out later. For this afternoon, sitting in my chair, I am going to laugh about it and a myriad of other things that aren't really funny. My swollen hands and feet. My fear of being a good mother. My refusing to pull the daisies, even though they are technically weeds. My paranoia for safety at home. This afternoon it has suddenly become funny. It is like the veil of seriousness has dropped and the only thing left is laughter. I laugh because it feels good. It is good to forget about the mundane tasks of life and to care about nothing. It is good to drop my guard. It is good to let life happen instead of trying to control every second of it.

Looking at my watch I realize I've been in the store for more than three hours. The cold groceries have surely spoiled. I will have to go back and pick up a few new, fresh items and toss the rotten ones. I need to hurry so that I can get home and put away our purchased food and prepare the salads for dinner. Dinner! Oh, rats. The slow cooker needed to be turned off an hour ago. Most likely it will be over cooked, probably burning now. I need to come up with a new dinner plan. I stand, too quickly, my eyes seeing black stars for a moment before steadying myself. I grab my pile of new books and my purse and give away a hug. The hug lingers, neither of us wanting to pull away. Inebriated by the scent that surrounds me; cake with buttercream frosting, now I am craving cake. I make a mental note to pick up a small cake when I return to the grocery on my way home. I say goodbye and promise to come back tomorrow.

I walk back to the car, feeling the warmth of the sun hit my face. When I unlock the doors I rummage through the bags of groceries in the back seat. The chocolate ice cream is melting and sticking all over the ketchup bottle and the bananas which are in the same bag. I remove the ketchup and bananas and place them in a different bag. I take the bag with the melted ice cream, tie a knot at its top and place it on the floor. That is one of several items I will need to replace. I glance at the clock again. I really need to get home and turn off the slow cooker. I need to come up with a new plan for dinner.

Oddly, the rush of stress coursing through my veins is nonexistent. The pain in my back has been forgotten. I climb in the car, click my seatbelt into place and hear the engine come to life. I glance in my rear view mirror as I pull out of the parking lot, smiling at the Black Cat Books sign. As I round the corner and find my way to Main Street, this time without a hitch, a twinge of anger toward my dad rises inside of me. Cheating? Lying? How could he do that to my mom? I reach the next traffic light as it turns yellow and instead of slowing to a halt I press the gas pedal, racing beneath it as it turns red. And with Blair? Blair Palmento, my fifth grade boyfriend's mother? The mother of the boy I first kissed, for that matter. Not to mention, Blair is also a married woman. I couldn't stop my mind from wondering how long the affair had been taking place. Had it been a one-time thing? Surely not, if they were found in Beativille. Going outside of town must have meant that my dad was trying to hide something. Obviously, trying to hide from my mother. The affair could have been going on for years, now that I thought about it. The Palmento's attended our church. Blair taught at Saint Ann's, where my dad was the principal, although they were both retired; another connection they had. This affair could have been going on for years right under our noses, without anyone having a clue. Come to think of it, the Palmento's always donated a lot of money to the church, something my dad always mentioned during my childhood. Why else would it matter who was donating large sums to the church? Why else would my dad make a point to say something about it? How ironic that my mom had always hoped and wished that I would end up with Blair's son, Chuck. The tangled webs we weave, well, the webs he's weaved anyway.

I am shaking my head at the craziness of all of this as I pull into the parking lot of the grocery store for the second time this afternoon. Despite my confusion and disbelief, I am still smiling. I've always thought my parents had as close to a perfect marriage as anyone can have. After all, everyone is on automatic these days and if the slightest thing goes wrong or feels wrong in a marriage, they simply file for divorce. What is the statistic? More than fifty-percent of all marriages will end in divorce. Are that many couples mismatched from the start? Or is it that marriage isn't always easy and so the easy thing becomes leaving it rather than staying in it? Is there even such a thing as the perfect marriage? Realizing what my dad's been up to recently and possibly been up to for many years, I am wondering if all marriages are set up to fail. What is the best life: one where you keep your commitment to your vows or one where you follow your heart, even if that means upsetting everything that is normal? Can you have both or does it have to be one or the other? I'd like to candidly ask my dad that right now. I wish I could call him up and tell him I know and have him confess everything to me. A good church going man. The former principle of a Catholic school. A father. A husband. A pillar of our community. How can someone who is all of these things also be a cheater and a liar? I've lived in such naivety, only seeing the world in terms of black and white. Right and wrong. Good and bad. Never daring to think that there is a blur between the lines. A light turned on inside of me when I stumbled into Black Cat Books today. It was like the moment in the Wizard of Oz when Dorothy goes from her mundane black and white world and walks into a beautiful world of color and newness. I learned that my father, who I'd always believed was nothing short of perfect, is a lying cheater (is there any other kind of cheater?). That revelation is the very thing that has oddly opened me to a new perspective. Life doesn't have to be black and white. It can be full of bold, bright colors. It can be blurred. It can be filled with laughter, even when we are in pain.

I kill the car engine and toss the keys into my purse as I exit the vehicle. I run through a mental list of the items I need to re-purchase, in addition to the small cake with butter cream frosting that I am still craving. I walk with my head held high and quickly dismiss any looks of sympathy that come my way, knowing I stand out like a sore thumb with my swollen belly and my chubby feet that are squeezed tightly into my unsightly soccer sandals. Dinner is certainly burnt in the slow cooker at home. I'm at the grocery store to re-buy items I've already purchased today, because I let them melt and rot in the back seat of my car while I played around, totally off task in a book store. My cell phone rings as I push a cart around the aisles in the store. Unknown number.

"Hello?" I answer softly, not wanting to broadcast a phone conversation inside. I always hate when people are screaming on their phones while walking through the store or even worse, while in the check-out lane, completely ignoring the employee helping them. I find it beyond rude and I don't want to be *that* person.

There is no answer on the other line.

"Hello?" I answer once more.

Only crackling and so I hang up and toss my phone

back into my purse. A seller? A familiar chill races down my spine, just as it always does when I sense danger these days. It was just a seller, I reassure myself. Nothing more. Nothing to worry about.

I find a beautiful, small round white cake at the bakery in the back of the store. It is topped with butter cream frosting. The cake is plain and primed to be personalized, written on with whatever message the buyer wants. I will be the cake's buyer and I don't want anything written on the cake. I prefer a blank slate. I lift the plastic lid from the top and breathe in its warm scent. I am happy I am buying the cake. I like this new world of blurriness and bright color.

Eight

ANTHONY

Present Day, 2017

I offer to share my bottle of Hennessy Black when Fred Welleby comes through the door. I suppose I've seen my neighbor in passing while coming or going to the house, but we've never so much as shared a friendly wave. Fred takes me up on the offer for a drink and I pour us each a small glass. He sits on the couch while I sit in the La-Z-Boy chair, my hand resting around my glass.

"You have a nice home." Fred gestures, trying to make small talk before announcing why he's really here. I know he is not being honest because our living room is a mess. Abigail would have a heart attack if she saw the many toys scattered throughout the house. But I am a single parent for the time being and between caring for Gideon, searching for my missing wife and going to work, cleaning up messes at home is the least of my priorities right now.

I force a small chuckle and answer, "It's hard to find time to pick up after our son between work and the search..." I let my voice trail. I am not wanting to chit-chat. I would rather he get to the point; tell me why he is here and what he has to say. I hope my silence will convey that now.

Fred places one arm up along the top of the couch and holds his glass in the other. He takes advantage of the silence between us to empty its contents, a satisfied look unfolding across his face. "Good stuff." He holds his glass in the air while delivering the compliment and then places it directly in front of him on the coffee table, choosing not to use one of the stacked coasters that sit just a few inches from his placement. He is enjoying the suspense; knowing he has my complete attention. His face is pale and his back rounded. His jeans hang loosely around his legs. I think he must be in his sixties or possibly older. The well-defined wrinkles on his face in combination with the tint of his skin tell me he must not get out much. I make a mental note to study the outside of his home next time I leave. He said he lives four doors down from us and by his appearance and demeanor I am beginning to think he is a recluse who keeps to himself and watches the comings and goings of the street from behind his thick curtains. I may be wrong, but I don't think I am. I wonder if he realizes how cruel a thing it is to have information on someone's missing loved one only to hold on tight to it, savoring the quiet instead of delivering the clue.

After a bit I clear my throat, "Mr. Welleby, what information do you have on my wife?"

He smiles and leans forward. "My there. Someone is anxious." He snickers and it sends a chill down my spine.

"You must understand, my wife has been missing for months and we do not have any clues to her whereabouts. If you have information that might help our search, we would be incredibly appreciative." I am to the point, but also trying to play to his heart, hoping he has one behind his now callous tone.

"What's in it for me Mr. Parker?" I see a light come on in his eyes. He is here for money. He wants a prize to deliver a clue. But how do I know he really has one? Should I offer him money? Should I speak to my lawyer first? I make a mental note to call Omar when the man leaves and have the private investigator check out Fred Welleby. Most likely he is just a lonely, crazy man, but I do not want to miss something obvious. With the police and media having lost interest in Abigail's disappearance, it makes Mr. Welleby's supposed clue even more tempting to grab. If he truly has a viable piece of information, the story will be reignited and the public will be reenergized to help search for my wife. After mulling it over, I decide to take the bait and hope Mr. Welleby has some helpful information to share with me.

"We don't have much." I gesture to the home, remembering how much Abigail hated the laminate floors that were made to look like hardwood. She'd wanted to have them replaced before Gideon arrived. I felt a twinge of guilt looking at the cheap linoleum now. "As I'm sure you know, I am desperate to find my wife. I'm guessing it's why you've waited so long to come to me with your information. You wanted to wait until I was hungry enough to offer you a reward. Well, Mr. Welleby, we don't have much, like I said. We are a young couple with a young child. I'm our only source of income and every extra penny we have is going to the search for Abigail in the form of printing flyers and buying newspaper ads, anything to keep her story, and hopefully her, alive." I am astonished at what people will do for money. How can you know something that could help find a missing person and withhold that information until you are paid? There is nothing ethical about this behavior, but I realize I am in no position to judge. I need any new information that can be found. I need a new clue. Otherwise, the case is dead and Abigail is somewhere in the world thinking I don't care enough about her to save her.

"Oh," he winks "I'm sure you can come up with something." After a few beats, he adds "Refill?"

Taken back by his audacity I shake my head. "Sorry. No refills today." My forehead wrinkles above my eyes and I roll my neck from side to side. Does this guy think he can take me for a ride or does he actually have something legitimate to tell me? There is only one way to find out. "Five hundred dollars is the best I can do." I stare at him, wanting it to be enough, yet feeling guilty to spend our money this way. I'd worked so many extra hours before Gideon was born and everything I'd worked for, all the time I'd spent away from Abigail while she was pregnant was only to pay for searching for her instead of getting on with our lives and building our beautiful family. Life can be surprising.

"Ah. You do have something to offer me." He presses his thin lips together. He knows he has all of the power and he loves it. I want to stand up and wrap my hands around his flimsy neck and shake the information out of him, but instead I restrain myself and sit calmly waiting for the rest of what he has to say. "Make it one thousand and you have a deal."

I pause, squinting my eyes at this measly man. Maybe I should tell him there is no deal and kick him out of my house right this very minute. I'll send the private investigator on a hunt to find out about this strange neighborly man. I know this is what I should do, but the temptation to find out what he knows immediately is too much. "Okay. One thousand dollars." I hear the words escape my mouth before I have fully decided that this is acceptable.

"Good boy." He chirps. "Money first, then I will share with you what I know."

"How do I know what you are going to tell me is going to be helpful to finding my wife?"

"I guess there is a bit of risk involved, young man." I don't like the game he is playing and instead of engaging in any further banter I stand and tell him I'll be right back with the money. I don't want him to know that we have that much cash in the house, but what else am I supposed to do? He won't accept a check, only cash. If I don't pay him now, he won't tell me what he knows. We have exactly one thousand dollars hidden in one of my socks at the bottom of the drawer. When we were first married and moved into our house, I placed it there and told Abigail about it. I told her it was our emergency money. I am sure she would agree with me, if I could talk to her right now, that this is an emergency. I am sure she would raid our emergency cash too, if I were the one missing. Realizing this my racing heart eases up as I dig through the drawer to find the hidden cash. It's a white sock, like most of the others. It is pushed in the bottom back corner on the left side of the drawer. I pull the sock out from beneath the others and reach inside to grab the wad of bills. Abigail would want me to do this for her, I remind myself. I press the bills into the palm of my hand and toss the sock back in the drawer and close it. My stomach is full of life as I turn to walk back out to the living room and hand our emergency cash to a stranger who tells me he is a neighbor and has information. A stranger who is making me pay for something he knows about my missing wife. Everything about this feels wrong, although I am trying to convince myself it is not. I am only trying to do everything I can to find Abigail and bring her home safe and sound.

Fred Welleby hasn't moved from his spot on the couch. Thankfully Gideon is with Omar and Lois for the night and he won't be woken by the strange man in our living room. I flash the money in my hand and speak, "Information first, then this is yours." I take a seat after speaking.

"No. That's not how it works. My information, my rules. Nice try Mr. Parker." He smiles. "Money first, then information. It's the only way I'll speak."

Difficult is an understatement in describing this conniving man. I toss the cash to him, what other choice do I have? He pulls his hands together to catch the folded bills and begins to count. It is quite possible that this man is pulling one over on me. He might take the cash and run out my front door. I realize this, but only sit quietly and wait.

"This is five-hundred dollars Mr. Parker. I asked for one thousand."

"It's one thousand."

"I may be old, but I can still count. It is five-hundred. Count for yourself if you wish." He tosses the wad of cash back to me and I quickly count it, which I had not done before. He is right. It is only five-hundred dollars.

I stumble on my words as my mind races. Did we use the emergency money for something? I am certain we didn't. If Abigail would have used any of it, she would have told me. She tells me everything. We don't have secrets between us. Even if Abigail had told Lois and Omar about our emergency cash I am positive they would never touch it. No one else could possibly know. I push through the contours of my mind, wondering if I used any of the money just after Abigail's disappearance, when I had to take some time off from work. But again, I know I didn't touch it. "You're right." It's all I can say at the moment. "It's all we have left." I try to stay focused on what Mr. Welleby might or might not tell me about my missing wife, instead of where the other five-hundred dollars has gone.

He eyes me, trying to see if I am bluffing. He must determine that I am not. "Fine. Another drink and five-hundred then." I fetch the bottle from the kitchen and refill his glass. "There was a dark car. A Lexus, I believe." He sips the drink. "It parked outside of your house while your wife was home during the day, alone. This happened on more than one occasion."

Is this it? Is this all of the information he has to share with me? Admittedly, I'd forgotten that Abigail had told me this same information. I've given him five-hundred dollars to be told something I already know. When Abigail was somewhere around eight months into the pregnancy she had become incredibly paranoid about her safety. Sometimes she thought people were following her, other times she thought there was a dark car with tinted windows sitting outside of the house. I had tried to be sympathetic to Abigail, but it seemed probable that her paranoia had been caused by pregnancy hormones. It was not normal behavior for her and I knew she had a lot of anxiety building up about becoming a mother. As the birth of Gideon neared, her paranoia of safety grew. I was sure it would subside once Gideon was born.

"Did you ever see the driver of the car? This man?"

"No. He stayed in the car. The car had tinted windows."

"Did you write down the license plate number?" I felt a small glimmer of hope. If Mr. Welleby has the license plate number, the police can investigate the driver of the car and find out why they were parked outside of our house and if they have anything to do with the disappearance of Abigail.

"Again, no." There is no remorse in Mr. Welleby's voice when he delivers his answer.

"No?" I cannot hide my rage at this point. He has led me on and without a license plate number, what good is this information? It's information I already knew. "Can you tell me anything else? Have I paid you five-hundred dollars for a bluff?"

"It's not a bluff Mr. Parker. I saw this car outside of your home on several occasions. It was a black Lexus, I'm fairly sure. Tinted windows. Only came when you were away at work."

"I need more than that!" I stand from my chair, feeling rage course through my veins. Every muscle in my body tenses.

"That's all I have to give. A *thank you* would be nice. We are neighbors, after all." He follows my lead and stands. I am several inches taller than him and when Mr. Welleby stands, the hunch in his back is more noticeable.

I grit my teeth and point to the front door. "I will not thank you for conning me this evening Mr. Welleby. That's not a very neighborly thing to do, wouldn't you agree?"

"It's not very neighborly to ignore your neighbors is it Mr. Parker?" He is stealing my money for a drop of useless information because I didn't wave hello to him while coming and going from our home? "I tried to be friendly to your wife and she looked right through me." He added. Mr. Welleby shuffled forward and pushed open the front door. We both became entranced by the slow creek it made while opening.

It is taking everything I have to physically restrain myself from killing this man. "You tried to be *friendly* to my wife?" I slam my fist against the wall and punch though it, creating a hole. Mr. Welleby rushes through the door and I want to grab his feeble arm and shake him. Friendly to my wife? Did he make Abigail feel uncomfortable in some way? What is he talking about?

"I've told you everything I know. I did not harm your wife. She *was* sure a beautiful woman." The emphasis he puts on the word *was* leaves me screaming into the night air. Mr. Welleby disappears into the darkness and I am standing in the doorway of our house making sounds I do not recognize.

"Yes, his name is Mr. Fred Welleby. He lives just a few doors down from us." I give the police officer his address. I called the station as soon as I could pull myself together after Mr. Welleby's visit.

I've recounted everything that happened twice now to the officer, in excruciating detail.

"Was Mr. Welleby drunk when he arrived to your home?" The male officer asks flatly.

"No. I don't know. Maybe? I have no idea. I don't have breathalyzer tests on me! I'm not a police officer, you are."

"Calm down Mr. Parker. I'm trying to help you."

"Are you? Are you trying to help me? Are you trying to help my wife? Because it sure doesn't seem like you are. No one cares about who has taken her or where she is. Everyone has given up on finding her, at least on finding her alive. People think I'm some kind of freak show and they want to tell me they have information on my missing wife, when really they do not..."

The officer interrupts me, putting an end to my frantic rant. "We are doing everything we can, as we've told you many times Mr. Parker. There is only so much we can do in the case of a missing adult. I know you are aware of this. Until we find evidence telling us that Abigail was kidnapped or..." he pauses, stopping before he was going to say murdered. I know it, he knows it, but we pretend it hasn't happened. He continues, "Until we have a viable clue to go from, we have nowhere else to turn. If you had a license plate number for the car, for example, we could investigate that. If you had a description of the person driving the black Lexus, we could look into that. But you do not." He clears his throat and hesitates before asking another question. "Mr. Parker, I have to ask, why didn't *you* tell us about the car parked in front of your house before now? If your wife told you she was scared and she had told you about this specific car, why didn't it come up when we first questioned you?"

I realize he is trying to be clever. He is trying to catch me in a lie. He is trying to make me stumble on my words, to pin me down for the disappearance of my wife. I won't let him win at this game. I am not guilty. I am the only one trying to find her. This officer, like all of the others, just wants to place blame somewhere and move on. I am not somewhere. I am not to blame. I am innocent. I am just a husband who wants to find his missing wife. Why is that so difficult for anyone to understand? Why does no one have empathy for me and for what I am going through right now? "I told you, I forgot."

"Forgetting can be awfully convenient."

"It wasn't deliberate, or convenient." I mock his use of the word. "We're on the same side. At least I hope we are. I know I am searching for my wife. If you claim that you are too, then we're on the same side."

"We are on your side Mr. Parker. Like I said, we just need a lead in order to keep investigating your wife's disappearance. Right now we have no suspects. Right now our best guess is that Abigail decided to run away."

"Run away? You said you couldn't find any evidence of that either, so why is that what you want to go with?" I am insulted. Abigail did not run away. But as I speak the words, I think about the missing five-hundred dollars in our sock drawer. Would she have taken the money and left? I shake away the thought as quickly as it comes. It is not possible. I would have noticed a sign. There would have been clues.

"You're right. I'm sorry for what you are experiencing Mr. Parker. We all are. I can't imagine how difficult this must be for you. Please understand that I am not one of the officers assigned to your case, but I am on duty tonight and know what I need to. I assure you, we all want to help you find your wife, but again, we need a clue. We need a lead before further action can be taken. There are over five hundred thousand missing people reported in the

United States each year." He is trying his best to be sympathetic and I appreciate this gesture.

"But you, meaning our local police department, are not responsible for all of the missing persons cases in the country. Surely you have time to focus on finding my wife." I tell him.

"Again, until we have a strong lead, we have nothing more to go on. We are bogged down with homicides, robberies, rapes, assaults, traffic issues and crime prevention in general. We are short staffed and unfortunately there are a lot of crimes, even here in little Waterford."

Abigail's case is considered low priority, that is what he is telling me. I hear him loud and clear. I respect the work that they do, but right now I am desperate to find my wife and I want them searching for her twenty-four-seven. I realize this is unreasonable, but my wife is missing and if I have not already completely lost my mind I am losing it now. "I understand. Thank you for your time officer."

"I have made a note about what you've told me tonight; about Fred Welleby and about the black Lexus. This will be added to the file in case any further details emerge. And Mr. Parker?"

"Yes?"

"Don't give up hope. I realize I don't know how

you must feel right now. It is unimaginable. But please don't give up hope. If Abigail is out there, we will find her. Somehow we will find her."

I appreciate the kindness he has bestowed on me just before we say good-bye and end the conversation. It is rare these days; kindness. After the night I've had I soak up his words like a sponge. *Don't give up hope.* Maybe he knows something I don't. Maybe the officers are secretly working on a lead that I cannot know about just yet. Maybe Abigail is alive. Maybe they'll find her. Maybe...

I can't sleep. Gideon is at the Atwell's tonight because I have work in the morning. The house is too quiet. I stare endlessly at Abigail's unused pillow and despite the officers hopeful words on the phone tonight, I can't stop beating myself up. I can't stop racking my brain for a clue; for an answer. I am a caged hamster on a wheel. I am going nowhere. I keep running. I keep trying. But nothing changes.

I pull out my phone and turn on the Internet. I search for facts about missing persons. The officer was indeed right on the phone tonight. More than half a million people go missing every year in our country. I learn that there is something called the "missing white girls syndrome" and that the media tend to place the most emphasis on missing beautiful young white women with blond hair because of societies supposed fascination with "damsels in distress". Abigail is young and beautiful, only she has black hair, not blond. Can such a small fact make such a big difference in the lack of exposure the media is giving her now that she's been missing five months? I admit, they shared her story nationwide when she first went missing. Her photo was all over the television. But not now. The story has faded. Would it still be alive if Abigail had blond hair?

I also learn while browsing the Internet that adults with drug and alcohol addiction, psychiatric issues and elderly suffering from dementia or Alzheimer's are generally the ones who are missing. None of these are my wife. Why was she taken?

When I read that there are more than forty thousand sets of unidentified remains in the United States, as reported by the medical examiners and coroner's offices, I shut off my phone.

I will work with our church to organize yet another volunteer search team to scour the local woods. I will hire another team of divers to investigate the waterways. I remind myself of another fact I read on the Internet tonight: a person cannot be declared legally dead until they have been listed as missing for seven years. Seven years. I don't want to wait seven years to find Abigail. And I want to find Abigail alive. I can hardly bear the thought of waiting seven more days.

Weary without the hope of sleep tonight, I drift in and out of thoughts. I replay Mr. Welleby's cold words again and again, searching for a deeper meaning, only to find none. When I replay the phone conversation with the officer, something clicks and I realize in my late night stupor that I had suppressed another memory of Abigail. I hadn't meant to omit the story about the car parked outside of our house and Abigail's paranoia while pregnant. That was an honest mistake. But this memory I knew I'd suppressed on purpose. Abigail and I had an awful fight two weeks before her disappearance. It was the worst fight we'd ever had and it seemed so out of the blue. I told myself then that it was because of the stress of motherhood. Gideon was not sleeping through the night, and therefore neither was Abigail. She hadn't bothered to put on her red lip stick or any makeup for that matter since Gideon was born. She dressed differently, too. Normally she was well put together, but with the birth of our son, she opted to wear sweat suits and pajamas most of the time. I'm not recalling this part of the memory because I minded. I couldn't imagine the pain she had just endured and the difficulty of raising a little one around the clock. She never got a break. I went to work and came home. She could never leave her work and I imagine that would make anyone feel run down. I tried to kiss her, wrap my arm around her and generally show her affection when I returned home in the evenings from work. Co-workers mumbled quietly that it took women some time to come around to having sex again after giving birth. I wanted to be respectful and give her the space she needed, while showing her that I cared and that I still found her wildly attractive. Anyway, I made the mistake one evening of telling her we should go shopping to buy her new clothes over the weekend, when I was off from work. She blew up at the suggestion. A few comments were said, but all I remember are muffles as I look back on this moment in our marriage. My mind recalls the conversation starting at the point where Abigail's eyes widen and I know this is no ordinary argument; rather, I have hurt her.

"You think I'm unsightly? Are you embarrassed by me? Have I let you down, Tony? Do I not meet your expectations?"

I shake my head, wishing I could rewind time and take back the shopping suggestion. Wishing I could remember those muffled words before Abigail's eyes filled with pain.

"Do you think I am a slob? It's not easy being here all day with him. You're off at work living the good life and I'm here changing diapers filled with poop, being spit up on..." she broke off in tears.

I tried to comfort her and she pushed my arm away. I'm not sure of exactly what I said but one thing lead to another and before I knew it Abigail was screaming. I told her she was going to wake Gideon, because normally we were so careful to tip-toe and whisper when he was finally asleep. She said she didn't care and she began cursing. I'd never heard her so much as utter one swear word until that night. But something inside of her broke, she was unhinged.

"You're beautiful, Abigail. I'm crazy about you. I know you know that." I tried again to move closer to her as we stood opposite of each other, in our bedroom.

"Shut-up Tony. Just shut-up. This isn't about what I look like. That's the least of my worries."

"What do you mean? What are you so worried about?"

"You don't ever pay attention do you?" She spat, tears pouring down her cheeks.

"I'm sorry. What am I missing?"

"Everything. You're missing everything." She turned and left the room, letting out a shriek as she slammed the door behind her. Gideon, of course, woke up amongst the chaos and began wailing.

I stayed in our room as I heard a glass break against the wall. Moments later the door to Gideon's room creaked open and I heard Abigail's normal, sweet voice speak to him. I imagined she was holding him and rocking him in her arms. I heard the soft hum of a lullaby as Gideon's cries quieted. She was magic with him that way.

Once the house grew quiet, I opened the door to our bedroom and walked down the hall, standing quietly with my back against the wall, watching Abigail sway Gideon back and forth and then placing him gently into his crib. She jumped when she left his room, pulling the door half way shut behind her.

"Are we okay?" I asked softly, looking into her sad eyes.

"Sometimes I don't know anymore." Her words were cold and sent a dagger through my chest.

"What don't you know Abigail? I love you. What more is there to know?"

My question was met with silence as we stood in the dark hallway outside of Gideon's room.

"Do you love me?"

She answered me with a nod, but left me wondering what she was really thinking. We were disconnected somehow and I needed to get us back on track. This happened two weeks before her disappearance. Had she run away because she was unhappy with me? Had she stolen the money from our sock drawer and left, just like that? Would she really do that? A flood of sadness swallowed me as I sat in bed, consumed with guilt and unable to make an attempt at sleep. Did she love me? Did she hate me? Did she regret having Gideon? Did she blame me for him?

I showered her with affection over the following two weeks, in the days that I had yet to know, were leading to her disappearance. She seemed to warm to me after a few days and things resumed to normal. I knew that didn't mean they were normal. Nothing about our lives now is normal. Had that fight been a coincidence? Or was she trying to give me some sort of warning? I lean my head back against the pillow I have propped against the wall behind me. And then I remember something else Abigail said to me that night, the night of our argument. She said, "We need to get the security system installed. The one you promised me, Tony. It needs to be installed soon."

Nine

ABIGAIL

2015

Our little peanut is the size of a pumpkin! Our baby is the length of a stalk of rhubarb. I decide to go with purchasing a small pumpkin for Tony and placing it on his chair for tonight's dinner. I've read that our little one is now reacting to sounds, clenching her fists. Connections are forming in her brain that will help her swallow. As amazing as it all sounds, I still have swollen hands and feet. My face feels swollen, too. I have off and on headaches. And I have stomach and lower back pain. My doctor has started to talk about preliminary labor pains. She's trying to make me understand the difference between labor and pre-labor. All I know for sure is that I am uncomfortable and I think it might be better to have the baby out of me, rather than in me, at this point. I dread the crying at night, the inability to sleep, but I'm not sleeping well now. I am anxious. I worry about what the delivery will really be like. Of course, along with my pregnancy "what to expect" research, I've accidently stumbled on some horror birth stories. Stories of mom's who have died in labor. Stories of babies who died upon delivery. Terrible things that I know I shouldn't be reading, but when they are dangled in front of me on the Internet, it is difficult not to click and read. My mouth is always gaped and I find myself holding my stomach while reading what I know I shouldn't be. Tony tells me I don't need to be any more paranoid than I already am. I know this, but pregnancy is strange and the thought of giving birth is frightening.

I'm still hoping for a girl; Merry Violet. Tony is still hoping for a boy; Gideon Simon. I think a little girl will keep me better company and will want to help me cook and clean. I'm not sure what I'd do with a little boy. How would I connect? Tony tells me I'll be a great mom and I hope he's right. I know it will be okay whether we have a boy or a girl. I do know this. But my nerves are high and I would like to have a girl so that I have someone I can relate to in the house. I know Tony and I are starting to drift apart, even though we are about to have our first baby together. We just feel so distant from each other. I know part of it is me. I am swollen and heavy and anxious about the arrival of our baby. Tony wants me to calm down. But it's not so easy for me to do. I have so many thoughts swimming in my mind. I want everything to go smoothly, yet I have no way of controlling it. We just have to take it day by day right now and sometimes that drives me crazy. He hasn't been to so much as a single doctor's appointment with me. I asked him last week if he planned to be at the birth. I asked kindly, but my words tasted bitter. He said, of course. And I thought, how nice. He'll show up at the end and act like a hero. I know he means well. He does. But my nerves are rattled and I am terrified of the birth. No matter what I read in books or online, no matter what the doctors tell me, I won't really understand until I have the experience. I know this. This is what terrifies me. It will be here soon; the birth. And we'll have a child to care for. I can only hope Tony will be more involved in helping to raise our child, than he has been in helping me through the pregnancy.

"It's just for safety." Tony tells me one night at the dinner table while we are finishing our meal of chicken parmesan. "You're always talking about wanting to feel safer. This is one way we can be safe."

"I'm just not sure that's necessary." I finally chime in. We don't talk much over dinner these days. I know that Tony is tired of my paranoia and lately he doesn't seem excited to share any stories from work. When we visit his mom together, once a month at the nursing home, we have that to talk about in the form of a brief review. Otherwise, things are fairly quiet. He doesn't ask about the pregnancy. He doesn't ask how I'm feeling or what I've been up to. I guess I've stopped asking much about his days, too. It didn't happen overnight, it's just been something that has grown throughout these last months of pregnancy. If I bring up the feeling of distance to Tony he'll only tell me I'm not in my right mind and that things will be back to normal once the baby is born. I know this, so I don't bring it up. I keep quiet and wait until the day our little peanut is born so that we can go back to normal. Only, what will be normal about our lives then? We'll have a third person living in our house with us. I'll have an entirely new routine. I draw in a deep breath and try to focus again on what Tony is saying. I've missed most of it and only nod my head on occasion to give the illusion that I am still listening.

"It's easy to do and it will give us a peace of mind. I think we should do it."

I throw my hands up in the air, giving in, as I always do to Tony.

"You don't have to do anything but sign a paper. That's it. It's that easy Abigail." His tone sounds outwardly calm; however, the frustration in the undertone of his words it's written all over his face, the one I know so well. He wants me to agree. I will agree. It's really not a big deal. I am annoyed with him because increasing our life insurance isn't a safety precaution to me. It's Tony's work and nothing more. He's so obsessed with his work; I wish he were half that interested in me these days. But I won't beg for his attention. He says he's working so much to save money before the baby comes. Will he still work this much once the baby is here? Won't it make him more anxious about money once he sees the bills for diapers, doctors' visits and the like? I don't see how any of that will calm him.

I'm not really agreeing with or arguing with Tony on this matter. "It's fine." I tell him, wanting to end the conversation. But he is not done yet.

"If, God forbid, something should happen to you during the birth, it's important that our life insurance policy is…" he struggles to think of the right word, "enough." He clears his throat. "I'll raise the life insurance policy on myself as well, you see. Abigail, if anything should happen to me, especially because you do not have an income…and I don't mean any disrespect by that" he quickly adds, "then you will know that you and our baby will always be secure and taken care of with this money." He raises his eye brows wanting me to show that I understand.

I fully understand. I nod to demonstrate this to my husband. "Yes. I get it. It's fine, Tony. Really."

"Really?" He sounds excited, as if he's worked hard to get me on board, when in reality I never cared either way. It doesn't make me feel any safer, although, maybe it should. He's right about the money being able to take care of me and our baby if anything should ever happen to him. It is smart. I get it.

"Yes." I agree, again. "It's a good idea." I force a smile and stand to clear our plates from the table.

"I'll bring the final papers home tomorrow night to sign and we'll be all set." He finishes the last sip of soda from his glass before I reach for it to take it away. "You see," he winks as I pull the glass from his hand and hear the clank of dishes when I set it on top of the two plates in my arms. "I am keeping us safe. I care about you Abigail. You know that, right?"

For the first time tonight we are looking into each other's eyes. Instead of answering, I say this, "And I'm doing everything I can to have a healthy baby and to be a good parent." I smile and take the dishes to the sink.

We are not fighting, although admittedly, it feels like it some nights. We rarely argue, but as I'm rinsing the dishes before placing them in the dishwasher, I think maybe that's the problem. Maybe if we argued we'd work out whatever this frustration between us is. I don't think I've done anything wrong. Tony hasn't done anything wrong. It's just this weird distance that lingers between us. When Tony comes home from work I still hug him every night, but the air in the house changes. There's a pressure that fills the invisible space between us and it's everywhere that we are. He just feels absent. You know when you see those couples out at a restaurant, you know the ones I'm referring to, the couples where one person is talking away and the other isn't paying attention in the slightest? Usually the person not listening is texting or looking at the Internet on their phone. Sometimes they just have that blank stare and they've gone somewhere else in their head. That's how I feel when I'm with Tony lately. If I bother trying to tell him something, he's not really listening. It's been going on for a while now so I don't bother talking much, because what is the point? Why keep talking when you're clearly not being heard? And now, I've taken notice of my own distraction tonight. Is it because we have nothing in common? Is it because we don't have date night? Maybe we should reinstate date night. It was never really something we did before; we were just together a lot more. Surely that's why we had more to talk about? It's at least worth a try. If instating a date night once a week makes the distance between us dissipate, it is totally worth it. Can such a simple change really help us? Or will it really be better once the baby is born? Maybe both? A girl can hope. Our little peanut will be here soon.

When I finish cleaning up the kitchen I wipe my hands on the dish towel that hangs over the sink and I head out to the living room where Tony is sitting in the La-Z-Boy. His eyes are heavy as he stares at the television screen. All of the lights are off and his face is tinted blue from the glow of the screen. His left hand holds loosely to the remote and that is when I notice that his wedding ring is absent. Hesitantly, I walk up to him and place my hand on his arm. I gently shake him. "Tony" I whisper, not wanting to scare him as he is drifting off. "Tony."

He sits straight up in his chair, fully alert. His eyes are wide. "What' wrong? What's happened?" I've startled him.

I urge him to sit back. "Everything's fine. I just wanted to talk for a minute." I pause, waiting for him to settle before going on. "If that's okay?"

Tony draws in a breath and shakes his head. "Sorry. I was starting to dream. I guess I fell asleep…"

I shake my head. "It's fine. Sorry to wake you." We are both full of pleasantries. Like I said, we rarely argue, but maybe that is the problem. Maybe it's okay to disagree and get mad sometimes.

"Is it about raising the life insurance policies?"

I shake my head, "No."

"Oh." He sits quietly for a beat. "Is it the baby? Do we need to go the doctor?"

"No." I shake my head again. "Tony…"

I watch him settle back into the chair and I move to the couch, across from him, so that we are facing each other. His eyes focus on me and then move back to the television. He grabs the remote and mutes the sound and then turns back to me.

"It's not a big deal, really." I start. "I just wanted to ask if you'd like to go out to dinner with me, like a date, on Friday?" My words sound stumbled and nervous, although there is no reason for them to be.

Tony opens his mouth to speak, but the sound does not follow at first. "My wife is asking me out on a date?" He smiles, his head tilting slightly to the side.

"I know, it's kind of silly. But I just thought it would be good for us to go out. To talk. To be a couple. You know, before the little one is here and taking up all of our time..."

"Yes, yes. That is a good idea." He agrees quickly. "But we do need to be careful with money right now." He winces as he says the word money.

I wait for Tony to continue, only I am starting to get the feeling that he is waiting for me to speak. He thinks it is my turn. We have been speaking in *you go, I go* format, however, I don't know what to say. Is he agreeing, but wanting to go somewhere cheap? Or he is politely saying no?

"You know I love you Abigail. Right?"

Does he think I didn't notice that he hasn't answered my proposal for going out? I nod. "Love you too." I say. The words are automatic, but saying them does not make the distance between us disappear. If only it were that easy. "So…" I want to ask if we are going out on Friday, but now it's awkward and weird. "Is there some place that sounds good to you for Friday? Anything you're craving?" I pick at an invisible thread on my shirt.

"Oh. Well…uh…" His words are broken. "Maybe, to save money we could just stay in? We can light a candle or something at the table and call it date night…that works for me." I understand being frugal, as we are a young one-income couple with a baby on the way. But will going out to eat one night at a low key restaurant really break the budget? It isn't about where we go or how much we spend, I just thought it would be nice to spend some time together outside of the house. I just thought it might bring us a little closer somehow. I crave to be closer to Tony. I need to know he is really here, with me, on my side. I need to know that we are a team before our baby is born. I want to know this; to feel this. We have dinner at home every evening, so if I light a few candles and place them in the center of the table I don't see how that is going to help anything.

"Okay. If that's what you prefer." I hear myself say as I stand from the couch to leave the room.

Tony grabs the remote and takes the television off of mute, the sound of the voices on the screen take over the space between us. As I head upstairs to wash my face and change into my pajamas I speak softly. "I also wanted to tell you that the dark car, the one that's been scaring me, hasn't been around lately." I know Tony couldn't have possibly have heard me over the television. My words are muffled and I say them more to myself than I do to him. The distance between us only grows as I walk away. And then I think, maybe a date night wouldn't have fixed us anyway because Tony doesn't realize there's anything wrong at all.

Ten

Present Day, 2017

It was at the Waterford Potato Festival where I asked Abigail to marry me. It was the first year they introduced rides to the festival and I thought it would be the perfect place to propose, as it had been where we went on our second date. They'd added a climbing wall, the Scrambler, Octopus, a small roller coaster called The Monster and a Ferris Wheel. I casually asked Abigail if she wanted to stroll around the Potato Festival that evening. I'd only asked her that morning, not wanting to tip her off to my big plans in anyway. Of course it did take some pre-planning, though. I enlisted the help of my friend Michael Wentwell and his girlfriend (at the time), Alice. I also asked for Abigail's parents to be there and help with my plans. Everyone readily agreed. I'd had the ring tucked away in a drawer at my apartment for a few months, knowing I was going to ask Abigail to be my wife. I just hadn't known when, as I wanted to come up with a romantic proposal. I knew we would tell this story a million times over the years and I wanted it to be a good one. So I'd held on to the ring until I figured out the best plan of action. And now I had it. I knew how and when I was going to propose. I wasn't just nervous, I was a walking embodiment of cold sweat that day. It's not that I thought she'd say no. We'd talked about our life together and wanting to have a family. I was fairly confident Abigail would say yes. I knew we wanted to be together. It was the act of asking the question in front of her parents and in such a big way; it made my stomach flip-flop with anxiety. Would she like the proposal? The ring? Would she be certain she wanted to marry *me*? There were so many emotions racing through me for such few words that needed to be spoken.

Abigail wore a pair of jean shorts that frayed at the bottom and a plain black tank top that somehow served to highlight her already beautiful brown eyes and long lashes. She wore a simple strappy pair of black Teva sandals and a thin silver bracelet; one that I'd given her after we'd been together for one year. I was pretty sure she was clueless that I would be proposing that night. When I asked her later, she confirmed my suspension. She'd been floored when I asked her, although when she told me this, she also admitted that she'd hoped I would pop the question sooner rather than later.

We held hands and walked past the various booths as we had the first time we went to the festival together. We stopped to try Freda's Popcorn and then to sample the potato soup at Blain's Food Stand, all the while holding hands and laughing. Abigail grabbed a sample spoon at the soup stand and placed it in my mouth while crossing her eyes and making me laugh. Laughing and taking in a spoon full of warm soup at the same times do not mix and because of that, the soup dribbled down my chin instead of down my throat. This only made us both laugh harder. Abigail grabbed a stack of napkins and wiped my face as we walked away and headed to the next booth. After a bit, I suggested we go on a few rides. I knew the Ferris Wheel was Abigail's favorite. We hadn't been on one together yet, but she'd told me stories of other festivals she'd gone to as a child and how she loved when her parents let her ride the Ferris Wheel. We rode the Octopus first. It's a black contraption that has eight long limbs coming from its center, made to look like legs. At the end of each leg is a circular area that can hold two people. When the ride starts the circular area where you sit, spins and the legs spin around the center giving a double spin as it goes up and down in the air. It's sort of like the Tea Cups but with the added twist of going higher in the air. Abigail held onto my arm and screamed as we spun around and the evening sky turned dark. As the ride ended I noticed all of the lights flickering on throughout the festival, brightening up the sky below the stars. We headed to the Ferris Wheel next and I checked my watch; perfect timing. Abigail's parents and Michael and Alice would be there ready to help with my plan.

We waited in line for our turn to climb on board and I must have checked to make sure the box with the ring was in my pocket at least two dozen times. I felt my forehead begin to sweat and tried to breath slow and deep to calm my growing nerves. As we climbed into our carriage and the operator closed us in I felt Abigail's head rest against my shoulder and gulped, hoping everything would go smoothly.

I reached in my pocket once more and pulled the box out, keeping it hidden tightly in my left hand. My eyes searched the ground and I felt my heart ease when I spotted my four accomplices with their props. All of them waving to me with wide smiles spread across their faces. I nodded back, not wanting Abigail to notice them yet. We went up one notch at a time as the operator unloaded passengers and loaded in new ones. After eight pauses, we were sitting still at the top of the wheel and I knew this was the moment. Abigail was still resting on my shoulder and I nudged her and told her to take a look at the view from the top. We could see all of the festival lights sprawled out below us and the bright stars danced above our heads. The air was cool and crisp on that autumn night, with the sounds of chit-chat and laughter humming beneath our dangling feet.

"It's beautiful" Abigail said when she lifted her head and took in the view.

I turned to look at her, and at that moment I felt like my heart was going to beat out of my chest. I was as nervous as a long tailed cat in a room full of rocking chairs. But I knew I didn't have much time before the Ferris Wheel moved another notch and we lost the full impact of our current view. "You know I think you're beautiful, Abigail?" I tried not to stutter on my words.

"Tony…" She batted her eye lashes and her face grew flush.

"I love you so much" I continued while taking one of her hands in mine. "And I want to spend the rest of our lives together. I want to have a family with you, buy a house with you, and grow old with you."

"You know I want all of those things, too." She answered bashfully.

"I know…and that's why I want to ask you to marry me. Look down there…" I pointed toward her parents and Michael and Alice.

Abigail clasped her hands over her wide mouth and I watched her eyes grow brighter as she spotted the signs they were holding. They were jumping up and down, giddy with bliss. Each sign said one word: WILL YOU MARRY ME? The Ferris Wheel sprung to life and we moved forward one more notch as I turned to Abigail and opened the box that contained the ring and properly asked her, "Abigail Victoria Atwell, will you make me the happiest man on Earth and spend the rest of your life with me? Will you marry me?"

I held the ring out toward her, waiting for her answer.

"Yes! Of course! Of course I'll marry you. Yes!" I carefully placed the ring on her finger and she leaned forward and kissed me. We both started laughing and once again the Ferris Wheel began to move. This time all of the new passengers were boarded and we were moving fluently in a circle. When we glided past the signs Abigail held up her hand to show off the ring and screeched, "I'm getting married!" and my four accomplices cheered, along with everyone who was waiting in line for the ride. When we reached the top again, still going in a steady flow, Abigail began to cry and I asked her if she was all right. She couldn't stop hugging me and said she was so happy.

When the ride ended we thanked the operator and told him we were now engaged and he congratulated us as he loaded the next passengers into our carriage. We walked over to meet Michael, Alice, Lois and Omar. No more than a half-an-hour later, the festival ended with a round of colorful fireworks. Omar shook my hand and congratulated us. Lois hugged Abigail and told her she would make a beautiful bride. At that moment, everything was right in the world. We were happy. We had our whole lives ahead of us and nothing felt impossible. We were madly in love and nothing would ever change that.

★ ★ ★

I am a good man. I go to church every Sunday. I pray every night. I am a rule abiding man. But I am also human. I am not resistant to temptation. When our secretary at the office flirted with me, I admit, I flirted back. I knew it was wrong but it felt good. I'd been working extra-long hours at the office, trying to gain more clients and generate more revenue before the baby was born. At home, Abigail had turned into what felt to be a robot. Our conversations had turned dull as her days were only spent cooking and cleaning, she had no stories to share. Not to mention Abigail's growing paranoia in regard to her safety at home. Some of my extra hours were not spent focused on work, rather, they were focused on flirting outside of my marriage. But it was only flirting, I told myself. What harm could it do? An innocent wink. A smirk. My racing heart. Her, batting her long eye lashes in my direction. Watching the shift of her legs cross from one side to the other. It was child's play, that's all it was. I swear. It was just a little game. Something to look forward to during the day.

Between Abigail's focus on perfection, her increasing neurosis, and visiting my mother in the nursing home, watching her suffer as she drifted aimlessly, unable to be saved, in that black hole of nothingness her brain had created; it was too much stress. I felt like a mere back seat passenger in my own life. I had no control over my mom's debilitating disease. I had no way to relate to Abigail during the pregnancy. I did not understand my wife's growing paranoia for her safety. I also did not understand why she felt the need for every little thing in the house to be so damn perfect. I didn't demand it be that way, in fact, I'd rather it have been a little messy if that made her relax and come back to me; to our relationship. Her mind was always on cleaning and cooking, if not on safety. I didn't know what to do with that. I just sat back and let things play out; hoping the weirdness would all subside once our little peanut was born. Although I was willing to take the back seat in my own life at the time, I still longed for laughter, for happiness. Who doesn't? When it's presented to you, especially in the face of pain, you would be crazy not to reach out and grab hold of it, right? That's all I did. I allowed a little light to come in through the cracks in my life.

Eventually, the light flirtation began to grow. It was slow, but still picking up speed. I didn't mean for it to happen. It just did. I was getting so used to being a passenger in my own life that I'd become complacent about little things, like this. Because that's all it was, really. It was a little thing. A blip on the radar. Coming to work and seeing Cindy's eyes meet mine lit a fire inside of me, one I hadn't felt in some time with Abigail. I could tell you that I pretended Cindy was Abigail, but that would be a lie. They are nothing alike. Cindy has straight bleach blond hair that, when worn down, reaches her hips. Cindy has light blue eyes and wears just a hint of makeup to enhance her features, such as her puffy lips, her wide eyes and her high cheek bones. Cindy has legs that go on for miles. Cindy works and has a life outside of her home. Albeit, she isn't married or pregnant. She dresses different than Abigail, too. She wears tight pencil skirts that never reach further than an inch above her knees. She wears button up tops, allowing the top buttons to remain loose. She wears large hoop earrings and tall high-heels. I love my wife. I love Abigail to the moon and back. All I am saying is that Cindy and Abigail are two very different people.

Cindy filled a void when Abigail couldn't. Understandably, Abigail was preoccupied with our new home and with carrying our child.

One night I stayed late after work as did Cindy. The lights in the office had been shut off, except in my small office where I kept a dim desk lamp lit. Cindy had a knack for computers and mine had been struck by an odd virus. She said she knew how to fix it and could have my computer running and back to as good as new if we stayed late. Otherwise, I would have had to contact I.T. the following day and been without a computer all day while they worked on it. It would be a loss of revenue for me, to have been at work without my computer; my lifeline. I ordered a pizza for us to split while Cindy worked her magic and salvaged my computer.

I should have felt terrible when I called home to Abigail to tell her I wouldn't be home for dinner. I knew she had it already prepared. But instead, I selfishly felt like a giddy teenager. Before the pizza arrived, Cindy grabbed my arm and I felt a rush crawl up my skin.

"I've got it!" She screeched, thrilled with her accomplishment.

I did not push her away when she gripped my arm with her delicate fingers. She lingered for several minutes, while staring at the computer screen as it scrolled through lists of numbers and letters that I couldn't come close to understanding. But she was elated with what she'd done and promised it was cleaning up the virus on my computer.

She had not let go of my arm when she added, "If I want something, I always find a way to get it." Cindy turned her blue eyes up to mine and smiled. I knew she was taking our innocent flirting to the next level. But still, it was harmless. I hadn't done anything wrong. My computer was being fixed. I was staying late for work reasons. I was laughing. I was happy. There was no stress in these moments and it felt good, as if I'd been given a time out on life.

"Do you?" I teased back, placing my hand on top of hers and feeling the heat of her skin mix with my own.

Biting her lower lip she nodded and slid back her occupied desk chair so she could look at me. We were merely inches apart. I sat on the deck, one leg on the floor, the other dangling just above it. Her legs were crossed, her feet bare as she'd kicked off her heels some time ago, while working to rid my computer of the virus. I watched her staring at the wedding band on my left hand. After a minute I pulled my hand beneath my leg and shifted my weight from one side to the other.

"No one has to know." She whispered, leaning toward me and running her hand up and down the outside of my pant leg, lingering on my calf.

Now I knew this was more that child's play. This

was flirting at its best. Any further and it would be wrong. I thought of Abigail at home, eating dinner alone and wrapping my plate to save for later. But a breath later my focus was back on Cindy; on the present moment. I couldn't shake her when she was sitting right in front of me, when we were alone in the darkness and she was practically throwing herself at me.

We were interrupted when the pizza arrived and I felt briefly thankful. When I returned to my dimly lit office, pizza box, plates and a small stack of napkins in hand, Cindy kicked a spare desk chair toward me with her bare feet, keeping her eyes on me as I sat. I placed the pizza on my desk and asked what she wanted to drink. That's when we both stood at the same time; I was heading for the small refrigerator I kept on top of the counter at the far side of my office. She was standing to grab a slice of pizza. We both laughed, stumbling over each other's clumsy feet.

"Sorry!" I winced, dancing back and forth on my feet as she did the same.

"No, go ahead, sorry Anthony." Everyone but Abigail called me Anthony.

The desk light flickered and one of the two bulbs went dark. The change halted us both as we stared at the little lamp and then back at each other and nervously laughed. Cindy's eye brows rose, crinkling her forehead with two tiny lines. Her eyes came up to meet mine and I am honestly not sure who made the first move because it felt like we both moved at the same time. Suddenly we were no longer stumbling on our feet awkwardly trying to pass each other. Instead, I leaned down and our lips met. I felt her hands grasp tightly around my waist as I let one of my own hands linger on the outside of her exposed arm. My stomach flipped and I did not pull away. Neither did she.

It never went any further than a kiss until the day I left work early. The day Abigail went missing. That was the day I let my hand run up Cindy's skirt. We were in my office at lunch. I locked the door and we kept quiet. Everyone else was out to lunch or busy with their own calls, in their own offices. No one paid attention to what anyone else was doing. It was our little secret.

After letting my hand touch her, the guilt set in. The flirting had gone too far. I'd told Cindy on more than one occasion that I was devoted to Abigail, that what Cindy and I were doing had to stop. But we always kept going. One look at her and I was putty. I wasn't in love with Cindy, but she turned me on. The subtle obsession I felt with our flirtations filled my insides, a hunger I hadn't known was within me. The world offers countless drugs and endless alcohol, but my drug of choice was not in the form of a pill or a liquid. It was in the form of lust. The lust took me away from the stress, from the pain, from the wounds. The lust took me away from anything bad and left me feeling high, always wanting more. It wasn't about Cindy. I think she and I both knew that. It was about the rush. When I touch Abigail I often hesitate, wanting to be careful, wanting to be right. When I touch Cindy, I touch her like I own her, like she is mine, although we both know she is not. Cindy showed me that there can be a wild side to an innocent face. She reminded me that when life gets tough, a simple look or a subtle touch can make all the difference. It is when that very thought hit my mind, after placing my hands on Cindy, that I felt sick to my stomach. Reality hit me like a semi-truck.

Cindy pulled her skirt down and kissed my forehead before running her fingers through her hair, unlocking my office door and going back to her desk for the remainder of the afternoon. She turned and said "Now that's more like it." And she winked at me. I forced a smile while gulping down the rising bile in my throat. What had I done? Not just now, but all the while with Cindy. Why hadn't I gone to my own wife? My wife who was waiting for me at home. My wife who was pregnant with our child. My wife who I am certain I want to spend the rest of my life with. My wife who hugs me each time I walk through the front door. My wife who massages my feet at night, who prepares meals for me. My wife. Why hadn't I gone to my wife? My head spun in circles, dizzying me. In a stupor I walked to my door and locked it again. Leaning my back against the far wall, I bent my knees and slid my back down until I was sitting on the ground. Hanging my head between my knees I choked back tears. I was a good man. A church going, rule abiding man. Was I still? Or did I taint myself? What the hell had I done?

As soon as I could pull myself together I left the office to head home, early for once. When I passed Cindy at the front desk, her wide blue eyes scanning me as I stormed across the floor, I did not meet her eyes. "See you later Mr. Parker?" She asked, trying to keep her professional facade.

I only shook my head. I would not see Cindy later. I was sure of it.

The police do not know any of this. No one at work ever knew about our…fling. I don't know what else to call it. I did not sleep with her. It was not an affair. Yes, it was wrong. But I ended it. I realize

I should have never started it. I should have never allowed myself to find relief or take pleasure in the innocent flirting. But I did. And one thing led to another. The good thing is, it's only between Cindy and me. No one else knows. They are clueless.

Cindy left for Argentina the next morning. It had been planned for six months. She headed there with a friend and they were touring the country for the next year. It was a relief to have her gone, to not have to look at her pouty lips or pencil skirts when I walked in and out of the office each day.

Since Cindy was gone, the police never thought to question her in Abigail's disappearance. Even if she'd still been in the country, she would never have seemed relative to the case. She was only a secretary at our office. She was not a friend. She was not family. Not a neighbor. She was just a twenty-three year old girl who'd briefly worked at our office.

Cindy knows nothing about my wife's disappearance, at least I assume she doesn't because she left for Argentina the morning after Abigail had gone missing. Reports of her disappearance didn't hit mass media for nearly a week later because she is an adult and local police wanted to investigate and question me, the husband, first, before they took our case seriously or even considered it a case at all.

Cindy couldn't have been so jealous of Abigail that she'd done something to harm her, right? It hadn't occurred to me until now, because I tried to pretend that I never knew Cindy, that she was only a dream. Could Cindy have kidnapped Abigail and taken her out of the country? Was that even possible? No. Or could Cindy have told Abigail about our...fling? If Cindy went and told Abigail, maybe Abigail ran away? But she wouldn't have run away without Gideon and she would have surely confronted me first, giving me a piece of her mind. But Cindy was still at work when I left early that final day, so she couldn't have told Abigail. Unless she called her? Or told her in a letter? Or told her the previous day? My mind is racing with possibilities. Why haven't I considered any of this until now?

On our wedding day, before walking Abigail down the aisle, Omar told his daughter that divorce would never be an option for her and that it was against her religion. Her own father told her that he would stop speaking to her if she ever so much as thought about it. Had Abigail found out about my...fling with Cindy and run away, not wanting to face the shame that would be brought on to her by her father? Had she wanted to leave me because of the…fling and feared that her father and I would not allow the divorce to take place?

Cindy and I hadn't contacted each other since that last day. Surely she doesn't even know my wife is missing. Certainly she had nothing to do with Abigail's disappearance, either from telling her about *us* or from kidnapping my wife herself. No. That was all too outlandish. Cindy was innocent, young and carefree. She'd known I was married and hadn't cared. She never seemed emotionally attached to me. Never clingy. Never wanting anything but stolen glances and touches. She was not capable of doing either act. I am sure of it. I nearly laugh out loud at myself in the midst of these maddening thoughts. Look who is paranoid now! Cindy had nothing to do with Abigail's disappearance, she couldn't have. She is only twenty-three and still naive about life. Abigail and I aren't much older ourselves, but I swear I've aged at least a decade since she's disappeared. I've been suffocated by overwhelming guilt in every imaginable way.

Against my better judgment, as always the case with Cindy, I decide I will send her a text message. No. On second thought, I should call so that our words are not on written record. Just in case. Unless the police have tapped my phone? If they still even slightly suspect me I shouldn't take the chance. They probably still think I'm involved in some way. Yet I find myself taking the chance and dialing Cindy's number. I need to be certain she has nothing to do with Abigail's disappearance. The phone begins to ring. I have no idea what I'll say. I have no idea of the time difference between Waterford, Indiana and Argentina and to be honest, I don't care. I just hope she answers. I need to know I am right, that Cindy has nothing to do with what's happened to my wife.

"Hey! It's Cindy." The voice recording comes on and I hang up before listening to it any further. I will try again tomorrow and the next day. I will keep trying until I reach her.

"Mr. Parker, we need you to come down to the police station."

"What has happened? Have you found Abigail?" I ask, feeling my heart nearly beat out of my chest.

"Mr. Parker, we have not found your wife. I'm sorry. But we have received an anonymous tip in regard to a sighting of her." The officer continues, her words firm.

"Where? Is she okay? Do you think it's her?" The

questions rush off my tongue without thought. When the officer is silent I add, "She's alive, right? She's alive?"

"Mr. Parker, this is really something that needs to be discussed in person."

"Officer, I've been waiting six months. Six long months for my wife to be found. And now you're telling me to wait even longer?"

"Please hear me, Mr. Parker, it is only a tip. We have not found your wife. We just want to share the information we've been given, with you."

"So share it now!" I am overly excited, but as I pled for information I am grabbing my coat and my car keys and heading out the door. When I close the front door behind me I realize I have forgotten Gideon inside.

"Like I said, we'd really rather speak to you in person. Can you come to the station now?"

"Yes. Yes, I just need to get my son- our son- ready and I'll be there in a jiffy." I am breathless as I rush back inside and rush to grab Gideon from the floor where he sits innocently playing with his toys.

"Drive safely. We'll see you shortly."

The call ends and I replay the word *shortly* in my head again and again as I place Gideon's blue and white Nike shoes on his feet. Shortly. We may find her shortly. I may see her shortly. Shortly. I breathe in, ready to hear what they have to say. I know I shouldn't pin all of my hopes on a random anonymous tip, but it's all I have now. I have to pin my hopes somewhere.

"Thank you for coming." Two officers, one male and one female stand before me as I hold Gideon in my arms, waiting for what they have to say. "Please," the male officer gestures down the hall, "follow us." I am certain he is wearing a bad toupee and find myself wondering if it will slip from his head before we make it to wherever we are going.

We walk down a long hall and I hear the sound of our shoes clicking against the floor as we work toward our destination; a small windowless room with a single table and four chairs. The officers sit on one side and tell me to have a seat across from them. I place Gideon on my lap, but he is squirming and wants to move.

"You can let him run around if you'd like. It's a small room." The officer is right. It is a small room and there is nothing inside of it except for us and the table and chairs we are sitting in. I place Gideon on the floor with only a brief hesitation. I put his bag down after him and pull out a blanket that I sprawl across the floor, silently letting Gideon know where he can play with his toys. He has three toys in the bag and I place those on the blanket, motioning for him to play. The toys include a book titled, *My First 100 Words*, a plastic block set and a Fisher-Price xylophone. I know the last one is the toy he will choose to play with and that it will be noisy. Surely the officers have children of their own at home and will understand.

"Thank you." I tell them as I help Gideon situate himself amongst his toys on the pale yellow blanket.

"To be clear, you have not heard from your wife, from Abigail, since her disappearance?"

"That's correct. If I would have, I would have phoned you immediately."

"You have not heard from her in any form, correct?"

"Correct. What is this about exactly?" I am growing impatient.

"Please, Mr. Parker, understand that we have to ask you these questions before proceeding. Remember, we are on your side."

I hear Gideon begin playing with the xylophone behind my chair. Instead of turning around, I stay focused on the two officers, blocking out the ringing of the bells my son is striking with brute force.

"No text messages? Visits? Phone calls? Letters? No contact at all, correct?"

"Yes, correct." My words are rushed.

"Okay then. We just wanted to be sure." The male officer finishes his questioning and then turns to the female officer. Both officers introduced themselves when we first arrived, but I have never been good with names.

The female officer begins to speak now. "Someone has called in an anonymous tip." She sits a bit straighter in her chair. "Mr. Parker, the caller told us they saw a girl meeting Abigail's description." She pauses, waiting for me to digest the information she has just delivered before she goes any further.

"Is it her?" My stomach is twisted in knots and beads of sweat form on my forehead. My palms are warm and I wipe them back and forth on my pants.

"The caller is adamant it is Abigail Parker. However, we're not so sure. They describe the girl as the same age and height as your wife. They said she has blond hair and blue eyes. It is possible, when people run away from their lives, for them to change their hair and eye color. So it is a possibility. However, it's important to know that with cases of missing persons, we get a lot of bogus clues. All too often it's a crazed member of society wanting to have their fifteen minutes of fame; getting on the news, saying they saw the missing person…that sort of thing." She pauses and pulls something from a file folder and pushes it toward me, across the table. "The caller did text a photo they snapped from their phone. However, it is blurry and you cannot see the individuals face."

I study the photo. She is right. It is incredibly blurry. A tree is in the forefront of the photo and in the background is a blond, thin woman with her head turned away from the camera. Her hair is straight, not wavy. It's blonde, not black. This person is thin. The last time I saw Abigail she was still carrying extra weight from the baby and was not nearly as trim as the person in this photograph. I am scouring the photo for a sign, for anything to tell me it is Abigail. But there is little to go off of and I do not find the blurry individual remotely recognizable. I bite my bottom lip, feeling my rush of hope leave just as quickly as it came. Why would someone think this is my wife? If it were her, surely I would recognize something about her, I would get a feeling that it truly was her. But I do not have that feeling and I do not see anything that says it is her. I push the photo back across the table to the officers and shake my head. "That is not my wife. It's a terrible photograph, but it is not my wife." Gideon has stopped banging on the xylophone and has moved on to his plastic block set while babbling made up words to himself. I am grateful for the sound he adds to the empty room.

"We didn't think it was much to go off of, but we wanted to show you the photo, just in case you saw something we didn't. We are sorry for getting your hopes up Mr. Parker. Please know we're only trying to help." She takes the photo and places it back inside of the file.

We sit quietly for a minute, only Gideon's voice filling the room. "Where was the photo taken?" I ask, wondering if the caller thought they spotted my wife in Waterford.

"Yes, of course. The call and the photo were taken in Ashville, North Carolina."

I shake my head and feel my fists clench beneath the table. "That's not my wife."

"We felt the same way, but again, we needed to check with you to be sure. We didn't want to miss something."

If the officers are looking for me to tell them that

I appreciate them bringing me into the police station today, I cannot bring myself to thank them right now. I swallow, feeling the heat rise to my head. My brief bout with hope was merely that. a brief bout. A bout that has given way to a rising anger. "Tell me this" I say to the officers, "Why are there so many crazy people in this damn world? Abigail wouldn't have gone missing if there weren't so many of them!" My eyes widen, allowing the tears to fall like rain against my cheeks.

The officers wait a moment before speaking again. "We agree with you Mr. Parker. There are a lot of messed up things that happen in this world. All we can tell you right now is that we'll keep you posted on any additional tips that might come in. We do have a call in to the Ashville P.D., to have them post flyers and an alert in their area for your wife, on the off chance that this photo is somehow your wife."

I press my lips together and push my chair out to stand. I'm not sure if they are done, but I am. I can't hear any more today. They have not found my wife and I am crushed. I pick up Gideon and his blanket and toys, shoving them into the bag and hoisting my son up into my arms. As I turn to leave I nod toward the officers who are now standing in front of their own chairs, poised to follow me out of the empty room. "Thank you." I tell them now.

As I place Gideon securely in his car seat and climb into the driver side of the car, turning the engine to life, I hear my cell phone ring and reach to grab it. It is not a number I recognize and after the meeting I've just had, a small jolt of hope rushes through my veins. I quickly scold myself, it is nothing. We are no closer to saving Abigail than we were yesterday or the day before. "Hello?" I answer on the second ring.

"Anthony. Thank goodness." It is Omar and I wonder where he is calling from.

"Omar, is everything okay?" I look back in the rear view mirror, deciding to stay parked until ending my conversation with Abigail's father.

"Yes. No. Hopefully…" His voice trails.

"What is it, what's going on?" I beg. I am tense after what I've just endured.

"It's Lois. Lois was at the church, helping set up for a lunch thing they have going on tomorrow after Sunday service. Anyway, she fell and somehow broke her leg."

"Oh. Oh, poor Lois." I gather myself and try to focus on what he is telling me. "Are they putting her in a cast then?" I want to tell Omar about my strange meeting with the police, about the crazy people in the world and how they frustrated me. I want to tell him how I'd had hoped for a few minutes this morning, hoped to find his daughter, but how it all was nothing more than a hoax. But now was not the time. Now he needed to stay focused on his own wife.

"If it were only a broken leg, we would be grand." He says, his voice shaking with each word. "The problem is, while we were here at the hospital Lois suffered an aneurysm. The doctors say it is rare to catch them in time and if we hadn't been here, she surely wouldn't have survived. So they caught it, the aneurysm, but she's in critical care now. They don't know how much damage has been done. They think she will survive, but she may not speak. She may not have full function of her limbs. We just don't know…" I can hear that he has used what strength he has remaining to tell me this.

"Omar, I am so sorry. I am in the car with Gideon right now. Are you at Ludwig Hospital?"

"Yes." He proceeds to tell me which waiting room we can find him in when we arrive and I tell him we are on our way. "Anthony" he adds, "I want Lois to see her daughter again. Please." I am not sure if this is a direct request to me, implying that I can bring her back at any moment I choose, or if he is simply overwhelmed at this moment, as I am.

Eleven

Tony won the name war. We had a boy! Gideon Simon Parker was born exactly one week ago. I was in labor for nine long hours. He weighed seven pounds, eight ounces and exactly nineteen inches long. I loved him from the first sight of his squishy face. After a week with our little guy, however, I am realizing that I thought I'd been prepared. I painted the nursery a gender neutral yellow. Tony assembled the crib one evening after work just two weeks before Gideon's arrival into the world. I stocked up on diapers and onesie's. Our church hosted a small baby shower for me and I was grateful for all of the extra supplies that I knew we would utilize in the coming weeks and months. But all of this preparing with material items had not readied me for what I now faced. I'd been incredibly naïve. Did every new mother get caught up in preparing the nursery and keeping a large stack of little clothes and fresh diapers on hand? Yes, these things are important, but what is really important now is survival, his and mine. And survival means breastfeeding, a total lack of sleep and an overwhelming amount of patience. Survival now means figuring out how to quiet my screaming son. I am undertaking what I've read to be called the *maiden days of motherhood* and there is no backing out now. I desperately wish Tony had taken paternity leave, even if just for this first week, to help me, as I think I'm in over my head. From what I've read and what other mom's at church told me in the final weeks leading up to Gideon's arrival, every mother feels this way and feeling overwhelmed is normal. One mom of four at church told me that becoming a mom means entering uncharted territory and that I need to remember to take one day at a time and to stay calm. She couldn't promise that I'd ever get a good night's sleep again, but she could give me her word that everything would balance out and that I would love being a mother. I am counting on the last part of her words right now as I stand in the yellow nursery rocking my son as he is red faced and screaming.

Every book I read said that I should sleep when Gideon sleeps, but I can't always do that. It's not that easy. I'm not one of those people that can just plop my head onto the pillow and fall instantly to sleep. Tony tells me I have a busy brain and he isn't wrong. I always have to read or watch television before falling asleep; otherwise I am consumed by my random worries. I've always been that way. Add to that, I am still recovering from labor and hoping my body will bounce back sooner rather than later. And I still have to clean the house, prepare dinner for Tony and make his lunches each day, too. Maybe it doesn't sound like much but learning to be a mother and keeping up with the other duties that filled my days before entering motherhood is a lot to process. I'll figure it out, but right now my head is spinning. I am tired. I always need a shower and the laundry has grown exponentially, which is crazy because we've only added one tiny human to our home. I know I need to call my mom and ask for some help, but I want to try and do as much as I can on my own before I go begging. I don't want her to think I am incompetent.

Who knew breastfeeding was so hard? Certainly not me. Is it a secret that everyone's keeping from me? I am rocking Gideon in the bright yellow nursery, his face red with anger because I cannot do this right. I am frustrated and so is he. I wish I had painted the nursery a different color, a darker one. Maybe navy blue. But I realize now that I won't have the energy to repaint, at least not for a while. That is not on my top list of priorities. What is, is keeping Gideon happy and quiet as much as I possibly can. I am having trouble getting Gideon to latch or to suck from me. My nipples are in pain. Last night, between feedings, rather than sleeping I scoured the Internet for relief and found a lactation consultant here in Waterford who I've requested to come and help me. She is supposed to come tomorrow, but I wish she were here right now. Tomorrow seems a million years away when Gideon is wailing like this, his fists are clenched, his mouth wide, eyes squeezed shut and tears running down his chubby cheeks. I feel like a failure asking for help to feed my own child, but there has to be a better method of doing this. I need to learn how to help him latch on and how to hopefully make this process a little less painful on myself. I am glued to this rocking chair and I'm beginning to think it's going to be this way for a while now. I need to bring a book or some magazines in the room to keep my mind busy while I'm rocking and feeding, that is, once we figure out the whole latching concept.

I've been trying to ask Tony to help out with Gideon by encouraging him to burp our little peanut, to wipe his face or to simply hold him. He has tentatively held him a few times, but mostly he treats our son like he is the plague. Why doesn't he want to be near him? I asked him directly last night and Tony only said that Gideon is so small he is afraid he will hurt him because he doesn't know how to handle him. I don't know if that was a genuine comment or if he simply doesn't want to be a hands-on dad when Gideon is so little. I'm sure once he is bigger and can toss a ball and go on hikes that Tony will take more interest in him. But for someone who has wanted children so badly, he doesn't seem to want to be a parent yet. Maybe he's scared? Maybe he's in shock? I know I am all of those things, but I have no choice but to care for our son. Someone has to.

When I can't get Gideon to latch properly I stand, cuddling him in my arms and swaying gently back and forth. I cannot be confined to this rocking chair anymore. At least not in this moment. I need to move. I am craving fresh air. Come to think of it, I am sure I haven't been outdoors since the day Gideon was born. That is, other than getting in and out of the car when we came home from the hospital. I need to get outside. Gideon is still crying, his face is as red as a lobster. I have him swaddled tightly in a baby blue blanket and I am holding him close to my chest, hoping that being near me will be enough to calm him, although this first week has assured me that will never be enough. I slip on a pair of sandals without bending down and head to the door. My hair is a mess, I have not brushed it other than running my fingers through it once, hours ago. I do not have any make-up on and I am wearing a loose fitting t-shirt and a pair of gray sweatpants. I don't care if the neighbors see me. Like I said, it is about survival now. Tears are welling in my eyes as I pull the front door open. I try not to let them pour out, but I am helpless to stop them. This isn't the first time tears have come this week. Being home alone most of the time, going day after day without sleep, listening to the constant crying, failing at breastfeeding time and again, it's all a lot to take in. I am trying. I am doing my best. I throw open the door and slowly take in a breath of fresh air as I let my shoes hit the outside ground. Gideon is still crying, but begins growing quieter as the sun hits his face. I bounce him in my arms and hum to the tune of *You are my Sunshine*. Finally, something is calming him. This only makes my tears grow heavier, but I don't care because I can hear the birds singing in the trees and I can hear the sound of my own breath because for what is the first time in a week Gideon is quiet. I do not want this moment to end. I continue bouncing him and walk through the grass and over to the side of the house where I've let the wild daisies grow. They dance on the breeze and I watch as they happily wave toward the sun.

I love my son but I feel incredibly used. He needs me for everything. While I am trying to survive, so is he. Overnight I have been reduced to a food factory. I am here to serve and nothing more. And while Gideon's appetite grows, mine is nonexistent. I am overcome with fatigue and exhaustion. I have trouble sleeping, although I do try when Gideon is resting. It usually doesn't work, but I still try. I realize I am moody and I have even apologized to Tony for that, although he is not here often enough to notice most of my moods. I am cooped up inside of our house. I am lonely and hungry for adult conversation. When Tony is home for dinner our dialogue merely consists of a list of occurrences and do's and don'ts with Gideon. There is no real conversation to be noted. It is all business these days. Like I said, *survival.* Last night Tony tried to tell me I am suffering from post-partum depression. He did not attend a single doctor's visit with me leading up to the birth. Who is he to diagnose me now? I smiled while gritting my teeth and told him that I disagreed. I know I am struggling to figure everything out, but I am a first time mother and I'm bound to be overwhelmed, especially when I'm home alone with our child day after day. He took that last part as a slight against him and became defensive.

"Your dream was to be a mom..." He was trying to tell me that I'd wished for this. I'd wished for a life without sleep and one of being glued to a rocking chair with a screaming newborn in my arms.

"Really, you're going to play that card?" I was exhausted and incredibly thirsty. I didn't want to use my energy on arguing with Tony about why I was tired. "Your dream was to be a dad. Do you remember that? But it's a funny thing, Tony. You dreamed of being a dad and having a house full of

children, yet you can't even be present for our son."
I had never spoken to him this way. We both knew
it, but I couldn't hold back. It rolled off my tongue
before I could stop myself and there was nothing I
could do to take it back. My words hung between us,
thickening the already dense air.

"Someone has to make money around here instead
of playing house all day." And there it was. He hadn't
spoken to me like *that*. We were suddenly throwing
darts at each other with deadly aim.

"You think this is play? Do you honestly think it's
fun to push a human being out of your body? Did
you even know that I'm still bleeding from the birth?
Do you think it's fun to never sleep and to have a
newborn attached to your hip every second of the
day and night?" When he didn't respond I continued,
I couldn't help myself. I was on a roll. I laughed, "I
guess you think this is fun and games. Yes, I wanted
to be a mother and you wanted to be a father. We
are. It's a dream come true. Look at us now. Is this
everything you pictured?" It hurt that he called my
work, *motherhood*, play. It was anything but play and
his weighted words weren't going to make life any
easier.

"I'm sorry." He muttered. Although I sensed his

sincerity, I was too tired and too crushed to accept his bleak apology.

"If anything is play, it's your work. You get to go and be out in the world. You collect a pay check. You don't have to work around the clock and you get to come home to a clean house, well, a fairly clean house" I corrected myself as I looked around the room and saw the piles of baby toys and a sink full of dishes needing to be washed. "You get to come home to cooked meals and a family who loves you. Talk about play..." I let my words dangle in the air as I stood, cradling Gideon in my arms. He began to cry at my movement and I walked back to the nursery, knowing I needed to glue myself back into the rocking chair and tend to our son.

Admittedly the first week with Gideon was rough. But the second week started out better. Tony sincerely apologized for our argument and told me that he knew what I was doing was hardly play. He said he took my role in our family very seriously and he wouldn't know what he would do without me. The next day he brought me a gift and said he was going to surprise me with a gift every week for the next nine months, as I had done for him with the gifts of fruit, showing him the size of our baby each week while I was pregnant. I appreciated the gesture and hugged him, grateful that things were starting to turn around. The first gift was a sterling silver charm of a baby rattle. He'd given me the charm bracelet before we were engaged and I'd always loved it, although I hadn't worn it in a while. The next week he had a fruit basket delivered one afternoon, an assortment of colorful strawberries, sliced bananas, blueberries and green grapes in the shape of a heart. I loved being showered with gifts. It made my days a little less stressful. It gave me something to look forward to each week, a surprise.

I don't know if it was because of the gifts or because I was finally beginning to understand the demands of motherhood. I became more experienced with each passing week, but despite the exhaustion, I began to feel lighter; happier. I began to become a proud mom instead of a terrified one.

Gideon and I fell into a groove. I made a point to walk outside at least once each day, often going over to the wild daisies to watch them dance in the breeze and reach toward the sun. Gideon always grew quiet when we were outside, too. We both needed the fresh air and so I made it a daily habit. Yesterday when I was changing Gideon's diaper for what felt like the tenth time that day, he looked up at me and we locked eyes. He smiled and my heart melted. His chubby cheeks transformed before my eyes. No longer were they simply begging to latch onto my body, but they were puffy and soft and each one brought the appearance of a thick dimple when he smiled. Oh, that smile got me each time. I started hearing my own voice transform from that of an adult to one of a cartoon character. I used words like "wiggle" and played peek-a-boo. Although motherhood hadn't come naturally to me, it was beginning to seep into my veins. I was becoming the mother I wanted to be and as I transformed, Gideon did the same. As I became happier, so did he. He still cried, of course. He still woke during the night. He still required a lot of diaper changes, but we fell in sync with each other somewhere along the way and I went with it, not wanting to look back on that first week together. Only wanting to look forward, to focus on what was going right. And there was a lot going right. Our son smiled at me. That was a big one and I longed for it to happen again and again. A simple smile turned my world upside-down. I even grabbed my camera and started snapping photos of Gideon, something I hadn't yet cared to do. Everyone told me that even when it gets hard, to make sure I savor the moments. I am starting to do that now. And I hope our bond will only continue to grow in the coming months and years. Even if we have a handful of other children, Gideon will always be our first and there is something magical about that. He is special and I want him to always know this. He is special for a million reasons, but most of all, because he was made from love. He was created by two people who love each other and who, despite the roller coaster that is marriage, will love each other, always.

Twelve

ANTHONY

Present Day, 2017

Doctors believe Lois will make a full recovery, although she has been in the hospital for four-and-a-half weeks. Abigail has been missing for seven months, I've lost track of how long my mom has been deteriorating from the dementia and our little boy, Gideon just keeps on growing. It's amazing how time marches on regardless of the events in our lives. Shouldn't we have a pause button when big things go wrong; a time out of sorts? If there is one, I have not succeeded in finding it. I cannot help but think that if we'd lost Lois, Abigail wouldn't have known. She wouldn't have been here and when she returns home, when we find Abigail safe and sound, whenever that might be, she could have come home without a mother waiting for her. How incredibly devastating that would have been. It will already be a lot for everyone to take in, but to have lost a parent too; that would have been unbearable. I know I am still sounding optimistic toward the prospect of saving Abigail. The police and the Atwell's private investigator have all told us that we should not get our hopes up; that after such a long period it is likely if Abigail is found at all, that she will not be alive. But I cannot bear the thought. I have to think that she is alive and holding onto hope. I have to think this way, although it isn't always easy. Believe me, I have my moments. My breakdowns where I simply lose it and collapse to the ground in my own pity. It is all too much to bear. Friends at church tell me that the Lord would not have put this burden on our family if we weren't strong enough to handle it. I've never questioned the teachings of our church, not once my whole life, until now. If there is a God, why would the almighty himself cause such harm to anyone? It doesn't make sense. It doesn't add up. My life doesn't feel real anymore. Everything is out of order and discombobulated. Regardless of a person's strength or tolerance, I am of firm belief that no one should ever have to endure this kind of pain. It's a pain that poisons you; it floods my veins a little more with each passing day. I am in absolute agony, this gaping bloody wound, a constant thorn in my side and I am helpless to stop the bleeding.

I can't stop searching for my wife. I won't. I can't just forget that our beautiful life existed before all of this chaos took over. Admittedly, sometimes when I look at Gideon, it is pure torture. He has her perfect little nose and her long eye lashes. And I know this might sound off the wall, as he is still a baby, but I swear he has her smile. While most parents melt inside when their child smiles at them, our son's smile only serves to stir a dark melancholy within me.

I hadn't remembered until now, but as I sit in the stiff rocking chair watching Gideon breathe peaceful puffs of air as he sleeps, I am flooded with the memory of my childhood pet, Daisy. Daisy was my cat; a gorgeous black and white long-haired feline. Daisy spent most of her time outdoors romping through the yard, catching field mice and moles and then leaving them, a sign of affection, at our front door step. At night she would return home and sleep at the end of my bed, always keeping my chilly feet warm on bitter winter nights. When Daisy was somewhere in the vicinity of twelve years old and I was just about to turn sixteen, she disappeared. One night she didn't come home. There were no deceased critters waiting for us on the door step that day. I called for her for hours that night, to no avail. I left a bowl of cat food on the front porch, hoping she'd only gotten lost and would be on the front door mat waiting for me in the morning with her wide green eyes. But the food was left untouched. Each night I called again and left another bowl of food on the door step for her. We lived on a plot of land in the country and my mom told me that it was possible coyotes had taken Daisy, but I didn't believe her. Daisy had been roaming the grounds for more than a decade; she knew how to outsmart the coyotes, surely. I was bound and determined to find her and I swore that when I did, she would stay safely indoors from now on; I would keep her safe and not allow her to be in harm's way. But Daisy never came home. The food bowl was still filled each morning, until months later when the raccoons and opossums found the food and licked it clean. My mom yelled at me for drawing the wild life up to our front door, but I still placed the bowl of food out every night, just in case. I still called for Daisy. I put signs up at the local veterinarian's office and at the grocery store, just in case anyone had seen her. I kept trying every night until years later when I left home. And even then, I didn't want to give up. Even then, I asked the neighbor to keep a bowl of cat food out just in case he found Daisy. Not knowing if she was alive or dead ate away at me. Thinking about it now, I realize it still does. It was so inconclusive, so confusing. I knew that odds were she hadn't survived. My mom was probably right about the coyotes. I shuttered at the thought. Maybe when things are terrible and horrible it's better not to know the facts. Maybe. I'd like to think this way, but I know that I would still rather know what happened to Daisy. She was a good cat. I'd rather know that there was nothing I could have done to help her and that she wasn't out there in the world somewhere lost, hungry and searching for help. Although it would be hard to hear that something awful had happened to her, at least knowing would provide closure.

Gideon is fast asleep and I should be, too. But right now I'd rather rock in this chair and watch my son, than be under the covers alone in our bed. Alone with my memories; the should have's, the would have's, the wishes, the regrets, floating in my mind like a deadly eddy in the river. I'd rather be sitting with the person who most reminds me of my wife, than crying and praying for a miracle that may likely never happen.

Sometimes I daydream of Abigail's return. I imagine getting a call from the police, telling me they've found my wife and that she is alive and well. I play out the details like a movie in my mind and sometimes I even tell myself that if I daydream this movie enough, it will come true. She will be found and she will be alive and we will be a family again. I imagine buckling Gideon in his car seat and rushing to the police station to meet my wife. I dream of touching her skin and wrapping her in a warm embrace, whispering in her ear how much I love her and how happy I am that she is okay and promising her that I will always keep her safe. I imagine feeling Abigail's lips pressing against mine, her big brown eyes speaking to me without the need for words. I picture climbing into bed with her at night and holding her while kissing her soft neck. I can still smell her scent on her pillow case, although it is becoming much duller now. Admittedly, I haven't washed her pillow case since she disappeared. I have washed the bedding, but not that one item. I have to breathe in her scent to keep hope alive. I don't know what I'll do when it's completely faded.

No matter where Abigail has been taken, no matter

what unthinkable trauma she has endured, I will find a way to make it better. I realize now that in the months leading up to her disappearance, I was not home as much as I should have been. I realize that my fling with Cindy is and was unacceptable; it makes my stomach churn. I realize that I should have gone to the obstetrician with Abigail. I should have asked how to help more when Gideon was born, I should have learned to be more hands on with him. I realize so many things now; as the saying goes, hindsight is twenty-twenty. I cannot change the past, but I can influence the future. But to have a future, we first have to find my wife and bring her safely home. I'm sure I am not the only one with regrets in life, with should have's and would have's. I think we all have that baggage on our shoulders. But when I have this daydream, this hope of Abigail being found alive and returning home, I realize most importantly that I have learned the lessons that many men don't learn until the end of their lives, when they're ninety- years old and taking in their lasts breaths, wishing they could have a redo. I won't be on my death bed wishing for a redo. I will get the redo. We will start fresh when Abigail is found. I will be more attentive to her. I have learned so much about raising Gideon and I will play a bigger role in this arena, too. I will learn to cook a few things, making dinner for our family some nights. I will work less hours, because what really matters are the people in our lives, not how much money we make. I haven't completely lost my mind, money is still incredibly important for a comfortable life, but I can't put money before loved ones. I can't and I won't. Not anymore. I tried that before and it didn't work.

Gideon puckers his lips and makes a soft sound. I stop rocking and hold my breath, not wanting him to wake. Once he settles again and I hear his breath return to a normal slow steady rhythm, I make my way quietly out of the room and back to my empty bed. I can't remember the last time I slept soundly through the night. Not since Abigail has been taken. Seven months without a good night's sleep is too much for anyone to endure. I stumble to the kitchen and grab my bottle of Hennessy Black, heading back to the bedroom with the bottle in my hand. I am not a drunk, but I need something to numb the pain, something to help me find a few hours of sleep before the sun rises and I live another day in agony, not knowing where my wife is; not knowing if we'll ever find her or if I'll ever hold her in my arms again. When I reach the bedroom I hold the dark bottle in the air, "To Abigail, wherever you are. I love you.

We will find you. I promise." I pull my arm from the air and take a swig from the bottle, feeling the liquid rush down my throat with a purpose. Between drinks I reach for her pillow and pull it close to my nose to breath in what's left of her scent. *My beautiful, innocent Abigail. I am so incredibly sorry for what I have done.*

I am still trying to reach Cindy. Each time I call I am delivered to her voicemail. How has she not noticed my number by now and called back? While I do not leave a message each time I call, I have left at least half a dozen in addition to a handful of text messages. In the last message I told her that it is urgent and that I need to speak with her immediately. I have not told her that my wife is missing. I've tried to be vague so that in case she did say something to my wife about our fling or in case she knows something about Abigail's disappearance, I won't scare her off. But I need to talk to her. She needs to return my call or at the very least, text. It's not like I can just fly to Argentina and find her on a whim. Although my gut tells me that Cindy doesn't have anything to do with Abigail's disappearance, her lack of returning my texts and phone calls is setting off an alarm in my head. She must be hiding something or surely she would contact me back. What is she hiding? What did she do?

Gideon said "dog" while we were out walking today. He spotted a small poodle mix, barking and wagging her tail at us from behind a fence while out on our short stroll. I was elated and encouraged him to say the word again. When we returned home I pulled out his stuffed animal toy of a German Shepherd and I barked from behind the toy. "Dog", he said again and I praised him on his new word. It would be a great time to go to the local animal shelter and save a dog; a dog Gideon could grow up with. But we will wait until Abigail is found; it's something we wanted to do together, as we'd talked about. Maybe we will adopt both a dog and a cat once Abigail is home. Like everything else in *normal life,* we will have to wait. We will keep waiting for Abigail's return and until then we have put our normal life on hiatus. But a hiatus is not a substitute for a pause button. Gideon is growing by leaps and bounds. Lois and Omar have each aged a decade in the last seven months. And my hair now has bands of gray highlighting the brown, just above my ears and in a spot above my left brow. I am still in my twenties and I am turning gray. If we don't find Abigail soon, she will not recognize me when she comes home. Each day she is gone, I imagine I turn a little more silver. I wonder if Abigail's dark hair has been overtaken by any gray strands. I shudder at the thought, shaking it away as quickly as it comes. I do not want to think about what she's endured or…is enduring.

After the walk we snack on blueberries, eating them straight from the plastic container. Abigail once put a blueberry in a tiny box and handed it to me over dinner, letting me know that Gideon was this size in her stomach at the time. It's incredible to think that our son was once the size of one of these small round berries. I'm careful to watch Gideon with the berries, realizing that the small slippery things could cause him to choke if he doesn't sit still while consuming them. Abigail, I think, would probably not allow him to eat blueberries just yet. But I searched online and found that it is actually okay for children his age to eat them, if careful. We're being careful.

Lois and Omar come to visit as we are finishing up our snack. Lois is moving slowly, but otherwise back to her normal self; although nothing is quite normal these days. I take the bin of blueberries away as the Atwell's come in the door. "Good to see you both," I say, watching Gideon's face light up at the sight of familiar family.

"Blueberries, really?" Lois scolds as she narrows her eyes in my direction.

I do not want to argue as she is newly released from the hospital, coming off of a miracle life-saving procedure. Omar nods his head toward me and waves to Gideon, all while keeping his arm around Lois, helping her enter the house and make her way to the couch. They are both avoiding eye contact with me and I am curious as to what has unfolded since we last spoke. I sense that they are about to tell me something I do not already know. I stand from where I am sitting on the ground cross-legged with Gideon. He grabs a toy and I pick him up in my arms and seat him on my lap as I take a seat in the La-Z-Boy. "It's good to see you out and about again Lois." I break the silence, although it isn't enough.

Lois settles back into the couch and crosses her arms across her chest, only to wince at what I assume to be pain in her body and grab hold of Omar's arm as she readjusts. Omar pats Lois's hand, reassuring her and opens his mouth to speak. "Anthony," he clears his throat.

I raise my eye brows, silently asking what it is he has to say. Gideon is surprisingly content for the moment playing on my lap, completely infatuated with his toy.

"Anthony, our private investigator has found something. I don't think you're going to like what we're about to tell you."

Thirteen

It is hard to complete any task these days. Gideon is three months old, graduating from newborn to infant status, and his demands are relentless. Everyone says the time goes by so fast with your children and I'm embarrassed to admit it out loud, but time feels anything but fast these days.

For a brief moment during the newborn stage, I thought I had started to bond with my son. Yet I still find myself wishing he had been a girl; that he had been Merry Violet instead of Gideon Simon.

Does that make me terrible? I would never voice this thought to anyone. It's too embarrassing to admit. And what kind of mother would that make me, to say that I wish my son had been a daughter?

Gideon has just started to clap his hands together and this usually makes us both giggle. In those sweeping moments we must look like the picture of perfection; the perfect mother and child. But I know we are not; we are far from it. I still take him outside every day. This morning we watched as two birds flew around the wild daisies on the side of the house, fluttering their wings and then disappearing from our view. Gideon likes the outdoors and I am thankful.

We are back indoors now and I am spending belly time with Gideon. Belly time is when I place him on his stomach, on the floor and today I am rolling a ball so that it stops one to two feet in front of him. The hope is that this activity will help with his coordination as he learns to reach his arm out to the ball. I've found a whole host of activities like this online that I introduce into our daily routines, to help aid in his development. Although I do not feel totally attached to our son just yet (I still have hope that it will click and I will one day), I love him with all of my heart and I want to help him in every way I can. I sing and talk to him all day long. I read short books to him, although I know he can't understand the words or the story just yet. I play peek-a-boo and I placed a non-breakable plastic mirror in his crib so that he can look at himself. I know he will grow up in a world full of technology, meaning that the ever popular "selfie" will probably never go out of style. I consider the mirror I've given him, his first attempt at selfie's. But in all seriousness, the mirror is supposed to help in his development, too. I may not be completely bonded with my son just yet, but I will not be accused of being a bad mother.

I roll the ball to Gideon again. He has not yet made an attempt to reach for it and I am growing bored. That's another thing about newborns, or rather, infants, while they can be quite adorable with their little smiles at times, they are incredibly demanding and not very thought provoking. I miss my books. I miss having a clean house, especially when I dare to move my neck and look around the house at the pile of dirty laundry sitting on the kitchen table and the toys littered across the linoleum floor. I roll the ball again and encourage Gideon to reach for it, to no avail. I realize I am playing a lame game of ball with myself. I leave the ball motionless on the floor, giving up, and reach for the television remote instead. I turn on the screen and find a cartoon, my head instantly pounding from the shrill voices that now fill the air. I know more Dora the Explorer and Doc Mcstuffins songs and sayings than I care to. Admittedly, there are some cute songs and good lessons to be learned from the beloved cartoon characters, but I am an adult and I prefer to read adult books and watch age appropriate shows. However, my life has been turned up-side-down since Gideon arrived. This is our life now; together. I long for conversation. I tear up incredibly easily these days; sometimes when I catch a glimpse of myself in the mirror. I tend to pick a trait in myself to focus negatively on. The bags under my eyes, for example, drove me mad all day yesterday. I wondered what I could do to help them. I told myself it was age, but I am still in my twenties. I am hardly old. And then I realized it was from a lack of sleep and there is nothing I can do to solve that problem. It seems that never again will I have a full night's sleep. So, I stared at the bags under my eyes, while Gideon took a brief nap. And I sobbed at the sight of myself. I know it's not good to focus on nit-picky negative things, but it's what I've been doing and it has become a nasty habit; tearing myself down until I break down in tears. Logically, I should try to reverse this cycle. I should try and focus on one good thing about myself each day, but I haven't been successful in that arena yet. Maybe tomorrow, I chuckle to myself knowing that maybe means never in a million years. It won't happen. Because I will be focused on other things.

Tony walks in the door while I am still sitting on the floor, surrounded by toys and Gideon, practically holding still on his stomach. I have lost track of the time and do not have anything prepared for dinner. I am still in my pajamas and not only do I not have any make-up on, nor have I brushed my tangled hair, I have not brushed my teeth. Instead of standing to hug him, my face turns red, embarrassed by the mess in the house and the mess that I am. I have not greeted him at the door with a hug for several weeks now. We have lost that tradition to my focus on Gideon. "Tony?" I say, nearly breathless as I glance up at the clock on the wall.

His eyes are scanning the room and I can tell he thinks the house is a disaster. I quickly brush my fingers through my hair, as if it will magically correct my lack of hygiene today. Tony is used to seeing me with make-up, a nice outfit, and a spotless house. But I am a very different version of me these days. Whatever Tony is thinking, at least he is kind enough not to say it at this moment. Maybe my frightened eyes are too fierce and have scared any words away that he might have wanted to say. Whatever the reason, I am grateful he remains silent about everything being unkempt, including his wife. "How are you Abigail?" Tony bends to our level and I am taken back for a moment, by his kindness. I am pleasantly surprised to be wrong. I had suspected he would be upset with me right now, although he's never yelled at me for being less than perfect. This is the first time I've not had dinner ready for Tony upon his arrival home.

I manage a half smile and look up at him with my weary eyes. "We're good." I reply for the both of us.

"It looks like you've been having a fun day together." Tony continues, no sign of malice or disappointment can be traced in his tone.

I nod, "We have." I look at Gideon and now we are both focused on our son who continues to be content on his stomach just in front of us. I can't help but wonder if we're both staring at our son because we don't care to look at each other. It's not that things are bad between us. But they do feel strained. They feel different and it is taking some time to get used to this change. Adding a new human to your house is tough; it changes the dynamic of things. There are shifts in our lives now that I never saw coming; like tonight, not having dinner prepared. I don't even have anything started. I can't believe I forgot. I feel unproductive. What have I accomplished today? I've fed and changed our son a handful of times. I've placed him in his crib to nap and held him when he woke. I've rocked him. I've cleaned him. I've made attempts to play with him, to sing to him and to tell him stories. When I tell you this now, it all sounds so easy; so incredibly simple. But I can do nothing else besides these things. They take all of my energy and then some. My mind is now programmed to respond to his every cry.

"We can order pizza tonight. If you'd like I can place the order?" Tony is being so kind. He reaches out to lightly pat Gideon's back and our son coo's, his eyes looking up at his father.

"Yes. That sounds great." I try to sound excited, knowing I won't have to cook, but I am sure that my words sound dull and lifeless.

"Okay then. I'll change out of my work clothes and place the call. Mushrooms?" He waves at Gideon and then stands, looking at me.

I nod. "Thank you." I tell him, meaning it.

"Oh, and I have something for you." Tony's hazel eyes light up and I realize for the first time in a while how handsome my husband is.

"What do you mean?" I have a basket in my arms and am trying to pile as many toys into it as I can.

"A present." He winks, bending down to kiss my forehead.

"What kind of a present?" We don't buy each other gifts, especially not since the arrival of Gideon. Tony was very clear about wanting to save our money. I begin to relax as I stuff the last toy into the basket and place it against the wall. It isn't until now that I remember the gifts he's been bringing me each week. Somehow I'd forgotten in the course of such an unproductive day. "Believe me, pizza is enough of a gift." I smile and meet his eyes this time.

Tony reaches into his pocket and pulls out a small box, handing it to me as he leans back against the La-Z-Boy and sits on its edge. "Someone is like a kid at Christmas!" He laughs. "Open it! Go ahead..." He urges.

I stare at the box wondering why he's bought me a gift; he's already given me one this week, a single red rose, two days ago. It's still on the kitchen table in a clear narrow vase, its smell sweet and fulfilling. I scan my mind to make sure I am not missing our anniversary or heaven forbid, my own birthday. But it is only an ordinary day and my husband has brought me a surprise gift in a small white box. I carefully open the box and lay my eyes on a stunning bright Swiss Blue topaz necklace. Tiny faceted rock crystal gems adorn the sterling silver chain where it meets the pendant and at the clasp. This is a carefully made hand crafted work of art and I know he did not go to a generic jewelry shop to purchase it. Just knowing that Tony remembered my love of handcrafted jewelry warms my heart. The necklace brings tears to my eyes and I am filled with a happiness I haven't felt in a while. "Thank you," my words are merely above the level of a whisper as I swipe my finger around the necklace.

"Do you like it?" Tony's smile is wide and proud.

"I do. I love it. Thank you Tony."

"Put it on." He urges happily.

I reach inside of the box and pull at the chain until I have it in my hand. Tony leans down and offers to help, placing the chain around my neck and clasping it behind my hair.

"You look beautiful." He stands back, looking at me.

"What is it for?" I can't help but ask. I am curious. And as I ask, I remember once again that I am still in my pajamas and I suddenly have the urge to change.

"Because I love you. I love our family. Our life…"

"It's beautiful, Tony." I tell him, meaning it.

"I'm so glad you like it." He leans down to kiss my forehead again before carefully walking around

Gideon and telling me he'll get changed and call for pizza.

My fingers fumble with the necklace that hangs around my neck and I can't help but wish I'd made it myself. I make a mental note to find some time while Gideon is napping tomorrow, to look up the shop's website and read about the owner. I know I will find myself wishing I was her, but I am only curious of my new necklace's origin. I appreciate good craftsmanship. If only Gideon had been born a girl, maybe one day we could make jewelry together and open a mother-daughter shop in town. I highly doubt Gideon, our son, will have interest in doing such things with me. I drop the necklace from my hands and feel the weight of it around my neck. It is stunning and I'm still in shock that Tony went to the trouble of surprising me with it. I reach out for Gideon and pull him carefully to my lap. "Are you ready to head to the kitchen big guy?" I hug him before standing, cradling him in my arms. "Your daddy's getting us pizza tonight." I tell him as I tickle his stomach and watch a smile creep across his chubby face. "Maybe it's not such a bad thing you made me lose track of time." I whisper in Gideon's ear as we head to the kitchen. "Maybe things are starting to look up!"

★ ★ ★

It is Sunday and after church we've decided to take Gideon to visit Tony's mom, Lily, in the nursing home. She hasn't met our son yet and although we know she will not understand who he is, it is important to Tony that she meets him. Lily is merely a shell of her former self. Her physical form is still there; despite her lack of recognition or memory, it will serve as a peace of mind for Tony, to see his mother lay eyes on our child. After all, her blood runs through him, too.

As we walk into her shared room, Lily is sitting slumped forward in a wheel chair, facing the single small window. Her roommate is missing and the room is quiet. The four plants on her window sill are brown and withered, no longer trying to beam upward toward the sun. The room is filled with the strong scent of bleach. There is no sign of a nurse or an aide and we stand in silence for a moment, watching Lily before making a move. It almost appears as if she is sleeping; she is motionless in her chair. I know that Tony is trying to hold back his tears. It is awful to see someone you love in so much distress. While Lily is quiet for the moment, this is not how anyone wishes to see their loved ones; isolated, alone, uncared for and confused. After a few moments I watch as Tony steps forward. Gideon is thankfully asleep in my arms and like Lily, is quiet for the moment. I am wearing my new necklace, a surprise gift from Tony, and Gideon's little fingers are clutching the left side of the chain in his sleep. My back is aching from standing with our son in my arms and I long to sit down, but wait until Tony makes contact with his mother. I do not want to startle Lily before Tony has had a chance to speak with her.

I watch as Tony touches his mother's shoulder and bends down to be at her side. How many times must Lily have woken Tony throughout the years and bent to his level. Now, her son is lovingly mimicking the same behavior. Maybe, I think, life isn't about our days, but instead, about what we create, about who we create. Lily raised Tony to be a kind human being and a devoted husband, just as I hope to be raising Gideon. If only Lily could make sense of her environment today, she would be immensely proud of her son; I have no doubt. Eventually Lily turns to her son and places her hand on his. For a moment, I think, she realizes who he is. But as quickly as the moment comes, it passes and she is visibly upset. She turns to face where I stand holding Gideon, near the doorway. "Who is in my room?" Her words are demanding and accusing at the same time.

I open my mouth to speak, but Tony interrupts before I can form a word. "Mom, it's Abigail. My wife. And we brought our son, Gideon to meet you. He is three months old, mom. And I think he has your beautiful long eye lashes." He smiles, trying to pretend this is a normal family gathering; only it is not normal for him or for us, now.

"I don't know you. I don't know any of you!" She shouts, tossing her hands around in front of her.

I step forward toward her and bend down to show Gideon to her, although I know this most likely will wake him. "Your grandson." I say softly, focusing my gaze on him and wanting desperately for her to do the same. I know Tony wants his mother to realize she has a grandson, even if only for a second.

"Help!" She looks above Gideon's head and becomes desperate for an escape. "Help, please! I need to get out of here!" Her eyes are darting back and forth frantically and I back off, standing up and moving slowly toward the open doorway. Gideon has woken, as expected and is crying quietly in my arms. I know the wails are coming, but right now it is a soft cry and not disturbing in comparison to Lily's outburst.

"Why don't you hold him?" I suggest to Tony. I tell him I need to use the ladies room and purposely leave the two men in my life alone with their own bloodline.

Tony nods and takes Gideon awkwardly in his arms. "Will he stop crying?" He asks before I leave the room.

"Yes." I lie. I do not know. He may or he may not. But when I come back I will take Gideon and settle him down if he is still carrying on. "I'll be back in a jiffy." I tell him as I exit the room, hearing the fading sounds of Lily's shouts and Gideon's soft cries as I head down the hall.

Fifteen minutes later when I return I see that everything has worked out beautifully. Lily is smiling and Tony has pulled up a chair next to hers, Gideon in his lap cooing and being a delightful version of himself. Lily may not understand who the two men sitting next to her are, but all three of them are happy and that is what matters in this moment. As I stand quietly against the door frame, not wanting to interrupt the peaceful scene that is playing out before me, I fiddle with my necklace and think happiness is all that really matters. Whether we're infants, adults or seniors with dementia, all any of us want on any given day is to be happy.

Fourteen

ANTHONY

Present Day, 2017

Lois and Omar are sitting on the couch as I hold Gideon. He is surprisingly content for the moment, playing on my lap, completely infatuated with his toy.

"Anthony, our private investigator found something. I don't think you're going to like what we're about to tell you." Omar narrows his eyes in my direction, sending a chill down my spine. I search for signs of sadness on their faces, but only find them laced with anger. If Abigail's body has been found, why haven't the police called to tell me? If she is dead, why are the Atwell's not consumed by tears? Have they assumed she's been dead the whole time, is that how they are coping with the news?

I gulp and kiss the top of Gideon's head before placing him carefully on the ground beside my feet. Leaning forward, my forearms resting on my thighs, I wait for what Omar will say next, although I'm not sure I want to hear the words.

"Why didn't you tell us?" His question is demanding and full of blame.

"I'm sorry?" I itch my neck and wonder what in the world he is referring to.

"I bet you're sorry. So sorry that you failed to tell our private investigator and the police about your affair with this young Cindy girl?" Omar's words hit me like a ton of bricks. I watch as Lois stares back at me, pressing her thin lips together. Her eyes look tired and her face is overrun with defeat.

"How could you?" Lois adds, her voice weak. "How could you Anthony?"

Omar pats his wife's leg but quickly turns his focus back to me. "Care to explain? Wait, no, don't. I don't want to hear what you have to say because it will be a lie. We know the truth and it's not because of you. We had to pay good money to find out that you were sneaking around with some young bimbo while our daughter was carrying your son? Wait," He pauses briefly in his fury and points his finger in my direction. "No, I do want you to tell us something Anthony. I want you to tell us what else you are hiding? What other secrets do you have? Did Abigail find out about the affair and you were embarrassed, you were upset that she'd found out so you killed her and buried her body somewhere? Is that how it happened?"

I can't stop shaking my head. "No, no! Of course not. Of course not Mr. and Mrs. Atwell. I would never harm Abigail!" I am pleading with them, but for what, I am not sure.

"An affair harms a person. Did you know that Anthony?"

I am still shaking my head. "Yes. I know. I know I should have told you, I should have told everyone about Cindy. I'm dreadfully sorry. I'm so very sorry. It was wrong of me…"

"Wrong isn't even the half of it!"

"No, I know. I'm sorry. It was wrong. But Abigail never knew. How did you…How did the investigator even find out? No, I'm sorry again. I don't need to know. That is the job, to find out things. I get it…" I cannot stop rambling.

"To say we're disappointed is a huge understatement. You have undermined all of us. We only came here today to let you know that we know and to ask you, to beg you to tell us what other secrets you have. Don't you think seven months is long enough to let us stew like this? Don't you think we've been through enough Anthony?" His face coils tightly and I can tell he can hardly stomach to look at me, let alone be in the same room. "We're taking Gideon when we leave. I don't want to hear a single word. Do not argue. You do not have a leg to stand on, you know that, right? We do not want our grandson staying with a murderer."

"Wait, please. This is all getting out of control…" I beg.

"This all went out of control a long time ago, Anthony. I think you should know that better than us. You lying sack of shit!" Omar makes an attempt to stand, but stumbles on his feet before attempting a second time and then reaching to help Lois do the same. Once Lois is standing I watch as Omar bends down feebly to pick up Gideon, who has now started to cry in the midst of all of the commotion. I had been excited to tell the Atwell's that Gideon said the word "dog" today. But now that news has been buried like an avalanche. They do not care that Gideon added another word to his small vocabulary. They do not care that I can't bear to wash my wife's pillowcase because it still contains a hint of her smell. They do not care that I regret my fling with Cindy and that I have been trying desperately to reach her as of late, on behalf of Abigail. They do not care about anything more I have to say at this point. Because now they see me as a liar. A cheat. They think I am full of secrets. They think it is not safe for our son to be with his own father.

And now I've just lost the only remaining family I have.

Now I am truly alone. I have no one. Gideon is parentless. The Atwell's are destroyed; I guess that's the only thing we have left in common. We are all destroyed.

Eight long wretched months, that's how long Abigail has been missing. At night when everything is quiet and calm I beg myself to let her go, to let it all go. It's just Gideon and me now and I need to get used to that. Only, Gideon has now been taken from me, too. It's just me. Me, alone. The Atwell's have had Gideon since the day they told me they found out about my affair with Cindy. They don't trust me and are insistent that I am full of secrets pertaining to their daughter and her possible whereabouts.

I called to speak with Gideon, so that he could at least hear my voice. I started out calling once a day, but it has dwindled to a measly once a week at this point. Each time I call I am met with acidic resentment as Lois or Omar hold the phone up to Gideon's ear or put me on speaker phone. When I'm done speaking briefly to my son, Omar always picks up the phone and adds, "Do you have anything to tell us yet?" I always tell him no, but he thinks one day I will tell him yes. He thinks that one day I will break down and tell him that I killed his daughter; my wife. He thinks I am a murderer and there is nothing I can do to change his mind anymore. A part of me wonders if they suspected me all along. What's that saying; *keep your friends close but your enemies closer?* Is that what they'd been doing with me? Maybe they had been waiting for a piece of evidence to drop in their lap so that they could vocalize the blame. Well, now they have it. Now they can point their aging fingers at me and maybe feel some sense of closure. But it isn't closure, is it? How is it closure if they don't have any facts or details? They can't prove that I killed my wife. They may be able to prove that I had an affair with Cindy, but they cannot validate that I had anything to do with my wife's disappearance.

Any remaining secrets I keep are not for the Atwell's to know.

Last week marked our three year wedding anniversary and I celebrated it completely alone with a bottle of Hennessy Black. How is that for depressing? I went to a little shop off the beaten path and purchased a bracelet for Abigail, although I don't know that I'll ever have the chance to give it to her. A man can hope; and that is what I am holding on to right now. Hope. The bracelet is one I'm sure she would…(*or will*) love. It is beaded bangle bracelet made of sterling silver wire. The bracelet has been buffed to a soft matte finish and the jeweler assured me that Abigail can wear it with other bracelets or as a standalone, so it is versatile. It is wrapped in a small navy blue box with a thin red bow tied neatly around it. I placed a small note beneath the ribbon saying:

Happy 3ʳᵈ Anniversary Abigail! I love you always. Yours, Tony

I wrote in 3ʳᵈ because I do not know how many anniversaries I will spend without her until we find her. Will the 4ᵗʰ leave me at home alone too? What about the 5ᵗʰ? The 9ᵗʰ? How long will this nightmare continue? How many gifts will I hide away before she is found?

To pile on to my pain, Abigail's birthday is next week. She will be twenty-seven years old. As with our anniversary, I will buy her a gift. In fact, I've already ordered it. Is that weird? That I'm buying my possibly deceased wife gifts? I'm beyond the point of caring what other people think of me. It's quite possible, actually, that I've completely lost my mind. I brush away that thought as quickly as it comes because of my mother. I haven't lost my mind and I should not joke about it, not even when I'm alone. She's lost her mind, literally. I am simply overwhelmed. I am tired. I am worried. I am nervous. I am filled with melancholy. I am alone. And I am terrified. I know the chances of Abigail being alive after eight months are slim to none. I know this. I've read the statistics and watched the chilling news stories of other, similar victims. Yet I am somehow managing to hold on to the tiniest inkling of faith that everything will go back to how it was. That Abigail will be found and alive. That the Atwell's will find a way to forgive me. That Gideon will return home, unharmed from the absence of his parents and the confusion of this whole giant mess.

Maybe hope and faith are making me delusional.

That's how it's beginning to seem to me as I sit alone in the La-Z-Boy chair and wrap myself in the maddening silence of my own chaotic thoughts. Is this the punishment delivered for my affair with Cindy? Is this what I deserve? Maybe so. I guess that depends on the jury. My affair was brief. I ended it. It's over and it's been over for a long time. Does that mean this horror that has become my life will end too? *And this too shall pass*…does that apply to me? Or will I finish out eternity alone and never truly knowing the answers that I long for?

Fifteen

ABIGAIL

2016

"Will you at least talk to your doctor about this?" Tony has grown impatient with me, but I will not give in to his demands.

"No, I don't need to." Finally, I am standing up for myself on something. "I'm fine." I add for good measure. Although I realize I am in my pajamas again today when Tony comes home from work and dinner is not made. I did brush my teeth this morning and I ran a comb through my tangled hair. I have a small bit of make-up on, too. But when you have a busy six month old it's not the easiest thing in the world to spend time on yourself. Gideon is throwing a lot of tantrums these days, but what's new? He is not a quiet baby, that much I know for sure at this point. I try to sing to him as I did when he was younger, but it isn't doing anything to help him quiet down at this stage.

"Abigail, please. I'm not saying this to upset you. I promise you that. I'm just worried about you and I want you to be okay. I want you to have everything you need. Won't you talk to your doctor about these moods?" His tone is calm and soft, but his words still sting. I do not need to talk to my doctor about my moods. I am a busy mother. Moods are normal. If I wasn't moody, that's when I would be worried about myself. I have a lot on my plate trying to figure out how to parent our child. I am practically a single parent and although I have not said this out loud to Tony, I am getting to the point that it will soon slip off my tongue unintentionally.

"I do not have postpartum, Tony. You can read an article on the Internet and think that you've diagnosed me, but you're wrong. You are not a doctor. And I do not have anything wrong with me. That is that." I pick at an invisible thread on my pajama bottoms as I wait in silence for his reply. He always gets in the last word, so I know there will be a reply.

Tony stutters on his words before forming a proper sentence. I told you, there it is, he always gets the last word. "You're taking this the wrong way."

"What other way is there for me to take it? Indulge me, why don't you..." I spat back, surprised at myself.

"As love. I care about you."

"You care about me so much that you would like me to go tell the doctor that I'm moody or depressed...something along those lines, right?" I don't pause to wait for his answer. "So you would like me, your wife, to be placed on medication? You would like someone to drug me so that I can be perfect for you? Is that it? Do I have it all about right? Do you think that's how you love and care for someone, by placing them on pills?" I am sickened by the thought that he merely wants me to smile and nod and be the perfect housewife. Not once since Gideon has been born, has my husband asked me how I am feeling. But now, suddenly, he's ready to diagnose me and ship me off to a doctor who will drug me into complacency. I won't allow it. I may be a submissive woman, but I will not be fooled into this.

Tony is standing before me, his mouth gaped open wide as he stares back at me. His eyes tell me he thinks

I have gone nuts. Or maybe it's more a look of shock that I have spoken up to him. After all, this is a rare occurrence in our household.

After a few beats I begin to speak again, starting where I left off. "I will consider going to a therapist. Or maybe we should consider going to a marriage counselor together?" I am well aware of the fact that Tony does not believe in the power of therapists. He has told me so on more than one occasion. But I still throw it out there to show him I am trying. I am willing to talk to a professional if that will make him happy. It won't do me any harm as I don't get much social interaction, other than baby talk with Gideon. At least I would have another adult to talk to once a month.

As expected, Tony disagrees and is not shy to voice his opinion. He squeezes his face as if he's just eaten something sour. "You don't need a therapist." He rolls his eyes. "*We* don't need a therapist!"

"You said I needed a doctor. A therapist is a doctor." I say quietly, unsure if he hears me.

"Abigail, if you won't go see your doctor...a *real* doctor that is your choice. But we're not spending money on a therapist. You can talk to me. I'm as good as any therapist."

It is all I can do not to roll my eyes. Not only

does Tony pride himself with the thought that he can diagnose me as a physician would, but now he's telling me he is just as good as a therapist. He's also telling me we don't need marriage counseling when everything about this very conversation is screaming otherwise. I say nothing in return to his comments.

"What you need is church!"

I go to church every Sunday with Gideon on my lap. Tony usually joins us a few times a month these days, but not every Sunday. Who is he to tell me that I need church when I'm always in attendance? Before I can tell him that I am the one who is there, with our son, every Sunday, he speaks again.

"I know you go to church, but you need more of it. Clearly. You need counseling from the church. I'm sure Father Henry would be happy to counsel you."

I walk out of the room and although Gideon is napping I head to his bedroom to wake him. I am done with this conversation.

It isn't until I'm holding a wailing Gideon in my arms and scouring through his room to find his tiny jeans, white top and fresh socks that I see my Swiss Blue topaz necklace on the top of the dresser. Ah, I get it. It hits me then that Tony bought me that necklace as an attempt to cure me. He thought by buying me gifts he could lift my mood. He thought that these small material items would pacify my moodiness, perhaps. The gifts weren't for nothing, they were very much for something. And now I know what. Now I know that he had been trying to boost my spirits with small gifts and when he didn't think that was working, he became frustrated and we are where we are now. Tony throwing a tantrum, wanting me to go on medication or to tell my every secret to our priest. It was all just a ploy to get me to be exactly how he wanted. Instead of thinking Tony is sweet for caring about my happiness, I feel played. I feel placated at the very least. I leave the necklace, lifeless on the dresser top as I change Gideon from his dirty diaper and oversized shirt into the fresh set of clothes I have now located. Despite my anger, I tell myself that once I have Gideon changed and quieted down (if that ever happens) I will rejoin my husband in the kitchen and act as if everything is normal. First, I tell myself, I will change out of my own pajamas and into a proper outfit. Then, Gideon and I will resume our evening as if my previous conversation with Tony had not happened. I think it will be best for all three of us that way. It is not healthy for Gideon to be around arguing parents and I am too tired to engage in disagreements any more tonight. I just want to pretend we are a family. Well, we are a family. But I want to pretend we are a happy one at the moment.

I am home alone with our son, as I should be at this hour. It is only nine o'clock in the morning and Gideon is in full swing. We are sitting on the red and brown checkered rug in the living room and I am making animal noises. Meow-meow! Quack-quack! Each new noise elicits a laugh from the little man in my life. Sometimes when I hear myself acting absolutely ridiculous to amuse or potentially teach our son, I feel embarrassed. Today is different, however as I do not feel this way. I am engaged and somehow embracing my inner goofy side. Last night when I gave Gideon a bath before bedtime I splashed my hands in front of him and he mimicked me, laughing the whole time. I called out to Tony to come and watch, but he did not hear me over the television and missed the whole thing. I never bothered to mention it to him once Gideon was asleep.

Gideon is at the stage where he loves to be on his stomach and then roll over onto his back. He is also attempting to sit up on his own and I know he will accomplish this task soon. To help Gideon strengthen his little chubby legs I spend time each day holding him under his arms and letting him stand with my assistance. Just as I am on the sound of *moo-moo!* I hear something at the front door. It is early and we aren't expecting any one. My parents always call before they stop by and we have not introduced ourselves properly to any of the neighbors yet. My heart skips a beat but then I shake my head and refocus on Gideon and our animal sounds game. After making the sound of a cow I move on to the sound of a pig, but I pause again when I hear something at the front door. Gideon halts his laughter and I don't know if it's because he hears the sound at the door and senses some kind of danger or if he is merely cueing off of me. Maybe it's neither. Maybe our game is over and the moment has passed. When I hear a shuffling at the front door again I push my back up against the far side of the couch, realizing that the large front window could allow for any stranger to look right into our living room, where we are sitting. I reach to grab Gideon from where he is on his stomach on the carpet and pull him up to sit on my lap, resting his back and head against my chest as we tuck ourselves behind the furniture. I pull my phone from my pocket and look at the screen. No missed calls or text messages. The door knob jiggles and this time I am sure someone is at the front door. I peak my head around the corner to watch the knob moving and feel my body tighten under stress. Gideon begins to cry and I whisper to him, begging him to be quiet.

I should have taken the self-defense class at the YMCA before we were married. If nothing else, at least it would make me feel safer to know that I knew some moves. But I don't know any moves, other than clutching my son and dialing 9-1-1. I am doing one of the two. I don't want to rush to judgment and place an emergency call though. I don't want it to come to that. Hopefully it's just someone who's coming home from a late night and they have the wrong house. Although the houses on our street were built twenty years ago, they all look rather similar in their exterior. Yes. Surely that's it. It must be.

The door knob jiggles again. My heart rate has sky rocketed and Gideon's cries have not quieted, but instead, only grown louder. I stare at the screen of my phone and choose Tony's name. I wait through four rings only to find that he is not answering. I hear his voice at the start of the message system and hang up from the call. After another few times the jiggling stops and everything is quiet with the exception of

Gideon who is not enjoying our new game of hiding from strangers in our home. Maybe he is only vocally expressing how I feel in this moment. I am terrified. Once the jiggling has been silent for several minutes, I poke my head around the corner of the couch and look first at the door and then to the window that is wide open, curtains resting easily at each side to let the light flood into our living room. Slowly, I stand and creep over to the edge of the window, holding Gideon tightly in my arms and doing my best to zone out the sound of his cries. I peek out the window and see nothing. There is no trace of anyone ever being outside my door. Although I'm certain they were. I'm sure someone was trying to get inside. Only, for what reason? My heart rate begins to slow as I realize whoever was there is now gone. I walk more confidently to the front door now and pull it open, leaving the chain lock in place for good measure. There are no flyers on the door, although if it had been someone selling something, there would have been no need for them to jiggle the door knob at all. I tell myself that it was definitely someone coming home after a late night; surely realizing after a bit, even in their hazy state that they were at the wrong house and that their key would not fit into the lock of the wrong door. That's all it was. Nothing to worry about, I try to assure myself. Just as I am doing this my phone startles me with a ring. I look at the screen to see it is Tony. There is no sense in telling him about this now. We are fine.

"Tony?"

"Hey, it's me. I just saw I missed your call. Is everything all right at home? Is Gideon okay?" He sounds genuinely concerned. "I was in a meeting. I'm so sorry."

"Oh, no. It's nothing. Everything is fine." I am pleasant, trying not to let on that I have just been spooked.

"Are you sure?"

"Yes. I'm certain. It's silly, really. I was just calling to let you know that Gideon used his hands to splash in his bath water. He mimicked me all on his own." I try to sound cheerful and upbeat, knowing that Tony will not realize that I give Gideon his baths in the evenings and not in the mornings.

After a beat, he responds. "Oh, that's great honey. Our little guy is really growing up, huh?"

"Indeed he is." I agree. "Well, I'll let you get back to it. I know you're busy."

"Okay hon. I'll see you both tonight." We both hang up the phone and go back to our lives. Gideon has not yet quieted down and I notice he needs another diaper change and we head to his bedroom to clean him up.

I go back to double check that the front door is locked, ignoring Gideon's impatient wails, before successfully making it to his room. We are safely locked inside of our own little simple world. There is no need to worry about anything other than caring for Gideon now. But sometimes the simple seems so complicated.

I wasn't quite at eight months into my pregnancy the last time I made love with my husband. I've lost track of time with a little one attached to my hip these days, but it has been more than eight months since we've touched. We've briefly held hands, on occasion. He kisses my forehead and I quickly press my lips against his sometimes when I say good-night. But even that is not a daily occurrence. I used to hug Tony every time he walked in the door and that too has fallen by the wayside. I am assuming all parents go through this phase. Our relationship is a roller coaster of phases, all centered around Gideon's moods and development.

I am ready to be intimate with Tony now. At

the very least, our marriage needs this. We need a boost to help us through the funk we've been in. I felt embarrassed to Google the topic while Gideon was napping yesterday, but I did it anyway and read that many husbands are afraid to push the topic of intimacy after pregnancy, not wanting to go too fast or to hurt the woman in any way. I wonder if that's what Tony's been thinking. He's probably been worried that I would turn him down and ask him to wait. He wouldn't want to face the humiliation of that. Never once, before the pregnancy, had I turned him down. Even when I didn't want to make love I never told him so. I complied and avoided an awkward argument. It always seemed easier that way. Not that there weren't plenty of times that I enjoyed myself, too.

My parents are watching Gideon tonight. He won't sleep overnight at their house, but I sent along his Graco Pack 'n Play in case he needs a nap. This is the first time they've had him alone at their house since he's been born. They were more than pleased to babysit for the evening. Meanwhile, I planned a much needed evening with my husband. I knew I needed to do something to get our marriage back on track. And I couldn't do what I needed to do with Gideon in the house. Not yet.

When Tony walks in the door after work I hug him and we fall into the old familiar pattern. It feels comfortable.

"Where's the little guy?" He gleams, tossing his work bag into the coat closet.

"My parents have him for a few hours." I wink and rub my hand up and down Tony's exposed arm.

"Oh, do they?"

"I thought it would be nice for us to have dinner as adults, instead of as parents. Just for tonight. We can go and pick up Gideon later. My parents are madly in love with their grandson, so there is no rush." I add.

"You look nice." Tony comments on my loosely fitted pink dress. I admit that I purchased it online as I can't fit into my clothes from before pregnancy just yet and I certainly didn't want to wear any of my maternity attire tonight.

"Thanks. How was your day today?" I fain interest in his work, wanting to skip dinner and follow through with my plan; the goal of the evening, to rekindle our marriage. Can it be done in one simple evening? I'm not sure, but I'm hoping.

"Good. Same old thing. Nothing exciting to report." He heads to the kitchen and I follow. "So, do you want to go out to eat tonight?"

"No need. I have dinner ready." I pull out his chair

and he takes a seat and watches as I bring our filled plates to the table. A cinnamon candle is burning between us, filling the air with warmth. We start with salad and then move to our plates containing chili-garlic grilled chicken with avocado-cherry salsa. The conversation is light throughout the meal. He comments on how good the food is and I tell him small things about Gideon. But we each speak in less than two sentences at a time, neither of us ever daring to go into any more depth than that. Although I'm not sure why we are both avoiding taking a stab at any real conversation. Nevertheless, our chatter is polite and friendly. When we both finish our meals I clear the plates from the table and bring Tony a glass of Hennessy Black. When he asks what we have for dessert I tell him, shyly that it's me. I am well aware that I am not good at this sort of thing. I don't really know how to throw myself at my husband, but I am trying.

He turns his head sideways and asks me to have a drink with him. I agree and drink straight from the bottle rather than pouring it into a glass. I rarely drink and when I do, it's never directly from the source. However, I realize I have limited hours with my husband and I am trying my best to be his wife; to make him want me. I think I'm doing this to help our marriage, but I'm beginning to wonder if a part of me is doing this to test him. Does he still want to touch me? Does he still look at me in that way? After all, he's seen me change in shape and size. He's watched me grow a puffy face and he's seen me screaming in the delivery room, pushing our son out of my own body. Is he still able to find me attractive or is the sight of me tainted after what my body's endured?

After sitting at the table taking turns drinking from the dark bottle, as if we are rebellious teenagers, I make another attempt to show him my intent. I grab Tony's hand and run my fingers across his. I stand and kiss his forehead, each of his eye lids, his nose, his neck and behind each of his ears. And then I move to his mouth as I use my hand to pull at his, begging him without words to go to the bedroom with me. Only, Tony does not budge. He stays seated. We continue pressing our lips together for a few lingering moments. When he pulls away, we meet eyes and as I stand in front of him I tug at his arm again. "Come on…" I smile, begging him to follow. Instead of standing he lets go of my hand and I realize I am walking out of the kitchen alone. "Tony?" I ask, confused.

"This is nice Abigail."

"I can make it even nicer." I whisper, beckoning

him to follow me to the bedroom as I motion for him with my hand.

Turning his head to the side he returns the smile to me, but I cannot see his teeth. He leaves his lips pressed together. "Abigail, you don't have to." He tells me.

"I'm ready, though. Really. I'm telling you I'm ready." It's difficult for me to say these words and heat rises to my face as they spill off my tongue and into the air.

"It's okay hon. We can wait. There's no need to rush…"

"Tony, it's been eight months. You've been more than patient. I'm fine…"

Our words dangle in the air like a roast on a string.

I kick off my shoes, and although I realize it's not the sexiest move I can make, I am still trying. "I'm yours for the taking." I spit the words into the air and hope that he'll give in. Surely he'll give in.

"Why don't we go out for dessert?" He suggests innocently, trying to avoid me. But why? "We can get ice cream sundaes from that place you like in town…"

I am fairly certain that an ice cream sundae is not going to give our marriage a boost. However, I am done trying. "Okay." I look down at my bare feet and walk toward him, placing my hand on his shoulder. "Are you sure that's what you want?"

He nods and I wonder how much weight I'll need to lose before he'll find me desirable again. "Hey," he grabs my hand and looks up at me from his chair. "You're my girl." I should be putty in his hands. Instead I am consumed with humiliation and doing my best to hide it behind a smile. "Put your shoes on and let's get out of here. What kind of toppings are you going to get?" He continues on as I grab my purse and he grabs the car keys, but I cannot focus on what he is saying. I have been rejected. I've never once put myself out there like this; I've never thrown myself at any man. I didn't think I would ever have to. But now I have and it's unsettling. I am unnerved by the way I've acted this evening. And then I realize as we're climbing into the car that sex isn't the cure all for the current flat line in our marriage. I'm not sure what is, but I'm betting on time. Time, surely will heal what's come unhinged.

Sixteen

ANTHONY

Present Day, 2017

Why did Cindy have to travel out of the country? Why not out of state, instead? I've left more than two dozen messages by now and to tell you I'm growing impatient would be a massive understatement. Does her silence mean that she knows something about Abigail? And if she knows something, what exactly is she trying to hide from me? I'm assuming that the Atwell's private investigator will attempt to track her down, even though she is abroad. I'm assuming he will successfully find her and determine if she has a secret. I say assuming because the Atwell's and I aren't on the best of terms these days. Ever since they found out about Cindy, any relationship we had, whether real or imagined, has dissipated and is strained beyond recognition. But Cindy is just a young girl, what could she have possibly done? What could she possibly know? Chances are that the answer to both questions is *nothing*. However, none of us will know for sure until she is found. It would be a start if she could return my calls or texts. I press call on my phone, attempting yet again to reach her. I am heating a Hungry Man dinner of meatloaf and mashed potatoes for one in the microwave only half listening to the rings as I wait for the inevitable answering machine to fill my ear. Only this time the call rings three times and goes silent. "Hello?" I say, breathless and wondering if Cindy has finally answered.

The phone is not ringing, but no one is speaking, either.

"Hello? Is someone there?" I hear the long beep on the microwave, letting me know that my dinner is ready.

Still, the phone is silent on the other end. Although I think I can detect the slightest sound of a breath.

"Cindy? Is that you? Say something if you're there. Are you okay?" I am overwhelmed with sudden worry. What if Cindy is with Abigail? What if they are both in trouble? I know this is highly unlikely, the two don't even know each other, at least as far as I am aware. But, what if?

No one answers again, but the line doesn't go dead either.

"Hello?" I pause briefly, waiting and hoping for a reply. Still nothing. "Cindy, if you're there...call me back. I can't hear you if you're talking. Maybe you can hear me? Please call or text me. I'd love to hear from you. I need to speak with you as soon as possible." I give the same rushed spiel that I always leave on her voice mail. I linger on the line for another moment longer, knowing nothing more will come of the call. I hang up and press my back against the refrigerator, staring at the face of my phone, begging it to ring. I stay like this for nearly ten minutes before daring to move. She's not calling back. I open the microwave and look at my dull dinner, a far cry from the meals I enjoyed when Abigail was here. She would be appalled to see me eating this junk. I place my finger in the mashed potatoes and feel that they are still cold. I heat my meal for another minute, letting the hum of the microwave lull my mind into a spell. Someone answered Cindy's phone. Was it Cindy? Was it someone else? What do they know? And why did they bother to answer and not speak?

The Atwell's share very little with me these days. Our brief conversations consist only of any updates on the search for Abigail and small tidbits of information about Gideon, as he remains in their care. I have no doubt he is wearing them out, he has a tendency of doing that to his caretakers. Regardless of this fact, they never let on that they are tired or overwhelmed with caring for him. I would imagine that a part of them probably feels like they are closer to their daughter by having Gideon in their home.

I've stopped going to church on Sundays, not wanting to see the Atwell's with my son in their arms; not wanting to sit on opposite sides of the pew. It would be far too awkward to stomach such occurrences every week. So I opt to stay behind, knowing they will certainly be there without waver.

My Sundays consist of watching television or staring at my phone as I blindly scour Internet pages in an attempt to numb my emotions. Today is no different. But it is nearly four o'clock and I assume the Atwell's will be home at this hour as it is after church. I haven't called to check in on Gideon in nearly two weeks and figure I should do that today. It's not the easiest thing to do; to call your wife's parents to check on your child when your wife has been missing for nine long miserable months and her parents don't trust the sight of you. But I am doing it for Gideon. I make the call because I know it is the right thing to do; although I admit, nothing seems right anymore. What does doing the right thing really matter anyway? Abigail always did the right things in her life and look where that's gotten her. She's missing and we may never find her. She may be...I can't say it. I can't go there. I am still clinging to hope that my wife is alive, somewhere; somehow. I may be low on faith, but I am still holding hope's hand.

"Mr. Atwell, it's Anthony." I've taken to calling the Atwell's more formally these days. Using first names hardly seems appropriate given their distrust in me.

I hear Omar clear his throat before speaking. "Anthony. Hi, yes. Gideon is doing fine." He spits out answers before I've asked any questions. I know that he wants to rush the conversation along. He probably wants to be off the phone before Lois enters the room and realizes that it is me on the line. I am well aware that I am a strong reminder of all they have lost; their one and only child, their daughter. I have no doubt that when they hear my voice they hold their breath, wishing they could shake answers out of me; wishing it was me who was missing instead of their own flesh and blood.

"Good. I'm glad to hear Gideon is well. I hope he's not giving you too much trouble." I add the last part for good measure.

Omar replies with silence. He has always been a man who has preferred to speak with his silence rather than his words.

"I...uh..." I am stuttering, not sure what I should say next. "Is Gideon there? Could I say hello?"

"Well, Anthony, now is not a good time. He's just waking up from a nap and being changed..." His voice trails.

"Okay. I understand. Maybe you could call later this evening and put him on for a minute or two so that he can say hello to his dad?" I am not trying to be snippy, but I do want to give Mr. Atwell a nudge. I want to remind him that I am Gideon's dad whether he likes it or not.

"Maybe. We'll see how things go. If he seems up to it, we'll place him on the phone for you." His words are curt.

"Well…before I go, I wanted to check in with you as well."

"With me?"

"I wanted to see if your private investigator has found anything else recently?" I say hesitantly.

"Do you mean, have any more of your secrets been discovered? Is that what you're asking me?" His words are charged with malice.

"No. Please, no. That's not what I mean at all. I've told you, I have no other secrets. I have nothing else to tell."

"You have nothing else you want to tell?" He questions me.

"Come on. You have to know…" I stop before I say something I will regret.

"What do I know, Anthony? Let's see. What I know…" he is growing angrier with each word. "What I know is that our daughter has been missing for nine months. What I know is that you came home from work early the day she went missing. What I know is that for all anyone knows, you were the last person, with the exception of Gideon, to see Abigail. What I know is that you had blood on you when police came to your home that night Abigail went missing. There was an open bottle of your favorite drink on the counter. What I know is that we had to find out from a hired private investigator that you had an affair while Abigail was pregnant. You failed to tell the police, the investigator or us about this affair and we know you have more to tell. We know you are full of secrets…"

I am stunned into silence. I set myself up for this. How had I not seen it coming?

"So when you decide you have something more to tell us, how about you call us then?"

"I…um…I…" I fumble on my words, unable to connect them into a sentence.

"Cat got your tongue?" Omar forces a chuckle. "Well, when you decide you'd like to share with us what you know, give us a call. We'll have our investigator and our lawyer present. You are welcome to tell us your secrets anytime. We're here, ready to listen. You just say the word. But, Anthony?"

"Yeah?" I answer weakly.

"Until then, don't call. Assume Gideon is fine. We'll call you if he's not. But he will be and he is. You don't have to worry about him going missing or anything. *Our* house is a safe one. Call us when you're really ready to talk. Is the message clear?"

My head droops at his question. I am defeated. I don't know how to muster up the strength to keep fighting, to keep searching for my wife. My family has been ruined. My home is empty. And the only blood relative I have left is succumbing to the deterioration of her own mind. My mom has no chance to come back from this. There have been miracle cures of those diagnosed with cancers, but no one has ever been cured of Alzheimer's or dementia. And I highly doubt that doctors will find a cure anytime soon.

"I'll take your silence as a yes." Omar adds, interrupting my conquered state. "I will tell you before I hang up that our investigator has not been able to reach your...Cindy. Also, there have been no leads in our daughter's disappearance other than a handful of criminals who are already in prison for other kidnappings. None of them will admit to the kidnapping or murder of our daughter, even when offered less time for doing so. So, although you think you don't have to talk...even though you think Abigail's disappearance will eventually blow over, I'm here to let you know that it won't. We won't let it. Gideon deserves to know what's happened to his mother. He deserves better than this. You, Tony, may have grown apathetic to the ongoing search for our daughter, but we never will. I can promise you that. We'll never stop searching for her. So when you're ready to talk, like I said, let us know."

I am still unable to talk, although my head is buzzing.

"We're praying for you." He adds, as if throwing me a bone. But I know that praying won't help. After all, I've been praying for months and my wife is still missing. If they're praying for anyone it should be for their daughter, not for me. But I know they think I hold a magical key; they're certain that I can give them an answer.

Seventeen

ABIGAIL

2016

Our little Gideon is crawling now. At eight months he is a chatty little man who is on the move. Our days are full of action and my nights are still fairly sleepless. Despite what I have accepted to be chronic sleep deprivation, I have gotten better at keeping a smile on my face. It is precisely because of my smile that Tony has stopped bringing me small gifts and I don't mind. The gifts were merely to placate me anyway. He was trying to cure the diagnosis he bestowed upon me: post-partum depression. Despite the increase in Gideon's activity level as of late, I've been much more attentive to preparing dinner in time for Tony's arrival home from work. I've been making sure to change out of my pajamas sometime before lunch, too. I brush my hair and put on a dash of make-up. The house, admittedly, is not always spotless. I think those days are long gone as it seems an impossible goal with a busy child at my side. Where a lack of connection with my child exists, I pretend. What else is there to do? Perhaps one day I'll feel a close bond to him, but for now I will feign for what I hope to be.

When we attend Sunday Mass each week I am flanked in the pew by the men in my life. From young to old they keep me close under their wings. Gideon sits on my lap, Tony is at my left and my dad is at my right, with my mom on his opposite side. We are the picture of perfection. We span three generations within a matter of a mere six feet of space. I actually find myself nodding off in church more often than not lately. It makes sense as it is the quietest, still time I have in my life now. But Gideon is always sure to jolt me back to life as my eye lids grow heavy and my mind spins into a blurry after thought. Gideon is always wanting to move, to play a game with me or have a new toy from the bag I keep close to us at all times. I try my best to be prepared for anything. Who would have thought a tiny eight month old could be so demanding? He is starting to understand the meaning of *no* and although at first I thought it was a good thing, I'm beginning to question my judgment. When I tell Gideon no, he usually begins throwing a fit. I think he's trying to see if that will help him get his way. He's testing me and as hard as it is, I know I can't back down once I've said the word. I may not feel tightly bonded just yet with my son, but I love him to pieces. Saying no and sticking to it nearly kills me. I hate seeing him upset and I hate trying to silence his cries when I know that giving him what he wants will silence them with a lot more ease on both of us.

After Mass today we go to my parents' house for a light brunch. My mom has prepared small bowls of colorful berries and bananas; a mini fruit salad. She has also made asparagus frittata. My mouth salivates as I smell the mixture of Swiss cheese, eggs, onion and asparagus. My stomach rumbles a beat later. I try to be patient as she places the food on the table and hands us individual plates and utensils. When my mom offers to take Gideon from my arms so that I can pile my plate with food, I gladly accept. I fill my plate and notice that she has also made fresh slices of cinnamon toast. The thin slices of bread are warm and the cinnamon has been sprinkled on top of a layer of butter and sugar. I reach for a helping of asparagus frittata as I hear my mom oohing and awing over her grandson. Her words are muffled to me, although I know she is kissing his chubby cheeks and telling him how special he is. She does this every time she sees him. Her faint words are intertwined with Gideon's babbling and then I hear it. I am placing a few berries in my mouth and I nearly spit them out at the sound. "Da-da!" Our son's first words.

"Abigail, Anthony...did you hear?" My mother shrieks with delight, no doubt proud to be holding her grandson during this monumental occasion.

I place my plate on the table and walk over to the other side of the kitchen where my mom is holding Gideon. "Da-da!" He says again and he is looking right past me, at Tony. My father and Tony are engaged in a political conversation of some sort, one that I do not care to partake in. They are slow to respond, but a few beats later both men are looking at Gideon as he smiles and stares at his father and repeats his first word three more times before returning to his nonsensical babbling.

"Da-da!" Tony repeats and looks first at my dad and then at me. "His first word, right Abigail?"

I nod and smile. I know I shouldn't be hurt by my son's first word, but if I'm being honest, it stings a little. I assumed his first word would be *mama* and that it would be when we were home alone, as we are the majority of the time. But Gideon chose a moment with our entire family instead. I can't help but feel a little remorseful at this fact as I am the one who tends to his every miniscule need. I am the one who cleans him and feeds him. I am the one who wakes every night to feed and soothe him. Yet his first word is the family member he sees least in his life. We are all laughing and praising Gideon for his big accomplishment when I return to the table to pick up my plate. I remind myself to smile and I answer the growing pleas from my stomach to ingest the food that is in front of me. I need to shrug this chip off of my shoulder and let it go. There is no need to feel hurt by my son's first word. I'm happy he's said his first word. *Mama* will probably be his next.

My mother says she is not hungry and will play with Gideon until I am finished eating. I have a seat at the table across from Tony and my dad who have gone back to their engrossing conversation. I sit quietly paying no attention to what they are saying. I am happy to be eating. I peek across the room several times, watching my mom play on the floor with Gideon as he shows her how mobile he has become. She is a proud grandma. When I've finished my two slices of toast and my bowl of fruit and I am preparing to take a bite of asparagus frittata the conversation between the men has come to a halt and when I look up they are both watching me.

"You're in your own world over there Abigail." My dad shakes his head and winks at me before turning to Tony. "She has always been a daydreamer."

I've heard this line from my father, the one about being a daydreamer, on more than one occasion. I never quite know what he's implying when he says it, but his tone is always one of love. And so I smile and raise my eye brows, waiting for one of them to clue me in on whatever it is they want to ask me. They can say what they want about me, I'm enjoying the moment of eating a meal without Gideon on my lap. I am sitting in a chair eating a warm meal. This moment has the taste of freedom written all over it and I am savoring it before it's over. While I know my mother adores Gideon, I know how taxing he can me and before too much longer she'll grow bored of crawling around on the floor with him.

"I was just telling your dad that I can't wait to have more kiddos." Tony fills the empty air with his statement and as I take a bite of the asparagus frittata I swallow too quickly and nearly choke on a chunk of onion. I quickly grab my glass of water and try to stop the coughing, feeling my face grow flush.

"More kids?" I raise my eye brows after putting an end to my coughing fit. My face cools down as I take a deep breath and reach for another sip of water for good measure.

"Oh, come on. You know you want more kids. You're so good with Gideon. He's already talking, he's crawling. You're a natural." Tony leans back in his chair and smiles in my direction.

"She learned it from her mother. Lois was a natural, too." My dad adds as they have a conversation about me across the table.

"We always said we wanted a lot of kids Abigail. Gideon will be a year old before we know it. It would be nice to have our kids close in age." I agree with Tony that we talked about having a large family; even before we were married we knew we both wanted this. But I'm not sure I'm ready to have another child yet. Tony may have forgotten that it takes some work in the bedroom to create a child in the first place. He hasn't laid a hand on me, not even when I threw myself at him. Society may call pregnancy and birth a *miracle*, but it's so much more than that. It takes work and it takes one specific act that we have not engaged in for quite some time. Despite the logistics of another pregnancy which I'm sure would be sorted out fairly easily, what's really bothering me now is the fact that Tony is bringing this up in front of my parents. This is a discussion we should have privately, at home. Yet, here we are sitting at my parent's kitchen table and I am listening to my husband and my father discuss the number of children I will conceive. The whole thing feels off-kilter. Then again, maybe I'm carrying around a tiny bit of resentment, feeling a little down because our son's first word wasn't mom. I need to get over it. He'll say mom sooner or later.

"They won't have any cousins, since neither of us have siblings." Tony adds, still leaning back in his chair, his arms comfortably crossed in front of his chest, his plate now empty. "I think now would be a great time." I see a light sparkling in his eyes and I know he is serious. He doesn't see anything wrong with having this personal discussion in front of my parents, or rather with my dad instead of with me.

"And you know Abigail, your mother and I are not getting any younger." My dad laughs and points to his spikey gray hair that only covers the sides of his head.

"I hear you in there!" My mother joins in the conversation from the opposite side of the room. "I love this little guy..." she looks at Gideon as he shoves his fist in his mouth and drools. "But it would be fun to have a little granddaughter too!"

I finish my frittata as the three of them continue their conversation. Although they are all laughing and chatting about the future of my family, I am not needed. When my plate is clean I finish my glass of water and stand to take everyone's dirty plates to the sink. I know that standing to clear the table means my moment of eating while sitting at a table without Gideon on my lap is over, but I'd rather tend to my son than sit idle in a conversation about what is best for me. It's not that I don't want more children. I do. Tony and I decided this a long time ago. But I don't feel ready yet. I need more time before I'm ready to endure everything that pregnancy itself entails, needless to say, before adding a second child to care for. I'm still trying to get my footing with Gideon. I'm still waiting and hoping for a few nights filled with sound sleep. After I've placed all of the dishes in the sink I make my way to the floor with Gideon and my mom. Gideon looks up at me when I sit. "Da-da!" He says his word again and I give him praise in the form of my over exaggerated expressions. I follow up with a soft kiss to his forehead. I am proud to be a mother and I love the way Gideon looks at me, his eyes so full of brightness and youth. Maybe, I think, our next child's first word will be mama.

"I want to have a smash cake. I've already found a local photographer who specializes in natural light photography of children and families. I just have to put the deposit down to secure our date. But I definitely want to have a smash cake. I was thinking a few green and blue balloons would be a nice touch too, for the photos. Our son is only going to turn one once!" I say to Tony as he walks in the door from work. I've forgotten the hug and the hello and instead I have gone right into my list of thoughts. "The photographer will come to our home; we can do the photos in the backyard near the line of mature pine trees in the back corner. Green and blue will be the perfect colors, too. They are Gideon's favorite colors."

Tony pauses for a moment as we walk toward the kitchen, I am following his lead. Gideon is napping and I am taking advantage of this rare quiet time to have an adult conversation with my husband. After a few moments Tony chimes in. "How much is this all going to cost? It sounds really expensive."

He is always thinking about money. And while I pinch my pennies and make the most of each dollar when grocery shopping, I think it's okay to loosen the purse strings sometimes; especially when our first child is turning one. I throw a number out to him and tell him it's not expensive, it's for our son. "We give half of that as a deposit to secure the date for the photographer and she'll bring everything along with her, the balloons, the cake…everything!" I'm doing my best to sell Tony on this idea but I'm not sure he is buying it. He is uninterested and fumbling through the refrigerator.

"We don't spend money on frivolous things…"

"My point exactly." Tony interrupts, still poking around inside of the refrigerator.

"I haven't finished." I don't normally speak up to him, but I really want to hire the photographer. "We don't spend money on frivolous things, so we should be able to do this for Gideon. He's turning one! And it's for me too. I admit, I'm a proud mom. I want to have beautiful photos to show off at church. My parents would love to have prints made and frame them. It's a good thing Tony." Tony grabs a piece of leftover pie and carries it out from the refrigerator, grabbing a fork from the drawer on his way to the table.

"Don't eat too much; dinner will be ready in ten minutes." I tell him as he begins eating the apple pie despite my warning.

"I don't even know what a smash cake is Abigail." He doesn't look up as he says this.

"It's just…it's just a cake that's for Gideon. He can make a mess of it if he wants. It's all his and the photographer captures it all on camera."

I watch as Tony looks up from his pie and raises his eye brows. I know he's not one to get excited about this sort of thing, but I am. "Couldn't you just make a cake and snap a few photos of him destroying it, using your iPhone?"

I pause for a moment trying to discern if he is being sarcastic, only to determine he is serious. "No. Not really. I mean, yes, I can make a cake. I can snap photos on my phone, but it's not the same Tony. I know you're not into art, photos or whatever…but hiring a professional is a much better option than going into do-it-yourself mode here. Trust me. The quality of a professional photographer is not even comparable to what I would do."

He finishes the apple pie after a few more bites,

placing his fork on the plate he pushes the mess to the side and folds his arms across the table. "Okay."

"Okay?" My forehead crinkles as I move toward him and pick up his plate.

He nods and smiles, looking up at me. "Yeah. If it makes you happy, let's do it."

"You'll be glad we did!" I assure him, kissing his forehead before taking the plate to the sink. His hand runs gently up my leg and I reach to squeeze his arm, surprised by his flirtation. We linger in the moment for a minute or two before a jolt rushes through my body at the sound of Gideon's cries. A mother's work is never done.

Eighteen

ANTHONY

Present Day, 2018

Our little Gideon is turning two years old without his mother. Will she be home before he is three? Not only is Abigail missing Gideon's birthday, she has now been missing from our lives for a full year. Twelve agonizing months. Three hundred and sixty-five days that have forever altered each of our lives in a negative way. Eight thousand seven hundred and sixty hours that have chipped away at us tirelessly, invading our dreams when we can find sleep and poisoning us with chronic worry and paranoia. Are we missing something? Did we do something wrong? Will we ever find her? What happened? Who took her? Where did she go? Is she alive? Is she dead? Is she trapped somewhere? The questions never stop. I say we as if Gideon were still by my side. But I have not seen or spoken to my son in months. The silence that consumes the interior of our home, only serves to flood my veins with fear. The unknown is terrifying. It's humbling. And it's bleak.

Unlike our wedding anniversary and Abigail's birthday, I do not buy a gift to tuck away in safe keeping for the occasion of her disappearance. This is an occasion that does not warrant a gift. It only warrants pain and heartache. I did not even buy a gift for our child on his birthday. Does that make me a horrible person? If that does not, I'm sure the fact that I'm no longer active in the search for my missing wife, does. There is no question there. I do not check the Facebook page or any of the social media sites or the website I built in an attempt to find my wife. I no longer hang flyers, buy ads in the local papers or harass the journalists and reporters to share Abigail's story. The whole world knows her story by now. Anyone could recognize her face, it's been flashed across every television screen in the county over the last year. I am at the end of my rope. I have lost all of my steam. I do not know where else to turn or what more I can do. The Atwell's must be stronger than I am because Omar assured me they would never give up the search for their daughter. I'm not saying that I'm giving up, but at what point do I move on? Do I ever? Is there even such a thing as moving on?

My somber thoughts are cut short when my phone rings. I pull it from my pocket and answer before studying the screen to see who the caller is. "Anthony Parker." I hear the echo of my own voice speak to the unknown caller.

"Yes, Mr. Parker?"

"Yes. This is."

"My name is Nancy Ultman, I'm a Registered Nurse. I work at Sunnyside Living Facility…" her voice trails as she waits for my recognition.

I do not know this nurse by name, but I know that Sunnyside is caring for my mother. They rarely call and the few times they have it's been due to my mother's severe outbursts, those of which have caused physical harm for herself, often warranting medical care. "Yes. Hi Nancy. Is everything okay with my mother?" I try to be polite but I am short with my words, unable to carry the weight of what has become my life. There are so many times when I silently pray to not be in silence when I sit in my quiet home, but hearing Nancy's voice I quietly scold myself. Be careful what you wish for, I think. Silence is better than bad news.

"Well…" her voice grows muffled as she gathers her words and tries again. "Not exactly Mr. Parker."

"Has she had another fit? An outburst?" I cannot remember what the nurses call it when she has these episodes.

"Mr. Parker, I'm afraid it's more than that."

"Is she okay?" I chime in, interrupting her words.

"Mr. Parker, your mother, Lily, was a very sweet woman. I'm sorry to have to make this call. I truly am. Mr. Parker, your mother passed away this morning." Her voice falls silent, the weight of her loaded words now placed squarely on my shoulders.

"Oh…" I cannot form any additional words. My heart feels tight in my chest and I raise my hand to cover it, pretending that somehow that will heal my pain.

After a few beats the nurse adds, "On behalf of Sunnyside, we are all incredibly sorry for your loss Mr. Parker. If you'd like to…"

Before she can finish I tell her I'll be right there. I'm beginning to think there will never be another occasion to celebrate again. The occasions in my life these days are only marked with sorrow.

As I grab my car keys and begin to drive to Sunnyside I am consumed with grief. I pull over to the side of the road twice on the short drive, breaking down in a flood of tears. Abigail would know what to say in this horrible moment. She would put her arms around me and give me her strength. She would hold my hand and tell me that my mother loved me and that she was proud of me. Abigail would find a way to reduce this impossible pain because she was full of magic. Magic that I didn't recognize until it vanished from my life.

Nineteen

ABIGAIL

2016

Better late than never? Our security alarm system is finally being installed. We fell behind with the birth of Gideon. But now I tell Tony we really don't need to pay for this sense of safety anymore. If we want to pay attention to our money, if we stay true to our tendency toward not being frivolous, then we do not need to pay for a security system installation. I admit there was a time when I felt we needed it, but we're okay now.

"We'll adopt a dog soon. We can get an adult dog

from the animal shelter; saving one who is already potty trained and who will keep us safe." I tell Tony.

He nods, soaking in my words. Most likely he is surprised that I am telling him I don't want the security system. I had been so adamant about it before.

"Really, I'm okay now. Promise." I add.

"Are you sure Abigail?" I see the concern in Tony's eyes and I want to let him know that I am fine. We are fine.

"I am. It was just paranoia. I mean, we live in a nice enough area. I don't think I need to worry. I keep the doors locked when you're away. We're okay." I assure him.

"If you're sure, then I'll call the company and tell them to cancel our appointment. I'm sorry it took so long. We should have had it installed months ago. It's just with my working extra hours and the arrival of Gideon...we've had a lot on our plate."

"No need to apologize." I say, meaning it. "We'll be saving money." I know that always makes him happy.

"I just want to be sure you're really okay. If you change your mind, we can always have it installed later." I love that his words are warm. He sounds genuinely worried about us; Gideon and me. I am aware that I live a pampered life. I am well taken care of. We are secure with money, we have good life insurance policies, I get to be a stay-at-home mom, we have a nice house. I know I am lucky.

"I will. I Promise." I wink at my husband and when he stares back at me my heart thumps an extra beat. He loves me, I know he does. And it is good to be loved.

I've slipped into somewhat of a comfortable routine now that Gideon is nine months old. Our little peanut will turn one year in January as we begin a new year and I try to stay focused on the celebration of both occasions. The photographer is booked for our smash cake session. I'm hoping we'll have snow as it would make a beautiful backdrop. If the weather doesn't cooperate we'll do the photos indoors. I'm sure no matter what they will turn out great. We've decided to go with the theme colors of green and blue, too which will compliment Gideon's light skin tone and bright eyes. We're still nearly three months away from the celebration.

Today I am tending to our busy little Gideon,

cleaning the house and preparing dinner. I've come to lean on the Crockpot on days like today. I can toss in the ingredients and let it cook for hours. It makes meal preparation much faster and easier. And today I need that. I'm making orange chicken. I whisked together the sauce ingredients of broth, orange juice, brown sugar, honey, vinegar, soy sauce, garlic, orange zest, red pepper flakes, ground ginger and black pepper. After placing half of the sauce into the Crockpot I placed the chicken in and then poured on the rest of the sauce. Now it is cooking and we'll have a nice dinner ready when Tony comes home from work. I'll throw together a salad just before he gets home, which will only take a few minutes.

I've been working with Gideon on sharing. I do my research on the Internet to see what babies should be doing at each stage of their development and I want to help Gideon stay on track. He is starting to be able to stand while holding my hands or onto the edge of the couch. Although he can't sit back down once he's standing, he usually falls on his bottom and cries. I am always there to watch him. I help him get to the standing position and let him stand and wobble for a minute or so and this usually thrills him to no end; he is all smiles and giggles, proud of his new accomplishment. To teach him how to share, I let him play with one of his toys and then I gently take it in my hand and hold it. He usually becomes visibly upset and cries. I hold the toy for a beat and then give it back to him and we repeat the cycle again. My hope is that he'll cry less as we continue this game. His absolute favorite toy right now is the stacking rings. There are five soft colorful rings in the set and he is fascinated with them. It is amazing how much he changes and grows every month.

This morning I've cleaned Gideon's room and vacuumed the house. I used the Swiffer mop on the kitchen floor and the linoleum floor in the living room, too. I even cleaned all of the windows. After feeding Gideon it is time for his afternoon nap. I am thankful that he goes down easily today as this is not always the case. I wave good-bye to him as I watch his tired eyelids grow heavy and he smiles at me. He loves when I wave to him lately. I smile back and softly close the door. I have not eaten anything since breakfast; I grab a banana and a handful of mixed nuts as I search the kitchen counter for my keys. I chew my food quickly, and jog to the hall to peek at myself in the mirror. I am wearing jeans and a fitted red sweater. My hair is down and loose, black waves falling just past my shoulders. I am wearing a hint of black mascara and eye linter and of course my favorite red lip-stick. The jeans I have on are just one size above what I wore before my pregnancy. I am happy to fit into them. A rush of adrenaline pulses through my veins as I take one last quick look at myself and head out the door with my keys and purse in hand. Gideon is safe in his crib and I am sure that he is asleep by now. Secretly, I've done this a handful a times and it has always been okay.

My heart thumps inside of my chest as I pull open the door of Black Cat Books. Every time I come it is the same feeling. It is a pure rush. Each time I leave I can't wait until the next time I can come back. My ring finger is bare as it hits against the closing door. I always leave my wedding ring in the cup holder of the car and make sure I don't have any traces of motherhood on my skin or clothes. This is my time to be Abby. This is my time to smile and giggle without forcing it. During these moments I don't have to be a mother or a wife. Instead, I can release the heavy weight that presses so heavily on my shoulders and I can breathe. I can be me.

"Hey Abby!" I love the way his eyes fill with light every time he sees me. My stomach flip-flops at the sight of him and I hold my arms out, awaiting our embrace.

"Gram…" I whisper in his ear as I throw my arms around him and rest my head on his shoulder.

"You look great today. Red is your color." He pulls back, although I'm still holding my arms around his waist. He makes me feel as if I possess some magical power; as if I can do anything I want to in this world. In his embrace I instantly feel secure and full of hope. I know with certainty that Gram would never leave me. I am the luckiest person when I am with him and I wouldn't trade this feeling for anything in the world.

"Thanks." A rush of heat hits my face. "You don't look bad yourself." I lift my right hand from his waist and pick at a piece of lint near his shoulder. After tossing the minuscule lint to the side, I let my fingers linger along the outer edge of his neck.

"Follow me…" He whispers, bending down and letting his lips linger on my ear. I am tingling from the tip of my head to the bottom of my big toe. I am brimming with the dizziness of this taste of freedom.

I know where we are heading and he takes my hand in his as I follow his lead. We jog to the storage room in the back of the building and he hits the lock button as the door closes behind us. In an instant Gram's hands are beneath my red sweater, caressing my sides and filling all the empty parts of me. My back is against the wall and he is pressed up against me. The simple touch of his hands somehow reach me deep within. I know what you're thinking. You're thinking I'm a horrible mother for leaving my son at home alone while he naps. You're labeling me as an awful human being at this very moment. You think that because I can do this, what you think is a horrible act by a mother and a wife, you think that every part of me must be terrible. But realize this; what we are quick to judge is inside each of us. What we voice our judgments about are the very parts of us that we fear the most. I am a better person and a better mother because of what I have with Gram. I've known that for a while now. He fills me with everything I need and things I didn't even know I longed for. This is not a ploy to find a high. This is real. This is more than a rush; it's more than a secret love. It's everything. I'd only found Gram just before Gideon was born, but knowing what I know now, feeling the way I do in this very moment as he releases the clasp on my bra and I open my mouth wide, waiting to be filled with his tongue, I don't know how I lived without him. Some mothers take a long bath and surround themselves with scented candles to brush off the mundaneness of motherhood, I spend time with Gram. He is the only thing that keeps me going. He's the only place I can find hope and the feeling of security all wrapped up in one. He makes me feel whole and he makes me realize that the sexiest thing a man can do to a woman is to crawl inside of her mind and make her imagination run wild and free, showing her with his gentle touch that she is perfect just the way she is in this very moment.

When you've moved on from judging me for this act of love between two human beings, you'll undoubtedly judge Gram for running his hands over a married woman's flesh. You'll call him a loser and a low-life. You'll hate him for what he has done to our family. If you judge him in this way, you're not seeing the whole situation. You are judging too quickly, before you have all of the facts. I told Gram I lost the baby. He does not know of Gideon's existence. Just as Gram is a secret from my life of marriage and motherhood, Gideon and Tony are secrets to Gram. At home I am Abigail, the doting wife and mother I was raised to be. But with Gram I am Abby, the passionate free spirit who has submersed herself in love. It had been an impulse to tell Gram that I'd separated from Tony. In reality, it wasn't far from the truth, emotionally anyway. Tony and I were not connected on any level. He was consumed with his work and I was submerged in the duties of motherhood. I'd told Gram that Tony and I separated because it was "too much stress after losing the baby." I'd never planned any of this. Honestly I never would have dreamed of kissing another man, not in my wildest dreams. I wasn't brought up that way. I was raised to be loyal to the church and to my man. But seeing Gram the day I discovered Black Cat Books by accident, lit a fire inside of me and I went with it. From the very start I told myself not to go back to the book store. Not to be lured by the nostalgia that surrounded Gram. I couldn't stop the pull. I couldn't stop thinking about him once I'd seen him. Although our relationship together had taken place years ago and had only lasted a brief seven months, Gram had filled me with electricity from the very first touch when our fingers grazed one another's while reaching for a highlighter in the supply closet at Saint Ann's. His hazel eyes cut through the exterior bull shit and saw to the core of my soul. Just being near him made me come alive in a way I never did with anyone else. It's as if Gram is full of electricity and if I'm anywhere in his vicinity I am drunk on the buzz I receive from him.

I admit that there are moments at home when Tony looks at me and he sees me, although those moments are fleeting at most these days. In those brief junctures I sometimes feel a flash of guilt. Yet Gram is everything Tony isn't. Gram is everything I need. We didn't work out before because I'd hesitated when he asked me to marry him. He was so hurt that we fell apart and we couldn't put the pieces of the puzzle back together at the time. Although he gave me everything I needed and he allowed me to be exactly who I was, I wasn't ready for that then. The feeling of freedom that came from being with him terrified me and I set out to search for something easier; something safe. That's how I found Tony. With Tony I didn't feel wild and crazy; I felt like the girl I was raised to be and at the time that felt more secure than breaking out of my shell and emerging into the person I really was. With Tony, I quickly fell into my submissive role and behaved much the way I'd seen my mother act before me. I'd foolishly convinced myself that the comfort of being who I was raised to be was worth the cost of sacrificing the real version of me, never fathoming the ramifications that would arise down the road.

Tony can never find out about what I have with Gram. I think he would kill me. Honestly, I never pegged myself to be a cheater or a liar for that matter. I was the goody-goody that followed all of the rules. I did what I was told. I went to church every Sunday.

I try to be the best mother I can. I've tried to be the best wife, as well. But my efforts there are to no avail as our marriage is a loveless one at best. My husband won't even look at me in *that* way. He won't lay a hand on me. To the Parker men I have become nothing but a baby machine and a care provider. Yet, I want to be more than that. I am so much more than that. I wish with all of my might that I could find complete satisfaction and fulfillment in the combined roles of marriage and motherhood, but I do not know how. I am a restless wild horse who has been tied up with heavy rope and sequestered to a tiny stall. I am itching to run free. I am desperate to live a life with the wind blowing in my hair and my eyes wide open taking in the ever changing scenery.

When I gave birth to Gideon I began wondering about personalities. I wondered if we are born with our likes and dislikes. Are we born with a certain level of compassion for others? Are we born with our mannerisms or are they developed by our environment and those that we surround ourselves with? An argument can be made for either side of the case. Yet I know that I am different than how I was raised to be. I am full of wild abandon. I long to rekindle the flame that nearly burned out deep inside of me. It never failed to flicker, but it had drastically dimmed. Yet with Gram I am brimming with brightness; a feeling I'd only experienced once before during our stint at dating years ago.

I've read enough books and quotes about love to realize that what I have with Gram is real. It always was. Somehow I've just been lucky enough to be given a second chance. The only problem is, when I'm with Gram, it all feels too good to be true. Is that idiom always right? If something feels too good to be true, is it? Or can some things just be good? Can some things be good and true? My jeans are in a puddle at my ankles, as are Gram's and at this moment I am certain that some things can certainly be both good and true.

A few minutes later we are replacing our clothes, although I believe on both of our ends it is unwillingly. But I have been gone for seventy-five minutes and I need to rush home before Gideon wakes, which according to his typical nap time, is any minute now. Gram hands me my red sweater and holds it out for me to place my hands and head in each slot before fully slipping it on. The sweater swallows my arms and neck and as I pull it into place I become a puddle of mush as Gram runs his index finger along my neck and kisses my chin and then the tip of my nose and the top of my forehead. He buttons his own pants and reaches down to press his lips against mine once more before I leave. We talk without words and in my world filled with babbles and cartoons, I am all the more grateful for dancing with the art of wordless communication.

"I love you" Gram whispers in my ear.

I pull back, both surprised and warmed. Maybe I do prefer words. We haven't exchanged this arrangement of three words since before I knew Tony. Before I was married. Before I had a child. Before all of this. "I love you, too." I whisper back, my eyes gazing into his as my head is held high to meet his hazel eyes.

"And it's not just because of...this" I know that he means our encounters. Every time Gram asked me out on a proper date I told him I wasn't ready to be seen in public just yet with another man, being that Tony and I were separated and soon to be divorced. He understood, not wanting to push me or make me uncomfortable in any way and so our meet ups were always like this. Make-out sessions in the back storage room of the book store.

"I know." I say shyly. Although admittedly, I love that he said it. I do know this is true, but hearing the words spill out of his mouth only makes this all more real.

"I'm serious Abby. I love you and of course I love all of this, but I hope you know I love *you*." I watch as his thick eye brows narrow and he places each of his hands on the outside of my arms, holding me in both his gaze and embrace, letting me know that he is real. This is true. He is not too good to be true. He is good and true.

"I don't know how I ever let you go Gram…" my voice trails as I brush a lock of wavy black hair from my face and tuck it neatly behind my ear.

After a few beats, Gram rubs my arms up and down. "We're here now. That's what matters, right?"

"Right." I agree and reach to the ground to grab my purse. I fumble around to find my keys and pull them into the palm of my hand. "See you tomorrow?" I smile and know that he will say yes.

"Of course. I'm already counting down the seconds." He smiles back with his perfectly white teeth sparkling back at me.

I toss my purse over my shoulder and give one last tug to my sweater to be sure it is in place before heading back through the store and out the front door to my car. "Me too." I turn my head over my shoulder and bite my lip as I walk away.

★★★

When I return home I hear Gideon babbling in his room. His babbles are following a happy tone and I breathe a sigh of relief as I rush to his room to pull him from his crib. I smile and wave hello and he laughs, his sweet giggles filling the quiet house. I kiss his forehead, taking in his distinct scent and place him on the changing table while grabbing a fresh diaper. "Mommy loves you little guy." I tell him in a sing-songy voice. "Mommy loves you lots, Gideon." He does not punish me with cries for my brief absence during his nap. Instead he showers me with his chuckles and I watch his chubby cheeks form spots of red as he stares up at me.

"Ma-ma!" He says proudly.

I nod as I latch the fresh diaper over his hips. "Yes, good job!" I repeat the word, "Ma-ma" and point to myself.

"Ma-ma!" He says again as I bring him upward to a seat.

I love that he is saying my name. He is becoming more interactive every day it seems. Yet despite the joy of hearing my name from our son, my thoughts are consumed by Gram. I replay our embrace today. I allow my mind to swim in the details of his every touch, his every look. The memory of today is still fresh on my lips and I let it all replay in my mind as if I'd hit the rewind button on my favorite movie. I can still feel his fingers on my skin. I can still feel the tickle of his breath on my neck. Although he is in one place and I am in the other, he is still with me. I can't let him out of my mind. I can't let go of the feeling of wanting and being wanted. I can't let go of him. He has become a life-preserver, appearing just when I thought I was drowning.

Twenty

ANTHONY

Present Day, 2018

The reception is horrible. "Hello?"

"It's me." She says.

I would recognize her light and airy voice anywhere. "Cindy?" I state her name as a question, following formality. Although I want to shout at her for waiting so many months to return my calls and texts.

"Yeah, it's Cindy." Her voice fades in and out on the crackling line.

"Are you still in Argentina?" I realize I need to take

a breath, slow down and ask one question at a time. With the shaky reception she won't be able to hear any more than that and I want to hear her answers.

"Yeah…"

"Did you get my messages?" A dumb question, I realize since she is calling me.

"Yeah, that's why…" the phone breaks up.

"Cindy? Are you there?" I beg, not wanting to lose her now.

"My phone is breaking up…" There is a pause before she continues and I hear the sound of loud music in the background. "I'm returning your gazillion messages…what in the world could be so important?"

"My wife. Abigail, my wife disappeared the day after you left. Do you know anything about that?" I wait to hear if she sounds shocked in any way, but the poor reception makes it hard to tell.

"What?"

I don't know if she didn't hear me or if she is confused. Maybe she's trying to play dumb to hide something. I repeat what I said two more times before she gets it.

"Get over yourself." She states flatly and for the moment the line has become crystal clear.

Now it's my turn to ask, "What?"

"You heard me jackass. Get over yourself already. You think I would have told your wife about what we were doing? Are you crazy?" Her tone is full of malice and I fear she will hang up on me now.

"I'm sorry Cindy. I am. We don't have any leads. She's been missing…" my voice trails as I realize my last hope has come to a dead end. I believe Cindy. She did not tell Abigail about our fling.

"I didn't even know your wife was missing. I thought she just had a baby or something?"

She isn't lying. I am certain. "She did have a baby, we had a son." I pause as if I'm waiting for her to congratulate me, but I know that is not appropriate at this time. I don't know what I'm waiting for. This conversation is too surreal.

"And seriously, you thought *I* took her? I weigh a whole one hundred and ten pounds. You think I'm strong enough to kidnap a grown woman? Needless to say, do you seriously think I would do something that crazy?" The reception on the line is still clear as I take in her words.

"No. I…I don't know where she is. She's been gone so long. I just thought…I thought maybe if I talked to you…if you told me that you told Abigail about us, maybe something would click. Maybe I'd realize something…" I shake my head, weary with defeat.

"It's not like we were in love." She states matter-of-factly. "Love is what makes you crazy. Not what we did. And for the record, I'm not crazy."

"I know. You're right. I don't know what I was thinking. I haven't been clear headed in a long time. Again, I'm sorry Cindy. I am…" I tell her, wondering if I should warn her that the Atwell's investigator will likely track her down and want to talk to her at some point, just to be sure. I decide not to tell her, knowing that she'll find out on her own sooner or later. I've gotten the information I needed from this conversation and there is nothing more to say.

"Anthony?" "Yeah?" I answer, wondering what more she could have to say.

"I really hope you find her; your wife."

"Thanks." I reply. "Me too."

We hang up from the call and I bury my head in my hands. There are no more leads. There is nowhere left to look. I've lost my wife, my son, my mother. I've lost the Atwell's. Everything and everyone in my life is gone in some way or another. And I am sitting here alone in my kitchen wondering what I did so wrong to deserve this.

I have taken a hiatus from work. I haven't left the house in twelve days. My mother's ashes sit quietly on the living room coffee table. I will scatter them over Newberry creek, where my father's ashes are, once I find the strength; although I fear that may be awhile. A part of me wonders if I'm waiting to scatter Abigail's at the same time. I keep the shades drawn tight, submersing myself in complete darkness, with exception of the light blasting from the television screen. I've lost track of how many bottles of Hennessy Black I've emptied. Today is day thirteen that I've holed myself in this dark empty shell of a house. And today is different. I don't know whether I've put myself in this new state of mind because of the staggering volume of alcohol I've consumed or if it's simply the fact that I've kept myself isolated from the world like a caterpillar hidden away in his cocoon. I guess somewhere deep down I had hoped to emerge as a butterfly on the other side of all of this; I'd hoped to surface a different man, a happier one. But things do not always turn out as we hope for or plan them to. Life is forcing this lesson down my throat. I want to scream to the universe, *I get it!* But the world keeps throwing heavy reminders my way. Life is what it is and it's how you react to the circumstances you encounter that make you who you are. I nearly laugh out loud at this revelation. What does that say about me? What kind of man am I that I have lost my wife and now my son and my in-laws? I have no family to speak of. How am I supposed to react?

Disgusted with myself, I stand from the La-Z-Boy chair and begin gathering the empty bottles and paper plates that I've tossed to the floor. When I finish picking up the garbage I have piled around me in my dark cave, I walk over to the large window in the living room and pull back the curtains, allowing the blazing sun to burn my eyes. I squint as I tuck each side of the curtains back. My eyes water from the foreign light that is flooding them. But I still see it, despite the blur. There is a black car parked in front of the house. The car has dark tinted windows. It must be the same car that haunted Abigail, I think. Consumed with a sudden burst of energy and anger I grab the handle of the front door and force it open, still not used to the flood of bright light. I use my hand to shield my eyes and march toward the black car, not realizing that I am only partially dressed. My feet are bare. My face is unshaven and full of messy stubble. I haven't showered in the dozen days, so I am sure there is a stench about me. I am wearing my red and black plaid boxer shorts and an old white t-shirt that is filled with various stains from the previous days. When I reach the car I tap forcefully with my fist on the passenger side window, impatient for an answer. It is still winter in Indiana and the frosty ground pricks its sharp needles against my bare feet. My arms are crossed in front of my dirty shirt and I can see my breath in small puffs hanging in front of my face as I try to stay warm. I hit my fist against the window again, this time much harder. The car is running; I can see the fumes pouring out from the exhaust. Someone must be inside.

A few beats later the window rolls down and I bend my knees and duck to look inside. There is a dark haired man wearing a nice suit sitting in the front seat. His dark eyes are flanked with deep creases making me guess that he is at least in his mid-forties. The man raises his eye brows and waits for me to speak.

I hadn't gotten this far in my mind. I'd thought he would say something when the window rolled down and now I'm not quite sure what to say to the stranger parked in front of my home. "May I ask why you're parked here…in front of my home?" I gesture with my arms to my yard and home.

"That's a rather personal question." The man's

voice is deep and raspy and I don't like that he hasn't answered.

"It is my house." I tell him, trying my best to be patient as I wait for an answer so I can ask my next question. I realize it is likely this man could simply drive away and so I place my arms inside of his car window, hoping that if I'm holding on he will feel that he must stay put.

He sighs and looks down at the screen of his phone before glancing back up at me again. When our eyes meet this time he seems both surprised and annoyed that I am still hanging inside of his car window.

I can't take it anymore. I've tried to be patient, but I can't do it any longer. Something inside of me breaks and I begin to scream, "Do you know where my wife is?" I realize I must look like a mad man screaming into a stranger's car window, wearing hardly any clothes in the middle of a bitterly cold winter. "She told me this car used to sit outside of our house and seemed to watch her. You must know where she is! Tell me where she is…I demand answers now. I have your license plate number and I have already phoned the police." I lie about the last part. As I gasp for air, shivering from the winter air, the man interrupts my shouts.

He is holding his hands up in the air in front of him

as if I am holding a gun. Yet I am only armed with words; with questions. "Hey man, calm down. I don't know what you're talking about."

"Calm down? Calm down! Who are *you* to tell me to calm down? Do you know where she is? You must know what she looks like. She is pretty, is that why you were watching her? Do you have a thing for pregnant women, is that what it is? I am banging my fists against his car now. "Answer me!"

"Hey! Hey! I don't know who you are…"

I cut him off before he can finish his sentence. "Yes, you do. I'm Abigail Parker's husband. I live here. I work during the days and she was always home alone. You know exactly who she is and you know exactly who I am. You're a piece of shit. Tell me where she is. Tell me right now!" I grit my teeth and yank on the door handle, finding it locked.

"Would you give me a second to explain?" The man screams back, matching the volume of my voice and grabbing my attention.

I stop pulling on the car door handle and become silent. My hands are shaking and now it is not from the chill in the air.

"Okay…" The man breathes in deeply, trying to gather himself before continuing. "Hear me out before you interrupt, man. Got it?"

I nod, reluctantly; my eyes burning into his.

"I don't know what this stuff with your wife is. Honestly, I have no idea what you're talking about man. I'm an investor. I've bought two houses on the street so far. I flip them and turn them into rental properties or I sell them. I'm looking at buying another house here, but I like to sit and watch the area at different times of day to see what the street is like; to get an idea of the neighborhood. It all impacts my profit, so it's important. Get it?" He scrolls through his phone and flashes the photos of two houses, each one with a professional sign in front of it. He then tosses me his business card. He's not bluffing. He's a real estate investor. His story is legit.

I begin to back away, this time I am the one with my hands up in the air. "I'm sorry. Truly. I've lost my mind."

"Do you need some help man?" He shouts from the window.

I shake my head. I know I'm way beyond help. There is no kind of help anyone can give me that will do me any good at this point.

"Can I call someone for you?" I realize he must have smelled the alcohol on my breath. Combined with my appearance and my insane rant, I can understand how he is thinking I'm a drunk. I bet he doesn't think a person like me in the neighborhood will enhance his property values.

I shake my head again, my hands still up in the air as I back away, feeling the frozen ground cut at my bare feet. "I'm sorry." I say weakly as I turn to return inside of the house. I was better off staying inside with the curtains drawn. I am no good to anyone anymore. I have hit rock bottom, or at least I hope this is rock bottom because I can't imagine things being any worse than this.

"Mr. Parker, Abigail has been found. She is safe." The officers' voice tells me on the other end of the phone. My entire body is numb. I am not sure whether this is a dream or if I am so drunk that I am hallucinating.

I am unable to bring myself to speak. Do you ever have the nightmare when you are in a terrible situation and you try to dial 9-1-1 and the phone won't work or no one will answer? I have it all of the time and it's always a gut wrenching, horrible feeling. You can't believe it is happening. That's how I feel right now. I can't believe someone is telling me, an official is telling me that my wife has been found and she is alive. I am dizzy with confusion. The words are so simple. They are the exact words I've waited to hear for more than a year. Yet they do not make sense to me in this moment. I am lost in a haze when I hear the officers' voice speak again.

"Mr. Parker, are you there? Have I lost you?"

His words, *lost you* echo back and forth in my mind. No, you have not lost me. I lost my wife. But you're telling me you found her. You're telling me she is safe. She is alive. You're telling me exactly what I've been waiting to hear, yet I am unable to reply. I open my mouth to try and respond, but have no luck. I cannot feel my arm that is holding the phone to my ear. My fingers are tingling.

"Mr. Parker?"

"Yes." I finally answer. "I'm here."

"You're wife, Abigail Parker...we've located her. She is alive." He tells me again.

This time his words register. "Abigail? You've found my Abigail?" I brace myself, knowing that I may have misheard him.

"Yes." He confirms. "We've found her. Your wife is alive." His voice is official and lacking emotion.

"Where was she? She's okay? Do you have her with you? Can I come and see her?" The questions roll out of my mouth like a tidal wave. I am overwhelmed with relief. I have been consumed by stress and worry for so long I do not know how to process what is happening. I use my free hand to pinch the skin on my thigh and I wince. I am not dreaming. I look down at my red feet, still frozen from my trip outside to scream at a stranger. I look at the trash can sitting in the kitchen and see it overflowing with my mess. I need to get everything cleaned up before Abigail comes home. A jolt rushes through my veins as I rush to the trash can and begin stuffing its contents down enough so that I can tie the bag closed and carry it out of the house.

"Mr. Parker, she is alive. She is safe."

"That's great! That's...this is perfect!" Although I'm still in shock, I am elated.

"We would like you to come down to the station and we'll explain everything in more detail once you're here."

"Is she with you?"

"Just come down to the station as soon as you can Mr. Parker. We need to talk. There are some things you need to know." The officer tells me.

"I need to get dressed and I'll be right there." I tell him. I want to go straight there but I need to shower and change out of my old clothes first. I can't let Abigail see me like this. We hang up from the call and I rush around the house throwing things under the couch or into corners, trying to at least clear the floor. I throw open all of the blinds and curtains, letting the light pour in so that the house will feel friendly and warm.

A pain stabs my heart, wishing I had Gideon here so that I could bring him with me to reunite us all together. Surely the police will call the Atwell's, too. I'm sure they will be at the police station and bring Gideon with them. We will all be reunited; we will be a family again.

I throw my clothes into the overflowing hamper and jump in the shower, lathering my body with Zest soap and shampooing my hair with vigor. I am in and out of the shower in under ninety-seconds and dry off even faster, tossing a pair of jeans and a sweater and running my fingers through my wet hair. I brush my teeth and place a dab of cologne on my skin before sprinting to the garage and turning on the ignition of the car. A million thoughts race through my mind as I drive to the station. My body is pulsing with excitement. A line of sweat forms at my brow and my heart is thumping hard against the wall of my chest. I'd never truly given up hope. I was certainly losing my mind, but I think that's because I didn't want to let her go. I didn't want to give up on hoping that we would find my wife. And now, not only has she been found, she is alive! Abigail will be shocked at how much Gideon has changed. Although I haven't seen him myself in some time, he is twenty-eight months old now and I'm sure he has only continued to grow leaps and bounds. She will get to hold her son in her arms again. I will get to press my lips against hers. At a red light, less than two miles from the police station, I decide I want to cook for Abigail tonight. I will make her dinner the way she used to always make dinner for me. I want to care for her. I want her to know she is safe and no matter who took her, no matter what she's endured, I want her to know that I will never let it happen again. I will find a way to work from home if need be. We can move to a different neighborhood if she wants. We can take a self-defense class together. Maybe she can take a jewelry making class once she settles back in. She always enjoyed making jewelry. If it will make her happy, she can do anything she wants. I just want her to be happy. I want her to be safe. And I want her to know that I love her and how terribly much I've missed her. I want to tell her that we are soul mates and that I would have never stopped searching for her. There is so much I want to tell her, but I realize I need to hear what the police have to say first. I need to hear what my wife has to say, too.

On the surface it appears as if my prayers have been answered. My wife is alive. She is safe. She is well. But when the officers tell me that Abigail doesn't want to see me, that she ran away to escape me, I know in my heart the gut-wrenching truth is that the brighter the light shines, the darker the shadow.

I don't know how to move on. It's true, I am now free of the chronic worry that plagued me for more than a year of my life, a pain I've grown used to in so many ways. But my veins are now filled with a new poison; a stronger venom, this time made of an amber agony that will stay with me until the end of time. I don't know how to begin to describe this new gaping wound, this pain that will surely never leave me the way she did.

I suppose there were signs I had ignored; things I should have paid more attention to, perhaps. I admit, I was in it for myself, although I never meant for it to be that way. I hadn't realized what I'd done. I was in our relationship for my image, my ego, my self-worth; it was all tied up into what we had. But I wasn't. Somewhere after Abigail got pregnant with Gideon and the initial excitement fell off, I did too. That's when we lost our connection. We used to tell each other everything. I knew Abigail's every thought, her every conversation; and she knew mine. This was not out of obligation in any way; it was out of genuine affection. We'd wanted to share those things with each other because we'd wanted to be close. But lost it little by little; it wasn't overnight. Suddenly it was gone. It grew too uncomfortable to be discussed. When that connection dissipated it was perhaps, I think now, looking back, the start of our downfall. Sure, we went through the motions, but *we* began to feel different. How did I not see all of this before? How did I not catch it in time? I silently scold myself now as I sit across from the two uniformed officers, stunned into silence, but not into a loss of haunting memories.

I don't know if Abigail had learned of my affair with Cindy? Had that sent her over the edge, perhaps? Or was it, simply, me?

The cold loneliness that exists inside of the walls of our empty house is what I imagine she felt before she left us. The tables have turned. Now she is the one with a life to talk about, a life to embrace and I am the one who's been left in solitude, worrying about her. The irony itself sends chills down my spine, although

I doubt she planned it that way; to make me feel what she had felt all along. Life is funny sometimes.

"Mr. Parker?" The officer's voice jolts me back to life. He smells like coffee. "Abigail has asked us to tell you she wants rights to visit with your son, Gideon, once a month. Although she said that she understands you'll want to be the primary caretaker."

"But Gideon's with the Atwell's...*her* parents. He's not even with me!" My reply is too stern, too panicked. I realize neither of the officers sitting before me has been in my shoes. At least I highly doubt that either of their spouses had ever run away. I try to refrain from stabbing my fists against the wooden table that sits between us.

"That's something you'll need to work out with Abigail herself or with your respective lawyers." The other officer's voice chimes in. Her voice is calm and soothing and she continues, telling me that I am also being served with divorce papers today.

Breathless and under the weight of the florescent lights, I sit across from the police officers and wrap my fingers around the edges of the wooden chair that holds me. I have to hold on tight to something right now, because I am consumed by the feeling that I am fading away.

Epilogue

ABIGAIL

Present Day, 2018

*"Like wildflowers; You must allow yourself to grow in
all the places people thought you never would."*

–E.V.

My tongue has bite marks on it from all of the
things I never said. Now it's time to heal. I'm healing,
at least I'm starting to. Now it's time to do things
right. My mind is a minefield of bruises and scars, and
like a forest with a trail that's been heavily traveled, I

need to let it rest. To let it grow in all of the places it has not previously been able to grow because of the repeated trampling of others that I'd allowed for so long. Being whole means taking control of my own words and actions. And that's exactly what I've done.

I will pay back the endless police fees, although it may take me my whole life to do so, or until my jewelry shop takes off. I did it, by the way. I opened an online store and I have a small studio here at home; my home with Gram, in North Carolina. Holy Grail Jewelers is the name of my shop. I'm officially a business owner.

When we left Waterford, it was all my idea. Gram had never used any sick or vacation days and so he took them all at once. Then, by the time we made our way to Kentucky he sent a letter through the mail, with no return address, telling the book store that he quit. No one knew about what Gram and I had between us; about our love. Gram never knew I had a child, and he didn't know that I was still with Tony. So when we ran away, he thought it was an adventure between two young lovers. I knew differently, of course, which is why I wore baseball caps and tucked my hair up anytime I went into a gas station or any place there might be a surveillance camera to find me. I had a blond wig I wore sometimes, too. When Gram asked why I put on that silly wig, I told him I was just playing around and laughed it off. He never asked about it again. I was careful to keep Gram away from the television and from newspapers as much as possible and luckily he never spotted any of the missing person reports that showed my photo. Five months ago Gram saw my picture somewhere online and I confessed everything to him; Gideon, Tony, all of it. I told him my reasons and he understood. When I asked him to promise not to tell, he kept the promise, wanting our life to continue growing together as much as I did. Once I confessed everything to Gram, we both agreed I needed to change my name, so I lost the *Abi* at the front of my name and I took Gram's last name and that left me with my new name, *Gail Nelson*.

How did the police find me? I had been considering calling them for the last two months, wanting to clear my conscience. But then someone recognized my face when I was taking a self-defense class in Raleigh, they snapped a photo with their phone and the rest is history.

Sometimes I miss my old life, but not for the reasons you might think. I miss the way our cape cod smelled like the cinnamon candles I kept in each room. I missed knowing exactly who I was expected to be, even though it wasn't who I wanted to be. There was an odd comfort in simply having to meet someone else's expectations, rather than blazing your own path and figuring it out as you went. I missed my parents and I hated knowing that I'd put them through hell the way I'd left.

My life in Waterford, Indiana had become like the tattered dirt brown La-Z-Boy chair I'd wanted to get rid of and replace with something new, the chair Tony told me again and again that he loved too much to let go. When I'd suggested at least having the chair reupholstered, Tony had thrown out the same line, the one about loving it too much to let it go. He didn't like change. He loved it just the way it was. And I suppose the same went for me. We loved each other in our own way. He loved me like that chair; too much to let me change in any way. And I loved him as the woman I was raised to be. But spending so much time alone in the house, I began to realize that I was something more than what was expected of me. I was different than I was raised to be. I didn't have to be confined to the views and desires of others. I could be who I wanted. Running into Gram reminded me of this and he lit me to life, like a fire in the dark of night. And so, little by little, I began searching for that person inside of me, for her. For Gail. And I'm glad I did. I'm glad I'm her. Because now I'm free. It may look like a giant mess on the outside, but I am whole on the inside, and that's a first.

Tony was always faithful to me, of that I am sure. I am aware that I am the one in the wrong here, but I felt so suffocated to be with such a perfect man. I didn't realize until I was pregnant that perfect wasn't what I really wanted. I wanted, instead, to live, not to be confined. I wanted to have experiences, not to be stagnant, caught in isolation. I realize that the police have told Tony by now that I am alive, that I have been found, that I am not coming home, that I am divorcing him. And I realize it may seem to you that I've traded a comfortable life for something else and in many aspects I have done just that. But what I've really traded is a life of complacency and rule following for one of love and fulfillment; for a life of freedom.

I admit, I asked Tony for a security system as a cover.

I wasn't sure at that point that I would really run away, but I daydreamed about it and in some ways it became a game to me. I'd taken five-hundred dollars from our sock drawer in addition to plucking ten or twenty dollars from Tony's wallet each week and hiding it away in the bottom of the hamper, just in case. My paranoia started off as real, I suppose it was the pregnancy hormones. But eventually I found the guts to walk up to that dark car that parked in front of the house and I confronted the man, only to find that he was an investor scoping out the area. He was harmless, I realized, after speaking with him once. Besides the cash I had stashed away, the only thing I took with me when I left were the earrings I'd made from the class I'd taken at the library so long ago. I wear them most days; the pair of petite dangle earrings made of blue Labradorite, the ones with the stormy appearance. The Labradorite faceted cubes dangle from the edge of the earring with a sterling silver daisy spacer and a tiny silver ball as the headpin. The small blue cubes catch the light when I place them into my ears, glistening and reminiscent of a late evening summer storm. Please understand, I didn't know any other way to breath. The only escape I could conjure up was to leave; to fake my disappearance. I never meant to hurt anyone, but I was hurting too much myself to do anyone any good any more.

Did you know that I once read that Abigail means "father's joy"? I may have been my father's joy at one time, that is, before I disappeared from Waterford. But leaving Indiana and forging my own path without adhering to someone else's rules that to me is victory. When Gideon entered my life I couldn't bear the thought of being ruled by three men; two had already been too much. I found myself wanting to breathe and that want grew into a desperate need. My middle name, Victoria, is said to mean victory. And realizing this during my isolated life, I took it to heart. I didn't have to be my father's joy. I could find victory, but first I had to define what that meant for me.

I am resilient. If you find yourself hating me for what I did, I am okay with that. It is quite possible you would have loved me if you met me in my former life, the one where I'd been married to Tony. You would have liked me because I made you feel comfortable, because I seemed every bit normal. But realize this, if you can dislike a stranger for making the choice to be happy and to find freedom, what does that say about you? Remember, we are quickest to judge that which we fear most within ourselves.

Do you find yourself judging me because I make you uncomfortable? Because I make you think about how quickly life can change? Like the green grass that graces this great Earth, I have found a way to grow and flourish, even when crushed by the unbearable weight of man's own creation; that of thick and heavy cement. Although it seems unlikely for grass to grow through the cracks in the tar, the strongest pieces do; they find a way to live, to stand tall and brave, to point themselves toward the light, and to dance in the warm gentle breeze and be grateful for all of its grace. No matter what opinion you have of me, I am the one who is free. I am free to make my own choices now, because I realized some time ago that all of the little choices matter. All the little choices make us exactly who we are.

"Catch on fire if you must, sometimes everything needs to burn to the ground so that we may grow."

—a.j. lawless

OTHER BOOKS BY STACEY RITZ

All the Little Choices

The Lost Years

ABOUT STACEY RITZ

Award winning writer and bestselling author, Stacey Ritz's novels are emotional dramas that delve into the complexities of relationships, families, friendships and secrets. Her books are published worldwide. When Ritz isn't reading or writing, she's likely spending time with animals, nature and family or watching Hallmark movies. Visit her at staceyritzbooks.com

Made in the USA
Middletown, DE
07 March 2019